ECHO OF LIES

THE LIES MYSTERY SERIES

CAROL POTENZA

PUBLISHED BY TINY MAMMOTH PRESS
www.carolpotenza.com

Publisher's Cataloging-in-Publication

(Provided by Cassidy Cataloguing Services, Inc.)

Names: Potenza, Carol, author.

Title: Echo of lies / Carol Potenza.

Description: [Las Cruces, New Mexico] : Tiny Mammoth Press, [2026] | Series: Potenza, Carol. Lies' mystery series.

Identifiers: LCCN: 2025921418 | ISBN: 9798986769097 (paperback) | 9798986769080 (ebook)

Subjects: LCSH: Women ranchers--New Mexico--History--20th century--Fiction. | Accidents--New Mexico--Fiction. | Women in science--New Mexico--Fiction. | Sex discrimination in science--Fiction. | Time travel--Fiction. | Self-doubt--Fiction. | Courage--Fiction. | LCGFT: Detective and mystery fiction. | Science fiction. | Thrillers (Fiction) | BISAC: FICTION / Historical / 20th Century / Post-World War II. | FICTION / Mystery & Detective / Amateur Sleuth. | FICTION / Romance / Time Travel.

Classification: LCC: PS3616.O8435 E24 2026 | DDC: 813/.6--dc23

EDITOR: RACHEL OESTREICH

PROOFREADER: GILLY WRIGHT

Cover Artist: Mia Sharp

Cover Design: Brandi Doane McCann

DEDICATION

For my mother, who, at age 18 (1951), was told by her parents they wouldn't support her dreams of college because girls didn't go to college.

She went anyway.

She earned a basketball scholarship, worked in the cafeteria to pay her own way, and graduated in three years instead of four. She did the hard work to change the culture around her—something we take too much for granted—and encouraged all three of her daughters to pursue advanced degrees.

Thanks, Mom. I miss you.

ONE

July 14, 1948
Capitan Mountains, Southeastern New Mexico, U.S.A.

A violent spark pierced the bright blue sky, tearing through the stillness and leaving ripples in its wake, like a stone disturbing the surface of a pond. Francie Cortez wrapped a hand around Orion's reins as the palomino shied, dust from the tree-lined trail rising beneath his hooves. "Whoa. Steady, boy."

The spark was heading straight for her father's ranch.

No. Not her father's anymore. Not since he ... She brushed aside the pang that came with remembering.

It was her Capitan Mountain ranch now.

Francie shaded her eyes with her free hand and tracked the object's descent—a brilliant lavender teardrop against the cloudless morning. It couldn't have come from White Sands Proving

Ground. The base and its testing range lay due west, and this rocket came from, well, directly above her. No contrail, no fuel burn or water vapor emission. Nothing she'd expect if another V2 rocket had gone off course. The object flashed again, unnaturally bright. A meteorite?

She calculated, relying on the memorized equations drilled into her by her father: *Velocity squared, v^2, equals initial velocity squared, u^2, plus twice gravity, $2(g)$, times height, h.* A meteor's acceleration would align with free fall.

But something about its trajectory felt deliberate. She'd almost swear it was aimed.

A bomb? Adrenaline shot through her. Her muscles tensed, hands gripping leather reins to turn Orion, to gallop away, escape the blast radius. But if it was like Trinity or Hiroshima …

Running would be no use.

Logically, whatever was falling onto her ranch couldn't be that kind of horror. When Trinity came, soldiers in trucks and jeeps rushed to homesteads with orders to clear out ranchers and their families. Food sat cooling on tables, clothes stayed tucked away in drawers and closets, no time to pack or say goodbye. They were evicted from their homes overnight.

Francie fixed her gaze on the object's path as it streaked toward the thickly wooded ridge above her. If her calculations were right, it would crash behind the row of tall pines lining the cliff—straight into the heart of her Capitan Mountain land.

This had to be military. A test gone wrong, an experimental rocket jolted off course. Maybe that was the new tactic. Let the hardware fall, then use the fallout as an excuse to claim whatever lay beneath it.

Even with the war over, the testing went on. Missiles and rockets took possession of the sky above desert plains and mountains, turning the land beneath their flight paths into off-limits danger zones. The people who lived there were forced off their land with little recompense and no recourse, their acreage swallowed up by White Sands. The military even blasted the freshwater springs, cutting off the only reliable water sources for families and livestock.

They'd already taken so much. Was her ranch—her refuge—next?

This ranch was home, where she'd been born and raised, where she'd retreated after everything fell apart. It was all she had left. If they took this, too ... Francie pushed the thought aside, but Orion shifted beneath her, sensing her disquiet. She patted his neck.

The bright object sped closer, flickering violet light jumping erratically along its path. It flared above the ridge and vanished beyond the trees. "Three ... two ... one—" Francie tensed for impact, ready to whirl Orion away.

And ... silence.

Nothing. No explosion. No fire. Only a slow, shuddering hush, as if every creature on the mountain had ducked for cover, settling into a silence too deep for the morning. Eyes on the ridge, Francie backed Orion into a copse of aspen, their leaves tremulous in the chilly morning breeze. Sunlight dappled around her in shifting circles of light and shade, and she shivered with an odd prickling anticipation, waiting.

Seconds passed, then minutes.

Orion dropped his head to graze, his jaw working steadily. Francie's grip on the reins loosened, her brows knitting in confusion. How was it possible that nothing—

A static burst hit her, quick and electric. It tuned her senses to the silence. Vibrations throbbed through her chest, expanding outward before rushing away in all directions. Then the whole ridge answered, echoing the hum in her bones. A hollow dog's bark broke the hush, thin and eerie from the ridge above. Her mind latched onto the sound, anything to wrench back control of herself.

Except she didn't own a dog.

The vibrations faded as quickly as they'd come, and the deep stillness broke, sound slipping back in. First the wind, stirring whispers through the pines, then the tentative warble of birdsong, then Orion's nervous snort, reassuring and real. Her shoulders loosened, and she filled her lungs with cool morning air ... and froze.

Movement on the ridge flickered at the edge of her vision. Slow, wary, Francie turned her head toward the top of the rise, eyes narrowing.

Purple sparks exploded soundlessly overhead, scattering like startled fireflies. Orion reared back, eyes rolling white. Francie's knees locked against the saddle, dread coiling in her chest.

Above, one of the tallest ridge pines shuddered before it groaned and toppled. The ground rumbled as it spun down the cliff, an explosion of cracking limbs and shattering rocks, spraying skeins of dirt into the gully below.

When the noise settled, she couldn't breathe. At the gap in the tree line, a figure stood silhouetted against the blue sky, swathed head to toe in a white, inflated suit. Its helmet was round and solid, visor blank and black—a window she couldn't see through. Nothing like the clear fish-bowl head covers on the spacemen from her father's *Amazing Stories* magazines.

Orion sidled left, nostrils flaring. Francie steadied him, her free hand brushing the rifle sheathed at her leg. The figure's black faceplate jerked back and forth, as if searching, before turning away and bounding beyond the ridgeline, out of sight.

Had he seen her? She didn't think so. She watched the gap in the trees, body taut. But he—or it—was gone.

She'd seen some strange things at Los Alamos, but nothing like this. Who was he? A test pilot who'd somehow ridden that purple light to the ground? There had been no parachute. Only that rumble, those sparks. No way to land safely.

Another troubling explanation crept into her head.

It was ridiculous. And yet ...

Just a year ago, the papers were trumpeting nonsense about

flying saucers on the plains west of Roswell, only to backtrack and claim it was a weather balloon. But it was too late. The first story had caught fire, and within days, the country had been infected with "flying disk fever."

But what if that first story was real—not a balloon, but something else? What if the military, the government, had lied and were hiding something not of this Earth?

Her instincts screamed at her to turn back, run for home and get help. But there was no one else. Since she'd come back to the ranch after her father's disappearance, there'd been nothing but silence for company. She was truly alone.

Unless she drove to Roswell for help. She could report what she'd seen, though she'd have nothing but her story, no evidence to give them. And without proof, who would believe her?

She bit her lip, gaze focused on the cut between the trees above. Her heart beat a rapid tattoo. Orion shifted, ears perked forward.

Proof could be waiting up there. On that ridge. On her land.

Francie squared her shoulders and kicked Orion into motion, guiding him toward the trail that led upward to whatever had fallen from the sky and trespassed on her ranch. Her hand reached for her rifle again.

If there was trouble—government, alien, or otherwise—she wouldn't let them take a single inch of her land without a fight.

Two

July 14, 1948
Roswell, New Mexico

Francie cut the truck's engine. Its soft metallic tick faded into the whine of cicadas swelling in the Roswell summer heat. The butter-yellow house shimmered in late-morning light, gingerbread trim casting delicate shadows over the porch steps.

She pried her hands from the wheel, realizing, with a pang, they shook. Enough. She brushed a gloved finger across her lashes, cleared away the start of tears, and unlatched the door.

Extending a stockinged leg, she grimaced at the sight of her shoes, ones she'd purchased in Albuquerque two years earlier—alligator-grained leather, serious but laced with a bow. She'd worried about that bow and that whoever she spoke to would dismiss her as just one more shallow girl, like they had in college.

She couldn't ignore what she'd seen that morning—not when it could change everything she understood about the world. Yet her doubt had grown during the precipitous drive from the mountainside ranch to the city of Roswell. Reporting it meant endangering the ranch, risking her home. The ranch was her anchor—the one constant in a life where even physics, once her trusted language for explaining the world, had failed her. In the rearview mirror, the Capitan Mountains loomed behind her. Anchors, she reminded herself, could drag you down, too.

She was caught between keeping silent and doing what was right.

If anyone could help her make sense of what she'd witnessed, it was Dr. Baer. In college, respected men like him dismissed her. Dr. Baer never had. He would listen, and he would help her.

Francie stepped off the running board into the street, but paused at the curb, drawing a slow breath to steady her nerves before she hurried around the truck, her gaze fixed on the house ahead rather than the crunch of gravel and the sidewalk's uneven rise.

The two-story Victorian housed the man who'd been her mentor, Dr. Eitan Baer, now retired and living a quiet life with his wife, Adelaide. Francie had once aspired to emulate his career as a physicist. Because of his guidance, she'd believed, body and soul, that she'd taken the right path.

Except she hadn't been strong enough. She'd let him down. And herself.

Regret and what-ifs dropped her focus to her shoes as they clicked down the leaf-littered concrete walk that split Dr. Baer's yard. Her skirts snagged on the ragged box hedge that lined the path. She lifted her head. Her pace slowed. Dr. Baer was an enthusiastic gardener, keeping his yard manicured to within an inch of its life, but now the hedges sagged, tufts poking past their cement border.

As Francie negotiated the stairs leading to the veranda, her frown deepened. The day sparkled around her—sunny, bright, and warm—yet curtains were drawn over every window in the house, their dusty panes reflecting distorted images of towering trees bordering the property.

Something wasn't right.

She paused on the veranda steps and swept her gaze over the rocking chairs and porch swing. The flower-printed fabric cushions were gone, and dirt filmed the tops of scattered tables. The Baers loved to sit outside in the evening, and when Francie had been in town, she'd sat and chatted and enjoyed lemonade and cookies. Guilt tinged with a touch of bitterness needled her. She hadn't darkened this doorstep since fleeing school, and then to pour out the heartache of her broken engagement.

*When two affianced people, i^2, break one (1) engagement, it becomes negative (–1), $i^2 = -1$. And the square root of negative one is the imaginary number, i—*as in Francie, whose present existence and importance felt equally debatable.

Her lips thinned. *Cut the sentimental nonsense and stop feeling sorry for yourself.* She lifted a hand and knocked.

The ornate front door, a fan of stained glass set above it in a colorful arch, opened. Dr. Baer slipped through, negotiating his arm into the sleeve of a black summer-wool suit jacket, his thick white hair mussed as if he'd awakened from napping in one of the two matching wingback chairs in the parlor. He squinted at her, his brow furrowing, before his wonderful smile blossomed.

"Francie, my dear! So unexpected, yet so welcome." His faint German accent brought each syllable to a crisp finish.

The world seemed to lighten around her. Her shoulders unknotted, and she dashed up the last step to be enveloped in a hug. *He'll make everything all right.* She pressed her nose into the shoulder of his jacket, inhaling the scent of menthol and root beer. The man was addicted to horehound candy.

Almost without thinking, she reached into his shirt pocket, tugged out his spectacles, and unfolded the thin wire arms.

"Always forgetting," she said, gently chiding. She rested them on his nose.

"At least they weren't on top of my head this time. An anchor is what they are, pulling me down to the depths of an age I do not wish to face." He waved a hand for Francie to precede him inside, eyes twinkling behind the lenses. "You have come at the perfect moment, my dear. Willa Mae has laid a proper morning tea, and *engelsaugen*. Yes, Christmas biscuits in July, but Adelaide would have them now."

Francie's gaze slid to a pendulum wall clock, her fingers knotting in her skirt. She was losing time, the ritual of tea and cookies a barrier to her urgency.

"Dr. Baer, I need to talk to you about—"

"Francie." He waved a dismissive hand. "I am sure nothing you need to say is so urgent. Come, say hello to Adelaide."

She bit her cheek, and followed him into the parlor with its familiar scent of orange oil and faded lavender. There she found Adelaide Baer sitting in her cushioned chair, hand beckoning. A lovely tray set with a silver teapot and paper-thin china cups rested next to a plate of *engelsaugen*—Angel Eye—thumbprint cookies, their apricot jam centers glowing a delicious amber.

"The apricots," Adelaide said, as if reading Francie's mind, "are from your trees at the ranch."

Francie's smile faltered as she bent to kiss her friend's soft, powdered cheek. Taller than her husband by half a foot, Adelaide Baer had diminished. Weight loss showed on gaunt cheeks normally apple-round and pink, the color now owing to a heavier hand with powdered blush. Yet her eyes were still lit a bright cerulean blue and sparkled with life. She often reminded Francie that she didn't need spectacles because her vision was perfect.

Francie perched across the low oval table on the green velvet settee, gloved hands tugging her dress over her knees. She slid off her gloves, stuffed them in a pocket, and accepted a cup of tea— one lump of sugar—and a cookie tucked on the saucer.

She held tight to her impatience, her mind on the ridge instead of caught up in small talk and gentle gossip about townspeople while sipping her tea. She ate a second cookie, her stomach reminding her she hadn't eaten much of anything that morning because she'd been so keen to ride up to the crash site. Except there'd been no spacecraft—only ... She stared into her cooling tea as the conversation ebbed.

Dr. Baer broke the lull, eyes behind his spectacles curious. "And to what do we owe this visit, for you are dressed for success. Not in your usual dungarees and boots, charming as that is."

Francie flashed a glance at Adelaide, who seemed to understand without words.

"Ah! You need to speak to Eitan. Top secret," Adelaide said, a faint tightness creeping into her smile. Francie shifted in her seat and looked away. "I will chat to Willa Mae about dinner in the kitchen."

The Baers' housekeeper appeared at Adelaide's side as if by magic. Dr. Baer rose as well, and together they guided Adelaide to her feet and steadied her.

"Stop fussing, Eitan, and give me my cane. Go sit down." Adelaide clasped her ebony walking stick with one hand and Willa Mae's arm with the other, her smile fixed in place, her face white and strained. "Would you join us for dinner, Francie?"

"I—I can't. I need to get back to the ranch tonight."

"Your animals." Adelaide chuckled. "How is your father's odd horse? Have that skunk and the other creatures reappeared in your backyard?"

"Orion's as arrogant as ever and has added a few more tricks to his bag of *let's mess with Francie*. And I haven't caught sight of any of the other animals." Her mouth pinched around a brittle smile. "Not since my father—"

"Vanished." Adelaide's tone slashed the air, sharp and cold beneath the surface lightness, as if the word itself were a knife.

Francie blinked, the change catching her off guard. Her hands clenched, nails digging into her palms. A year ago, Adelaide's comfort had been a balm. Now, "vanished" felt like an accusation. As if her father riding into the forests above the ranch, with only Orion returning, were a magic trick. As if he'd chosen to abandon his life and daughter without a word or reason.

He would never have done that.

Francie swallowed the retort that pressed against her teeth, saying instead, "Before he ... disappeared, he told me about a beautiful red fox after I called him wanting to know more about the Brazel crash."

Adelaide perked up. "A fox. Is it still there, at your home?"

"I haven't seen it."

"I wonder ..." Adelaide studied her, something unreadable flickering in her bright eyes. Then her expression smoothed. "Let me disappear so you can have your talk."

When the door closed behind her, Francie's anger faded, replaced by a nagging sense that Adelaide's words hid something deeper.

"Dr. Baer?" Francie gestured after his wife, but he shook his head.

"I'm afraid Adelaide wishes her health to remain private for now. Know she is getting the best care available." He sat across from her and clapped his hands on his knees. "Now, Francie. How can I help you?"

She met his faded blue eyes and straightened, her equilibrium restored. Coming to him had been the right thing to do.

"I saw something." Purple sparks in the sky; the jolt that had passed through her chest spurred her on. "This morning. A—a bright light. At first, I thought it might have been a missile from White Sands, but there was no contrail. It landed behind a ridge on my ranch."

His expectant expression slipped into a frown. "You think a missile crashed on your land? Hm. Possible. Two V2 rockets have gone off course from the proving grounds. Perhaps—"

Francie shook her head, more vehemently than she meant. "No. Not a missile, not a rocket. If it were military, they'd already be swarming my ranch. What I saw was ... different. Strange. It landed, but there was no crash. No explosion, no sound. Something I can't—"

She sought words to explain what had followed—the silent vibration, the white-suited figure. All she managed was, "I rode up to the ridge to investigate."

"And what did you find?" he asked.

"At first I thought it might be something like—like they found at Roswell," she said, the words sounding foolish even to her own ears. "Or... something otherworldly."

Francie searched Dr. Baer's face for any sign of understanding. But his expression—skepticism edged with pity—left her throat uncomfortably tight, a feeling she knew too well from university and again after her engagement ended.

"*Please*," she begged. "I'm telling you the truth. What I found doesn't belong on this planet. An alien artifact, I'm sure of it. A metal spear. And when I touched it, it turned on, lit up, and ... and ..."

A hollow opened in her stomach. She couldn't say it. Couldn't tell him. If what she'd said so far sounded like something out of a dime novel, what had happened *after* she'd held the alien spear would turn him away from her completely.

But what she'd seen was *real*. And after what she'd experienced, the world was no longer the same.

Dr. Baer didn't speak, his face shuttered. His silence made the room colder.

SCHOOL OF MINES
FALL SEMESTER, NOVEMBER 19, 1946

SOCORRO, NEW MEXICO
One year, seven months, and twenty-five days ago

Francie lifted her fist and rapped three times on Professor Standley's office door, clutching her heavy textbook like a shield. She inched back into the chill hallway with its mud-colored paint, stomach quivering, and wrinkled her nose against the tang of freshly waxed linoleum, her reflection a distortion flickering in the pebbled glass beside the door. Inside, the rustling of paper stopped, followed by the creak of a desk chair and heavy approaching footsteps. She composed herself, smile set and hands firm on the spine of the book.

The door swung open, blinding sunlight streaming through the windows.

"Yes? What is it?"

Francie's smile wavered. "Professor? I'm in your nine o'clock freshman physics course, and I can't tell you how much you inspire—"

He stared, brows furrowed. "You sit in the back of my class."

Her gaze sank to the floor as her fingers fluttered over her collar, smoothing imaginary wrinkles. She inhaled, willing her hands to stop trembling. Maury had told her not to approach Standley. That it would be a mistake.

"He's a right old bastard, Francie, and I heard he doesn't like women." Then he'd leaned over the cafeteria table, his gaze shifting around the crowded room before he lowered his voice, a sly smile on his lips. "Rumor is he's a homosexual."

"That's nobody's business, Maury," she replied primly. "Besides, what does that have to do with teaching physics, anyway?"

But her cheeks had flamed with embarrassment over the word.

Maury sat back and shrugged, losing interest. "Don't say I didn't warn you."

"Young lady." Professor Standley enunciated each syllable. "What is it you need? If it's help on today's lecture, come back during office hours."

"Oh! No, sir. Sorry. I ... I want to apply for the tutor position next semester. You see—" She tugged her exams from the pages of her physics book and held them out, her diamond engagement ring catching the light.

He took the papers and frowned. "You're F. P. Cortez?"

"Yes, Professor. Based on my test scores, I'm at the top of your class." Her smile came easier, the pride of accomplishment giving her confidence. "If you'd like to check with my other professors, you'll see that my grades are top-notch. I'm having no difficulty academically."

Her arms tightened around her book. Sure, she was doing well in her coursework, but the real challenge was everywhere else on campus—the sidelong looks, the snide under-the-breath remarks, the constant reminders she was one of the few girls in the college. During the war, women had been welcomed into mining programs because the draft had drained qualified men into the military. That open door had encouraged Francie to aim for a physics degree. Now, with GIs streaming back into civilian life, everyone and everything seemed intent on driving women back into the traditional role of wife and mother—

"Hold out your hand."

Her gaze snapped up to his cold gray eyes. "Excuse me?"

"Hold out your left hand."

She hesitated, then extended her hand. He grasped her ring finger, his touch cool and firm. Heat crept up her neck.

"You're engaged. Who's your fiancé?"

"Maurice Duncan. He's a junior, returning to finish the degree he started before he was drafted. Physics, like me."

The professor sighed. "I know him. A marginal student, but he'll find work once he graduates. Unlike you."

"Unlike *me*?" Her voice caught. "But the only reason Maury's passing is because I tutor him. And he's in upper-division physics. I'm much—"

She stopped, not wanting her pride to sound like bragging.

He let her hand go, and she hid her fingers in her skirt.

"Why are you wasting my time, Miss Cortez? Your seat in my class could be filled by someone with a future in this field."

"I d-don't understand."

"Yes, you do. Your intelligence surpasses most of your

classmates—even your fiancé's. But that won't matter once you're married. Do you think your husband will allow you a career? And if he does, who'll take care of the children and the house?"

His words struck her like a blow. "You don't think I can have both a career and a family? Elizabeth Graves—she's a physicist—had a baby after Trinity. And Leona Marshall married and has a son. And—"

She stopped. Her mind went blank. She couldn't think of another example to bolster her case.

"Look, Miss Cortez, I'm not unsympathetic. But the path you've chosen is difficult, and the women you listed are rare exceptions. Believe me when I say that someday"—he met her stricken eyes, his filled with aloof impatience—"I hope conversations like this go the way of the dodo."

He handed her the exams, then stepped back into his office. "The tutor position is no longer available. Good day."

Francie stared at the closed door, her certainty fraying. A draft in the corridor slid under her collar, and the walls felt a little closer. For the first time since she'd arrived at the School of Mines, it felt as if she didn't belong here at all.

THREE

July 14, 1948
Roswell, New Mexico

Silence stretched between Francie and Dr. Baer, broken only by the ticking of the pendulum clock in the hallway. He adjusted his glasses again and leaned back in his chair as if easing away from her words.

Her fingers curled into her skirt, gathering the fabric in her lap. She forced herself to loosen her grip, then smoothed the creases with deliberate care.

"Oh, my dear." Dr. Baer shook his head, his expression shadowed with distress. He stood and shimmied around the coffee table to sit by her side on the settee, picked up one of her hands, and patted it. "I am sure your perceived discovery is but a manifestation of anxiety. Though the war is over, such disquiet remains. The world is changing so rapidly, and that bomb, oh, that bomb. *So ein Fehler.* Such a mistake."

The scientists had nicknamed it the Gadget, as if to diminish and defuse its threat. And Francie had traveled from Site Y—they'd renamed it Los Alamos Scientific Laboratory that year—to the

Trinity Site with Dr. Baer and Adelaide to be part of history, only to have her childlike excitement swept away by the apocalyptic devastation she'd witnessed.

"Every day, someone comes forward to report strange anomalies in the skies," Dr. Baer said. His smile placated, his tone almost jovial. "Flying disks over Oregon, Washington, Texas. Even last year's incident with the weather balloon, here, of all places. People see what they want to see."

Dr. Baer didn't believe her. He wasn't going to help.

A dull ache took root inside Francie—one she knew well. She kept her features composed, determined not to let the distress show, but it took her a moment to squash her disappointment and shift to the conversation's new direction.

"Do you think that what crashed on the Brazel ranch was a weather balloon?" Francie had, until that morning.

The tight lines around his eyes relaxed, and he smiled and patted her hand. She'd followed his lead to safer ground, retreating from a difficult situation—again.

"Military secrecy runs deep," he said. "The crash, I suspect, involved classified technology, and the initial extraterrestrial explanation appeared to be a deliberate deception. They corrected themselves the next day, but it added to the craze, this flying disk frenzy. I never suspected you, of all people ..."

He rubbed at his temple. "Francie, you had—*have* so much potential. So much brilliance. But these kinds of claims ... You must understand they can ruin reputations. You can not afford that."

She dropped her gaze to the rose-patterned rug beneath her shoes, tugged her hand away from his, and rested it in her lap. "Of course."

"My dear." His voice was gentle yet firm. "I know how difficult it is for someone like you—a young female pursuing physics—to be taken seriously. I've seen how hard you've worked, despite your losses. But for women who dare to challenge it, our world is unforgiving."

Our world. He meant a man's world. Awkward silence fell between them. She tried to swallow her frustration, her anger, but the sting refused to fade. She'd idolized him, had relished his role as one of her mentors. He'd stood behind her dreams ... up to the moment she buckled beneath the strain. All she ever wanted was for him to believe in her, in what she was capable of, and—

Then she remembered.

Francie sat up straighter and let the last of her hope shine. "But I have proof. The metal spear."

His eyebrows shot up. "And where is this proof?"

"I hid it. At the ranch."

His spark of interest faded. He adjusted his glasses.

"Ah. You did not bring it with you." His polite smile hurt more than outright dismissal. "My dear, you saw something that has a logical and earthly explanation. What you encountered frightened you, and you became a little ... overexcited, eh? It was nothing, I am sure. A high-flying aircraft or another weather balloon. If you had brought this ... proof."

He sighed and met her gaze. "Francie, for your own good, no more. To humor you in this story any further—"

The phone in his office off the parlor jangled, and relief flashed over his face. "Excuse me while I answer this."

Francie stared after him, breath burning in her chest, as Dr. Baer hurried away and closed the office door behind him.

If a man she'd trusted and revered didn't believe her, would the military even listen? She'd be just another "hysterical female" chasing flying saucer headlines and notoriety, especially after last year's Roswell mess. She could see it. A room full of men in uniform, ribbons and shiny medals of valor from their war service pinned to their chests as they smirked and dismissed her as over-wrought—or worse, a liar.

But if they did believe her, her life might become much worse. If they came out to investigate, and she showed them the artifact, they wouldn't stop at the ridge. They might decide her land was too valuable to leave in civilian hands. She'd wanted to do the right thing, had weighed the possible consequences, even told herself she could defend her ranch alone, but she hadn't been strong enough to challenge Dr. Baer. The military would bulldoze her because the artifact she'd found was *real*. She'd felt its unnatural weight, the strange pulse when she touched it. Her palm tingled, and she rubbed at the sensation. Whatever it was, it didn't belong here. But leave it alone, and trouble would come looking—for the artifact and for her.

Second thoughts about her decision to report the crash piled high in her mind. There had to be a middle ground between Dr. Baer and the Army base commanders—someone who would take her seriously without taking everything. Her jaw tightened. She needed someone to investigate, but how could she convince them without risking the ranch? She'd have to choose her next step with care. One wrong move, and her refuge would be gone for good.

The kitchen door swung open behind Francie, and Willa Mae poked out her head.

"Miss Francie? Miz Doctor Baer wishes to speak to you." Willa Mae swung the door wide, and Francie passed by her into the bright blue-and-white kitchen, the lingering scent of baked cookies teasing her nose.

Adelaide sat at the scrubbed wooden table, a cutting board in front of her, orange carrot slices piled next to cut celery. She laid down a rather wicked-looking knife and beckoned. "Sit with me for a minute."

Francie pulled out a white wooden chair and sat. Adelaide nodded to the carrot slices, and Francie picked one up and crunched into it.

"As well as my superior eyesight," Adelaide said, "I have extraordinarily good hearing, which makes eavesdropping on your conversation with Eitan child's play."

Francie managed a smile. "Then you know he doesn't believe me."

"Of course not! Like most men, he is easy to read, and your story is too strange, too illogical for him to accept. He thinks this rash of flying saucer sightings is nothing but mass hysteria. Fear and anxiety over the shifting power after that awful war. I, however, believe there is more beneath the surface."

Adelaide's voice softened, but every word was edged with steel. "He is afraid for you. Like your father, he wants to shield you from this world. The bomb's development and deployment shook him to his core. I had to stop him from signing the Szilárd petition by sheer force of will. Such short-sighted *fools*. How do they not understand that weapon allowed us a future?"

The last was hissed, bitterness tainting every syllable. Francie's breath hitched as Adelaide lifted her head and smiled, the darkness in her features clearing. "They don't realize how lucky they are that I was there. Poor Eitan does not know it, but I wear the pants in this relationship. Without me, he will be lost."

Francie returned Adelaide's smile, careful to hide the shiver behind it. Adelaide had always been a hard woman, forged in situations Francie could only imagine.

She needed that same steel. Francie hadn't known such armor was necessary when she'd entered her degree, but had learned quickly that her smallest steps at boldness were too often met with cold dismissal. Adelaide's toughness wasn't just temperament. It was a shield against a world that kept women at home and in the shadows.

If she ever found the courage to leave the ranch and try again, she'd be stepping back into the same hard world that had driven her out. School, the ranch, all of it would demand more stubbornness and grit than she'd ever had before.

Doubt pricked her. She'd already run once.

Adelaide lifted her brows. "Since Eitan will not help you, I will. I want you to report what you saw to the military."

Francie focused on her tightly clasped hands. "If Dr. Baer doesn't believe me, then the military won't either. They'll laugh at me."

Just like her classmates had when Dr. Standley tore apart her equations or cut off her arguments—and Maury had sat silent, offering no support at all.

Her thumb brushed the bare skin at the base of her ring finger, and she blinked back the sting behind her eyes. So much for gathering up her armor. She'd never be able to stand up to—

"*Francie*. Stop *wallowing* and listen," Adelaide hissed, then muttered, "My God, you are so like your father."

Francie jerked upright, her eyes snagging on the blaze of annoyance banked in the sharp blue of Adelaide's gaze. Yet Adelaide's smile followed a moment later, practiced and brittle, as if she were trying to smooth away her impatience.

"It's been over a year, dear. You need to move on, or you will miss your chance at life. At a future. Yes, you will take your observations to the military, but not to Colonel Blanchard or Major Marcel at the base. They will dismiss you outright. Or worse, use it as an excuse to confiscate your land under the guise of national security."

Adelaide's words landed like a punch, and Francie drew back. "I know. But I don't—I can't—"

"Listen to me!" Her friend closed her eyes, jaw working, then breathed deep before lowering her voice as if sharing a secret. "You must speak to Sergeant Mitchell Ward instead. He works at the recruiting office downtown, but he is here because of the flying disk crash last year."

"But it wasn't—"

"Yes, yes, but he will know what to do. He will help you, act as a liaison, a shield between you and the Army. That is what you want, is it not?"

Francie stared, unsettled. Although hard, Adelaide had been a voice of comfort, someone who replaced the mother she'd lost so early in life. Now there was something urgent—almost desperate—beneath her words, and Francie couldn't shake the sense that her friend's advice was about more than helping her.

Still, she couldn't ignore what she'd seen, nor could she risk the ranch. And she did need help. Dr. Baer had dismissed her, like Professor Standley, like Maury. But Adelaide believed her without hesitation. Resentment against the men in her life, gratitude for this woman, bubbled up in her chest.

Holding her gaze, Adelaide's hand settled over hers, warm and deliberate.

"Trust me, Francie. Find Mitchell Ward."

Four

Francie set off for downtown Roswell and the Army Air Corps recruiting office. Its glass-paneled door sat neatly in the angled corner where two sidewalks met, catching foot traffic from both streets. She tried the knob, but it was locked tight.

"Well, well. Francie Cortez. Long time no see." Marsha Hellerman strolled down the sidewalk, wearing ridiculously high heels and a skirt as tight as the smirk on her face.

"I need to speak to Sergeant Ward."

"Me, too. Thinking of enlisting?" Marsha snickered at her own joke as she sashayed past Francie and around the corner. "He might be at the shoe store getting new wingtips."

She gestured down the street but didn't deviate from her strut, wobbling through a pirouette at the end of the block to meander back.

Francie frowned. "You're waiting for him? Is he your beau or something?"

"Not yet." Marsha's mouth curved into a slow smile. "Some fellows just need a little extra ... encouragement."

"What's that supposed to mean?"

Marsha side-eyed Francie as she passed her again. "Let's just say I'm not blowing my chance at a life outta this ratty town like *you* did."

Francie gasped, wide-eyed, and sputtered, "I-I did *not*—"

"Yes, you did." Marsha rolled her eyes. "You don't get it. I look at my future and see a dead-end job until I get married and have a half dozen kids, and, if I'm lucky, an overnight trip to Albuquerque and dinner at the Harvey House as the highlight of my year. If this guy's my ticket out, then I'll do whatever it takes." This time, Marsha's turn was much smoother, and her triumphant smile held smug satisfaction.

"You'd compromise your reputation for—"

"Whatever it takes. And stop being such a prude, Francie. He's single, I'm single. Just because *you* wouldn't—" She stared straight ahead. "We all know why Maury broke off your engagement. Now you're stuck here. *I'm* not going to end up like you."

The words hit like a slap, and in the quiet that followed, Francie wilted inside. It was a different lie than the one her ex had told his buddies at college, but just as self-serving. Maybe Marsha was right. Maybe she was stuck. But she couldn't let herself believe it—not yet. She was doing something, at least, trying to make sense of what had happened on her land instead of pretending nothing had changed. Marsha was scheming for a way out. Francie would fight to hold on to what she had left.

She clasped her hands together and sighed, a thin thread of envy curling through her words. "Don't sell yourself short, Marsha."

Marsha's sneer faltered. She slid her eyes away before resuming her walk.

Francie spun on her heel and hurried toward the shoe store, but Sergeant Ward wasn't there, either.

Mrs. Peters, the septuagenarian clerk, told Francie the sergeant had left about fifteen minutes ago. She tittered something about wishing she were ten years younger and unmarried because men like Mitchell Ward came along once in a lifetime.

"So charming and handsome! Very much like your fiancé—Oh!" Mrs. Peters's fingers covered her mouth, and her wide-eyed gaze fell to Francie's gloved left hand.

Francie forced a polite smile. "Do you know where he went after he left?"

Mrs. Peters directed her to the garage down the street. *Dear* Sergeant Ward loved to tinker with engines.

Spine ramrod straight, Francie strode to Fred's Garage. She was fast losing patience with the simpering smiles and gooey-sweet voices that seemed to come over every woman in Roswell at the mention of *dear* Sergeant Ward.

But the men at the repair shop weren't much better. Hearty chortles and back-slapping about how Mitch was the best man with a carburetor they'd ever seen and could change a tire faster than pit crews at Indy, and was probably at the Woolworth's diner counter because he ate pretty early in case men on lunch break came to his office to be recruited.

"Hell of a guy. A lot like your Maur—" The name appeared to clog Everett Beadle's throat. He exchanged a panicked glance with the other men, who all looked anywhere except at Francie. "'Scuse my language, Miss Francie. My wife would skin me alive for talking that way around a nice girl like you."

Francie, face burning again, thanked them, turned, and strode out of the silent garage, shoulders squared and head high, the rhythmic tap of her heels on cement keeping pace with her heart.

It had been over a year since she'd pulled off her engagement ring and left it on the cafeteria table at college. Maury was a charming cheat and liar who'd controlled the story surrounding their breakup to make himself the victim. If Sergeant Ward was anything like her ex, he'd be the kind of man who smiled too easily and thought the world would excuse him because he looked the part.

Well, if that's what she found waiting, no way would she be caught off guard again.

She was here to speak to Mitchell Ward about something astonishing, something that could change the future—for her, and maybe more than her. And she'd make certain what mattered—her ranch and her future—stayed in her own hands, under her control.

Francie shoved open the door of the F. W. Woolworth's, the string of bells above her jangling discordantly. Back-to-school sundries packed the shelves—Ticonderoga #2 yellow pencils, Pink Pearl erasers, Crayola crayons, Big Chief tablets—and the air was redolent with something savory mixed with apple pie spice. She laid a hand over her stomach in a vain attempt to suppress embarrassing growls of hunger and negotiated the maze of product racks with resolution until she popped out at the luncheonette with its chrome finishings and red vinyl stools. One man sat at the counter, his profile to her.

All the information she'd gleaned from the townspeople coalesced under her disapproving glare. Sergeant Mitchell Ward wore a crisp tan shirt that stretched over broad shoulders, its trim waist tucked into belted, razor-creased olive wool slacks whose cuffs topped spit-polished patent leather lace-ups. A matching wool jacket hung with precision on the chair next to him, a detail that spoke of a man who valued his appearance. Overhead light picked out the sheen in his black hair, a wave combed to one side and held fast with the liberal application of pomade.

He leaned over the counter, head tilted, lips curved into a teasing half-smile as he chatted up Barbara Jane Stevens, the café's waitress, whose too-long fake lashes batted so fast there should have been a breeze.

And Barbara Jane should know better. She was just married in May, and here she was flirting outrageously with Sergeant Ward.

He swung his stool to follow her journey along the counter, giving her the kind of once-over that ought to have left fingerprints—and wasn't Barbara Jane loving it? This man was a regular wolf, plain as day, and no one seemed to care. Unless he hid it from the townspeople, who spoke of him like he'd hung the moon. Francie gritted her teeth. When they'd compared Sergeant Mitchell Ward to Maury, it was truer than they realized.

A bell rang in the kitchen, and the cook, Louis White, called out the order and clinked the Buffalo China dish on the metal-lined pass-through. Barbara Jane simpered and batted her lashes some more before she turned to grab the plate brimming with steaming meat loaf, boiled spinach, and mashed potatoes with cream gravy. She slid it in front of the sergeant.

That's when Barbara Jane spotted Francie. She flushed bright red before she hurried to the pie carousel and pulled out a slice of chocolate piled high with cream swirls. Barbara Jane's downcast eyes and furtive glances behind him snapped Sergeant Ward's back straight. He spun on his stool, his gaze colliding with Francie's. A fleck of gold in his green eyes caught the light, and her cheeks warmed despite herself. His smile faltered, then gentled into something softer—almost wonder. His brows arched in a silent question as he studied her face, taking in every detail. Francie's breath hitched.

Oh, that smile.

Heat prickled across her skin, sudden and unnerving. For an instant, the light around him seemed to shimmer, as if the air stilled in anticipation.

Oh, no. Absolutely not.

She felt the tug and wanted no part of it, irritated as much with herself as with him. Francie pressed her lips together, willing her feet to stay planted, to not drift closer. She refused to be drawn to this ... this—

His expression changed. Francie's unwanted curl of attraction skidded into a chill wariness.

The smile remained, but his eyes cooled to an appraising focus. A flicker of unease shivered up Francie's back. The spaceman on the ridge flashed in her mind—the fear, the sense of trespass.

But she'd overcome the need to flee and faced down that unknown. She wouldn't let this Mitchell Ward chase her off, either.

By the time she'd lifted her chin in defiance, a genial, curious expression had replaced his cold regard. Doubt assailed her as she met his gaze. Her disquiet a moment earlier must have been an illusion.

But his Hollywood movie-star face was no trick.

"Hello." He tipped his head, one corner of his mouth quirking. "Have we met before?"

His deep, resonant voice drew her to him like iron to a lodestone. Her feet betrayed her, closing the gap until Francie stopped scant inches away. Her gloved hands clutched each other at her waist, resisting the urge to brush back a lock of hair fallen from his too-long pompadour to curl against his wide brow. But that thought dissolved under the intensity of his green eyes—startling, lake-deep, impossible to look away from.

There was something in the way he tilted his head—an echo of a memory she couldn't quite place, as if they'd stood like this before. He felt familiar down to her bones.

Barbara Jane slammed the slice of chocolate cream pie onto the counter beside him, shaking Francie from her reverie. Frustration simmered. Anger at Dr. Baer, at Maury, at herself for being so easily rattled.

His smirk reminded her of another man who'd once held her gaze—before letting her fall. That was the reason he felt so familiar. The only reason.

A flashy smile and handsome face wouldn't make a fool of her this time.

"Sergeant Ward? I've been looking for you all over town." His smirk deepened. "I—I mean, I need you—"

His eyebrows raised. "You *need* me?"

"Yes. *No*. Not in *that* way."

"What way?"

She scowled, cheeks burning. "I need to *speak* to you about—"

She shot a glance at Barbara Jane, who wiped the countertop in slow circles, ears perked and eavesdropping.

"Can we go somewhere private? Alone. The two of us." Francie winced. That didn't come out right at all. She scrambled to regain her composure.

Barbara Jane paused, eyes sly. "Why, Francie Cortez! Are you that desperate since Maury Duncan jilted you?"

Francie, tired of the lies, snapped, "That is not true, Barbara Jane. *I* broke off the engagement."

Barbara Jane's eyebrows rose. Francie clenched her fists. She'd just handed the gossips more to chew on.

"At least I now know the name of the woman who needs me." Mitchell Ward grinned, mischief dancing in his eyes.

Francie's gaze flew to his, and the roiling turmoil inside her quieted. *Woman.* He'd called her a woman. Not a girl.

His teasing gaze never left her face as he lounged on the stool, relaxed and stupidly, ridiculously handsome and charming. He settled his broad back against the counter and spread his elbows to rest on either side behind him—

To sink one right into the chocolate cream pie.

With a muffled curse, he yanked his arm away but hit the side of the pie dish. The dish flipped end over end, sailing over his shoulder to land cream-first in his pristine olive drab–encased lap. He jumped to his feet. The pie slid, the plate crashed, shards clattering as chocolate spattered his spit-shined shoes. Dancing away from the mess, he swiped at his trousers, sending a hefty dollop from the cream still clinging to his elbow arcing into the air. It plopped onto the wave of his pompadour and began a leisurely slide down his forehead. He grabbed for it—too late. His goo-smeared fingers only dragged chocolate-and-cream stripes across his right eye, brow to lashes.

Francie released an unladylike snort, eyes widening at the sound as she covered her mouth with her hand. But it didn't stem her laughter. She dissolved into giggles, shoulders shaking. Sergeant Mitchell Ward had finally stopped moving, perhaps realizing that anything he did coated him further in pie. A deep red flush crept up his neck.

Barbara Jane stood behind the counter, mouth agape, blinking, the damp rag dangling from limp fingers.

A strange boldness swept through Francie, spurring her forward. Perhaps it was a reaction to his mocking confidence, which still hung between them like a challenge, or the sense that, splattered as he was, they now stood on equal footing—woman to man. Whatever the cause, a reckless courage settled over her, clinging to her like the chocolate cream now plastered to Sergeant Mitchell Ward from head to toe. The sweet, heavy scent of pie mingled with her rising audacity.

She strode to the counter, snorts slipping out despite her best effort. Tugging off her glove, she plucked the rag from Barbara Jane and tiptoed through the worst of the mess to stand before the sergeant, her mouth curving into a smirk that matched his own from moments earlier.

"You have some chocolate right"—she dabbed his forehead with the cloth, fingers tucking that lock of hair back into his pompadour—"here."

His gaze blazed with mortification, the green of his eyes deep as a shadowed pond.

"Oh, yeah? What about"—he thrust out his goo-coated elbow —"here."

Francie tore her eyes away from his and surveyed his elbow with mock consideration before blotting away the cream. When she finished, she raised the rag and, thrilled by her boldness, said, "Anything else?"

He pointed a rigid finger at his chocolate-smeared eye.

She inched nearer, turning the rag to find a clean spot. In her heels, she was nearly eye to eye with him, his mouth right above hers. She dabbed away the pie from his eye. He blinked and swallowed, the movement of his throat pulling her gaze.

"Here," he murmured, pointing to his lips. "But you need to come ... closer."

Her pulse skittered. Indeed, a perfect drop of chocolate, placed like a Hollywood beauty mark, sat above the corner of his upper lip. It looked ... delicious. She caught herself leaning—then remembered the kind of man she suspected him to be.

"No?" His thumb swept the drop away, and he slipped it past his lips.

Time hung still. Was it possible to swoon over a chocolate smudge?

"So. Miss Cortez." Mitchell Ward's gaze lingered. "Why do you ... need me?"

Barbara Jane's gasp jarred Francie out of her dream state. Her face burned. He'd done it on purpose, this seductive show. Turned her hostility into dewy-eyed quiescence. And in front of an audience, because not only was Barbara Jane looking on, her mouth open like a landed trout, but the cook peered through the pass-through, grinning as if his team won the big game.

Francie met Sergeant Ward's smile with one of her own and sidled closer. Her hand, still clutching the sticky-sweet rag, held on to his shoulder. She lifted her face to his, tilted her head to the side, her lips close to his ear. He turned to follow, and Francie shivered at the gentle heat grazing her cheek.

"I heard you're in charge of alien landings," she whispered. "I had one on my ranch this morning. And I have proof."

His sudden intake of air made her mouth twitch in fleeting triumph. She drew back to savor his reaction, but her smile vanished when she locked eyes with him.

His icy glare chilled her to the core. Francie held his gaze.

The spark between them shifted—no longer just attraction, but a contest of wills. For a moment, the diner faded away, leaving the two of them in the charged air between disbelief and possibility.

He leaned in, lowering his voice so only she could hear. "You know what, sister? I don't believe you."

He grabbed his jacket and marched toward the exit. Francie stood, mouth agape, until the discordant jangle of bells jolted her out of her frozen disbelief. Her heart kicked hard.

"Oh, no. I refuse to be dismissed like I'm a—a lying *child* again." She ground out the words and darted after Sergeant Mitchell Ward.

FIVE

"Sergeant! *Sergeant Ward!*"

Francie chased the man down the bustling sidewalks, dodging lunchtime pedestrians, trying to match his long strides, but was forced into an unladylike skip now and then to keep up. As he passed the bank, she caught up and grabbed his arm, only to let go when he stopped and, scowling, swiveling to face her.

"Stop following me, Miss Cortez."

She backpedaled a few steps, blurting out, "I won't. You need to listen to me. I saw a strange purple light in the sky, and—"

"There's always some strange light in the sky from the air base or White Sands." He turned and strode away from her down the sidewalk, tossing over his shoulder, "What makes your light so special?"

Francie hurried after him. "Because my light has a space—"

"*Shush*," he hissed, and slowed at the next corner, raising a hand to signal for her to stop. He gave her a side-eye and pressed a finger to his lips. Francie frowned but nodded and stilled as he crept toward the edge of the building and peeked around it.

Unable to resist, she shimmied closer until she hung over his shoulder.

The tap-tap of high heels ricocheted down the street as Marsha Hellerman, her hips swaying with deliberate precision, patrolled her self-assigned beat. The woman still lay in wait.

Sergeant Ward turned his head toward Francie and mouthed, "Go home." Before she could respond, he darted to the door, the heels of his shoes muffled by the large rubber welcome mat outside the entrance to the recruiting office.

He kept one eye on Marsha's retreating figure as he pulled out his key. Francie held her breath as footsteps slowed near the pivot point at the end of the block. The lock turned with a faint snick. He slipped inside and—*now or never*—Francie dashed, heart thumping, for the closing door, slid in beside him, and locked the door behind her.

Sergeant Ward grabbed her wrist, the scowl back on his face. "Miss Cortez—"

"*Shhh.* She'll hear you," Francie whispered.

They stood motionless in the dim light striped by shuttered venetian blinds. When Marsha's steps again faded into the distance, Francie's shoulders eased.

Without a word, the sergeant released Francie and disappeared behind a door at the back of the small, sparsely appointed front room. Her wrist tingled where he'd gripped it. She rubbed it, the impulse to retreat tugging hard, before pressing her palms against her forehead and closing her eyes.

Had she done the right thing?

And yet, she couldn't believe she'd *imposed* herself on this man, gathered her courage, and made sure she wouldn't be rejected again. She forced herself to relax, studying her surroundings for insights into Mitch's—she set her teeth—*Sergeant Ward's* personality.

A large scarred wooden desk faced three chairs arranged in a cozy semicircle. Francie's fingers brushed the chair closest to a box of tissues on the desk's corner. For the mothers, when they came with treasured sons to sign enlistment papers. She lifted the lid on a cylindrical candy tin half full of lemon drops. For fathers, their throats tight as their boys committed to a calling from which they might never return.

Her gloved finger traced the desktop then a venetian blind slat. No dust. Paperwork, blotter, inbox—all squared with military precision. She'd already seen the Don Juan behind those ruthless eyes. Yet ... the room spoke of strictness and compassion.

The door behind her opened, and Mitchell Ward reappeared in olive drab summer fatigues, his trousers belted around his lean waist and tucked into black lace-up combat boots. He looked every inch the soldier now, alert and ready for trouble.

The man before her was a study of contradictions. A flirt and a warrior. A winsome smile under cold, hard eyes. Charm mixed with lethality. A chill of anticipation ran up her spine.

"Would you like to hear what happened before we go?" Francie pulled out a chair to sit down.

He didn't sit. But he did scowl. "Go where?"

"To my ranch so you can see, um, assess. Help me get rid of whatever landed."

Mitch raised his brows. "I'm not going out there with you."

She clutched the chair back to stop herself from swaying in shock. "But you haven't even heard my story."

"Do you know how many people come to me with their *stories*, Miss Cortez? Little green men." Eyes mockingly wide, he waved his hands in the air. "Flying saucers over El Paso. Strange sounds behind the shed. I've got enough on my plate without chasing after your light in the sky."

He glanced at his watch and sighed. "I've got paperwork to do. I'm sorry I can't help."

Francie gripped the chair, her nails digging into the wood. She'd promised Adelaide she'd try, and she'd seen sparks of real competence behind Mitchell Ward's charm—the calm scan of the street, the meticulous office, eyes that missed nothing.

She wasn't about to let him write her off with a shrug.

She squared her shoulders and marched to the front door. "If you won't help, I bet Marsha knows someone who will." Francie's fingers hovered over the doorknob, her meaning unmistakable.

A muscle jumped in Mitch's cheek. But before he could answer, heavy footsteps pounded on the stoop, and the door handle rattled. Francie yanked her hand away and stepped back.

Marsha bleated, "No, Daddy, no," and a gruff voice boomed through the windows: "Ward. Open this door."

So, this was Marsha's plan all along. Well, maybe Francie could use it as a little extra encouragement, too.

"That's Mr. Hellerman, and he's got quite a temper." She rested her hand on the lock. "What's it going to be, Sergeant? Help me ... or should I let him in so you can meet your future father-in-law?"

The pounding grew louder. His eyes narrowed, just a fraction. "We'll leave out the back. Follow me."

He ushered her through an inner door and into a room that resembled a barrack. Like the front office, everything was neat and clean—except for the uniform smeared with chocolate pie hanging on a coat rack. The sergeant's eyes darted back to the shaking door as Mr. Hellerman's shouts echoed behind them. He strode to a metal cabinet, pulled out a belt with a holstered sidearm, and buckled it around his waist. He placed a firm hand on Francie's elbow and practically shoved her to the exit before grabbing a backpack from the floor.

As they hurried down the alley, he met her gaze, jaw muscles bunched.

"You won this round, Miss Cortez. Where's your car?"

"Truck. Parked down the street."

His hand stayed clamped to her arm. "Don't think I buy your story. I just don't want to borrow trouble from Hellerman today."

"You can thank me later. I'll take a slice of pie." Her legs still felt shaky—from the close call, and from the dangerous thrill of holding her ground. "Why is Marsha pursuing you?"

"I let her into the office a couple of times out of politeness. I didn't realize she'd decided I was her ticket out of Roswell, or that she'd recruit her father to push it." They stepped out onto the main street. "Which way?"

Francie pointed down the street. "That's a horrible thing to say."

He marched her down the sidewalk. "Right now, marriage is about the only respectable future anyone will admit women to, with soldiers taking their jobs back. Besides, it sounded like you were diving headfirst into the matrimonial pool yourself at one point. Which truck?"

"The green one across from Binn's Mercantile. Women can do other things, you know. Like attend university. And my engagement is none of your business. I'll ask that you not mention it again."

At the truck, Mitch scanned the street, muttered, "Let's get this over with," and climbed in, dropping his pack to the floor.

Francie gripped the wheel, trying not to show her relief—or her nerves—and started the engine. She'd gotten what she wanted, but the cost of his reluctant help was written all over his face. This wasn't trust. It was necessity. And it could unravel at any moment.

The truck rumbled out of town, the silence between them thick.

She cut Mitch a sharp glance. "You'll see," she said, more to herself than to him. "You have to."

Francie drove up the two-lane highway out of the Pecos Valley, foot heavy on the gas, waiting for him to start his questioning. But he said nothing. Not even polite conversation about the beauty of the rolling hills, the deep green of the rugged Capitan Mountains, or the heat of midday. Past the small town of Arabela, she turned right and continued into the mountains. The pavement ended, her truck bumping along the dirt road to her ranch. Still no response from the man next to her.

She risked a glance at him, hoping for a question, a comment—anything that might show he was taking her seriously. But his head leaned against the window, eyes closed, arms folded.

When he snored gently, she almost gaped. He'd fallen asleep.

Like she didn't exist.

The hush in the cab pressed in, too familiar. She'd sat in this kind of silence before—back in college, sitting beside Maury. Pretending not to care when Maury dismissed her, called her boring for working so hard, and accusing her of holding back when she'd said no.

She could see it as if she were there. Bent over her physics homework, Maury slouched next to her, his textbook sliding from his lap with a thud to the floor. He stretched, checked his watch, and sat up straight.

"Jeez, look at the time. Bill Pyle's having a house party tonight. Come on, let's go."

She'd flipped her pencil around to erase an error. "His parties are always so wild, and there's so much alcohol. I'd rather stay here with you."

Maury's smile turned wolfish. He slid his arm around her back, nuzzling her neck. "Then let's ... stay."

"Stop it." She pushed him away. "That's not what I meant. I told you, I want to wait. And we have exams next week. It's my first semester, and I want to do well—"

"God, Francie. All you care about is school. What about me? I could've died on the battlefield, but that doesn't matter to you. *Other* girls— Forget it." He'd jumped up then and stomped to the door. "You obviously don't want me, and right now I don't want anything to do with you."

He'd called her boring for wanting more from her life than he did. How he'd left, slamming the door and erasing her with his indifference.

The same hurt twisted now. She pressed the accelerator harder, as if speed could outrun it.

Well, she was done twisting herself to fit someone else's convenience.

The truck topped a small rise—not quite airborne but close enough—and she braced for the hard bounce, correcting the slithering tires as they hit the powdery dust of a straightaway. She almost laughed at the exhilaration, stomach swooping and soaring. The bushes and trees flew by, sweeping away the last bitter dregs of her memory. When she pulled into the packed dirt yard in front of her house, she cranked the steering wheel, letting the truck skid, before she stomped the brake. It would serve Sergeant Mitchell Ward right if he slid off the seat into a heap at her feet.

He didn't budge. Instead, his lips twitched into a smile before he stretched his arms, yawned, and uttered his first words in almost two hours.

"It doesn't matter that you dragged me out here," he said. "I don't believe you."

Francie's hands locked around the steering wheel. The faint sweetness of chocolate cream pie in the cab soured as she stared out the front windshield at her long, low ranch house. If even he didn't believe her, who would?

No. She wouldn't give him that.

Four porch posts, peeled and carved. Five bowls of scarlet geraniums, swinging on the metal chains. Four plus five equals nine. Nine windowpanes separated by white wooden slats turned soft blue in the shade.

If he pushed, she'd push back. Equal and opposite forces. That, at least, was a law she could trust.

Francie uncurled her fingers from the steering wheel one by

one. The truck's engine sputtered into silence as she turned the key.

"If you don't believe me, then why didn't you just leave me at my truck and keep walking?"

Sergeant Ward lounged beside her, a lazy smile on his face. The man might have the looks and charisma of a movie heartthrob, but she refused to be impressed like the vapid females—and males—in Roswell.

"Strategic withdrawal from hostile elements," he said. "Besides, I needed a nap. Navigating half a dozen matrimonial-crazed women every day is exhausting. I like your truck. It's vintage, but something's going on with the engine. Did you hear that skip? Pop the hood. I'll take a look."

Francie blinked. On the drive, she'd been staring unseeing at the road ahead, the truck's mechanical sounds fading as her own thoughts drowned them out. She faced him, answering with as much scorn as she could muster.

"You are the most full-of-yourself man I have ever met, and my truck is two years old. My father bought it brand-new after the war."

She opened the door, marched to the front of the vehicle, reached for the hood latch—

His hand closed around her wrist, thumb pressing the edge of her white gloves. Their eyes locked. Heat rose in her cheeks.

"Uh ..." He swallowed. "Don't want to get these dirty. And ... you can call me Mitch ... if you want."

He let go, pulling a pair of oil-stained mechanic gloves from his satchel. Under his breath, she thought she heard, "What am I doing?"

He propped the pack against the front tire and raised the hood of her truck, eyes averted. "Key in the ignition?"

He didn't wait for her reply, submerging his head under the truck's bonnet, trousers molded over his backside.

"Yes." She caught herself staring and looked away, biting her cheek. Equal and opposite, indeed. "And ... call me Francie. When you're done, come on inside. I'll get you some boots."

"I'm wearing boots." He buried himself deeper in the engine, the hood above shading the top half of his body.

"Those won't work for riding."

"Riding?" His head thunked on the truck's hood. He rubbed his scalp, a hint of panic in his eyes. "You mean a *horse*?"

Francie swung open the front door, inhaling the comforting aroma of the lemon tea cakes she'd baked yesterday evening.

"I can't ride a horse. I've never—"

"You wanted proof." She smiled, her voice softer. "Then you're going to have to trust me, Sergeant—um, Mitch."

Six

Capitan Mountains, Southeastern New Mexico

Dressed in well-worn cowboy boots, dungarees, and Kelly-green blouse, Francie ducked under the split-rail corral fence and walked unhurriedly to a half-gentled mare she'd named Venus. She spoke in a low, soothing tone, tart red apple slices in one hand and a lead rope looped in the other. The pretty mare perked her ears and ambled forward, neck stretched, searching for her treat. Her chestnut coat shimmered in the sunlight, and her nostrils flared as she scented the offering, then lipped the fruit from Francie's flattened palm, crunching into its juicy flesh.

Francie clipped the lead to the mare's halter and led her to the fence. The young horse stood docile as Francie threw on a thick black-and-red blanket and a light training saddle. She cinched the girth, then checked the animal's legs, running her hands down each one to lift a hoof before tightening the girth again.

The ranch house's screen door creaked open. Mitch clomped over the flagstone porch in his borrowed boots, lips flattened in irritation. He sent Francie a narrow-eyed glare before tramping toward the turnout and the bright red barn.

"These don't fit right," he announced, and raised a foot, inspecting the scuffed leather. He'd tucked his fatigues into the boots, giving them the look of riding breeches. She half expected him to look a little silly, but he didn't. Her stomach fluttered. He looked ... good.

Francie swapped Venus's halter for a bridle. "That's because you aren't married to them," she said.

"Married?"

She secured the horse's reins to the top pole of the corral, lips twitching with a smile.

"Boots are a commitment, Sergeant. As you live with them, ride with them, you form a union. And once they're yours, they'll never let you down." Francie headed toward the barn doors, ducking into the shadows and the comforting scent of fresh-cut hay and sweet feed. Mitch clonked in behind her.

"The waitress at Woolworths said you'd been engaged. Was he the owner of these boots before you kicked him to the curb?"

Francie's jaw tightened. She traced a pattern on the wood rail and counted prime numbers under her breath.

"The man I kicked to the curb, as you so charmingly put it, was a townie before he was drafted. He didn't know which end of the horse to feed. Those belonged to my father."

Orion nickered, hooves thunking across the thick floor planks. She unlatched the gate to his stall, pushing the horse back as he sniffed her shirt pocket for an apple slice. Francie ran her hands over his chest, withers, and back, making sure he'd cooled down from that morning's ride home.

Mitch folded his arms over the top of the stall, resting his chin on his hands.

"Your ex came back from the war and asked you to marry him."

"We were engaged before he shipped out to Hawaii—a year

after I graduated high school." She grabbed a hoof pick from the hook, keeping her eyes on her work.

"And you sat under the apple tree—"

"I had a job."

"At the five-and-dime?"

He smiled down at her, trivializing her, just like her ex-fiancé. A tight knot of anger and frustration twisted in her stomach. She wanted to shake him up, surprise him. Impress him.

Francie moved to Orion's back leg and picked up his foot. "During the war, I worked at a place called Project Y."

She held her breath, watching his face, waiting to see if the name meant anything to him.

His smile vanished, his hand frozen mid reach toward Orion's head. He drew it back slowly.

"You worked at Los Alamos labs on the Manhattan Project."

"Not directly." She ducked her head. "Clerical staff. Secretary to Professor Eitan Baer—a physicist—and his wife, Adelaide. Family friends from Roswell. They were recruited out of retirement."

Mitch hesitated, then nodded, a new respect in his silence.

Francie moved around Orion's rump but didn't pick up the next hoof. "I'm curious. How do you know Adelaide Baer?"

A frown clouded his expression. "I don't."

"That's odd. She encouraged me to contact you about my experience. I think she worries about me being here on my own since my father's disappearance." Francie hesitated, then met Mitch's gaze. "He was a physicist, too."

"Your father disappeared from Los Alamos?"

"From the ranch. Last summer. He rode out on Orion one morning and never came back." She cleared her tight throat. "We've never found him."

Mitch's fingers whitened on the stall door. He stared past her, jaw tight, as if her revelation meant something to him. Had he lost someone, too?

Francie finished Orion's feet. When she hung up the pick, he said, "Your fiancé comes back from war, you come back. But you didn't marry right away. Why not?"

Francie clipped a rope to Orion's halter and guided him into the barn's central breezeway, Mitch matching her steps. He was interrogating her, plain and simple. If it helped him believe her, then fine.

"We didn't marry right away because we couldn't afford to. Maury needed to finish his degree at the School of Mines, and I went, too."

"You worked at the college while he attended classes?"

There was nothing unusual about his question because most universities had few women students, but his assumption still stung. She lifted her chin and led Orion through the open barn doors and into the afternoon sun.

"I pursued a physics degree."

Mitch paused mid-stride as if her answer had moved the ground between them. He took a half step back and studied her. "Your father encouraged that?"

"He and Dr. Baer. And Adelaide. None of my girlfriends did. My high school didn't, either. But it worked for me." At least for a while.

Francie smoothed the saddle blanket over Orion, waiting for Mitch's next question. He still hadn't asked about her morning encounter—the whole reason she'd blackmailed him up to her ranch.

"That couldn't have been easy, pursuing science with the kind of sexism tolerated in this era," he said.

She shot him a surprised glance. That kind of understanding caught her off guard—especially after coming home to a chorus of I-told-you-so's.

"It wasn't. The professors were condescending. The men in my classes didn't know what to do with me." She rubbed dust from

Orion's saddle, searching for words. "But I had mentors who supported me. Leona Marshall, from Enrico Fermi's group at Los Alamos? She said he didn't know what to do with her at first, so he had her take notes for his research team. And Maria Mayer? When she came to America, she couldn't even find a job teaching physics."

Francie hesitated, her hands trailing over the smooth leather on Orion's saddle before she hoisted it and turned to the horse. "My father championed me more than anyone. He taught himself physics, then taught me. He even has a lab tucked behind his workshop. He always believed I belonged as much as any man." Unlike her ex-fiancé.

She swallowed and braced for the familiar grief of losing Maury, but a new truth slipped in. The loss of his love hadn't hurt as much as the small-town whispers and how much it stung not to belong.

"You broke your engagement. Why?" Mitch asked quietly.

She didn't want Mitch to see the confusion in her eyes—a confusion she'd just recognized herself. Head down, Francie focused on the work. She gave Orion's cinch one more tug, the leather biting into her palm.

She'd left so much behind. The textbooks, the lectures, and the sense that her world could stretch beyond the ranch. She'd told herself it was healing, coming back home. But maybe it was easier to quit than fight for a future that shrank a little each time a professor forgot her name. Easier to blame Maury's betrayal, to let his leaving be the excuse, than admit she'd run from more than just him.

Francie pressed her hand against Orion's warm side. Choices that had seemed so solid—so simple—had blurred. Yet standing here, with the government's shadow creeping over her home, she knew she wasn't the same girl who'd run away a year ago.

But if not, who had she become?

"We need to get going," she said, her voice clipped.

Mitch nodded, but he loitered in the barn's shadowed doorway, frowning at something in his palm.

"What's that?"

He slipped the object into his pocket.

"Nothing important." His gaze slid to her, his mouth opening ... But he closed it, his throat bobbing, as if he'd swallowed a question he wasn't ready to ask.

"It'll take an hour or so to reach the site of the incident and my proof," Francie said, taking up the reins. "I'd like to get home before dark so I can drive you back to Roswell."

She handed Orion's lead to Mitch. "He's gentle—mostly. He has a few tricks. I'll try to keep him in line."

Francie scratched under the horse's chin. "Will you promise to be nice to the sergeant, Orion?" Orion tossed his head up and down as if answering, "Yes."

"Promise not to scrape him off on a tree?" The horse flicked an ear, utterly noncommittal. She hid a smile at Mitchell Ward's wide-eyed stare.

With any luck, Orion's tricks would keep Mitch's attention on the trail ahead and away from the questions she no longer had answers for.

Because her old explanations didn't work anymore.

Seven

The summer sun shimmered above the bordering trees, striping the dusty trail in bright shifting streaks, the warm air holding notes of sage and pine. Scrub jays, wind in the branches, and the rhythmic clop of hooves filled the silence —until Mitch's voice broke it.

"So do you have cows on the— Hey. *Hey!* This demon horse is trying to kill me again." The note of panic in Mitch's complaints had risen with each bend in the trail.

Francie touched the rein to Venus's neck, and the mare turned in a delicate pirouette to cast a critical eye over the man straddling the "demon" horse. Orion had drifted off the narrow strip of compacted dirt they were following and into a stand of pines. Francie leaned over her saddle horn and sighed. This guy qualified as a real tenderfoot and was no match for Orion, who ambled right up against a tree trunk. The rough scraping sound and yelp were accompanied by Mitch pulling on the opposite rein. Orion curled his long golden neck to one side and continued his path through knee-high bunch grass.

"My father sold all the cattle a few years ago. He told me he was getting too old. Watch that low branch," Francie called.

Mitch's "Whoa—*stop*" didn't halt Orion. The horse ambled underneath a horizontal bough right at shoulder level. But Mitch didn't duck forward. Instead, he leaned back in the saddle so far that he pulled the reins tight. Only then did Orion stop, his rider contorted under the tree limb.

She nudged Venus closer to Orion, who snorted loud enough to sound like he laughed. She fished a lead rope from her saddlebag, clipped it to Orion's bridle, and led both horse and man back toward the trail. Except Orion balked at a fallen branch and bunny-hopped over it. Mitch, who'd relaxed, bounced twice, then landed flat on his backside in a mound of dirt piled by some burrowing animal.

Francie kicked her boots free of the stirrups and slid to the ground. "Are you okay?"

He shot her a look, cheeks ruddy, grass in his hair—annoyingly handsome even as he glared.

"Fine, but I am not getting back up on Satan's pony. I'll walk the rest of the way."

She offered her hand, steadying him as he rose. The space between them vanished. They were face-to-face, his uniform brushing her shirtfront, the scent of dust and soap and something unmistakably *him* filling her senses.

Too. Close. She could count the dark spikes of his lashes, the emerald-green flecks in his eyes. His gaze touched her mouth, and the world narrowed to the heat between them.

"It's too far to walk," she croaked, and cleared her throat. "I'll make Orion behave, I promise."

"And how will you do that?" His voice turned low and rough around the edges. Goose bumps shivered along her arms.

She forgot about the crash, about Maury, about everything except the way Mitch looked at her—as if nothing else in the world was worth noticing.

Venus snorted, and the spell broke. She stepped back, heart tapping hard against her ribs.

"Orion's a handful, but my father always said a clever horse keeps a rider honest. He trained Orion himself, adding tricks over the years." The memory swirled, bittersweet.

Mitch's thumb whispered across her palm as she pulled free. She rubbed her hand on her jeans, but the tingle only transferred to her stomach.

"I gave Orion permission to play with his rider—you—at the ranch. I'm sorry. I'm usually nicer."

"Haze the greenhorn?" Mitch's lips quirked.

"You're not angry?"

"I expected it, honestly. It means you're reacting to me. That's my strategy with—" He stopped, his smile wavering, a shadow of something like regret flickering across his face. "I've gotten used to the culture here. Sometimes I forget."

Francie adjusted Venus's tack, using the task to steady herself. "Your strategy?"

He hesitated, then admitted, "With women, flattery and charm get me information faster than—" He broke off.

"Than treating us as equals?"

He didn't reply.

Dappled sunlight rippled through the surrounding pines as she called Orion to her with a click of her tongue. He ambled over, mouth full of grass.

Francie smoothed Orion's mane. "I'd rather see how that equality thing works, for once."

She touched the horse's cheek and nose, back and forth, then turned to Mitch. "No more tricks. But you need to ride with confidence. He'll follow your lead if you act like the boss. Want to try again?"

Mitch's eyes held a hint of uncertainty as they slid between Francie and Orion. He gave a curt nod and slipped his boot into the stirrup. She guided the placement of his hands, and he swung into the saddle with more grace than he had the first time he'd mounted at the ranch. She adjusted his posture and form with gentle touches and murmured instructions, doing what she should've done before they started. He didn't crack a joke or offer a smile—just listened—following her lead with a seriousness that felt new.

She'd set him up for failure, punishing him for his bravado. Now, Francie saw past the charming leading man act he'd put on at the diner to someone trying hard not to show he was out of his depth—and trusting her not to let him look the fool.

Francie stepped back, hands on her hips, surveying her work. "How's that feel?"

Mitch sat taller, his demeanor now a blend of military bearing and newfound confidence. "Better," he admitted, a hint of surprise in his voice.

Francie climbed onto Venus and reined her horse beside him. "Ready?"

"I am," he replied, and gave her what she considered his first genuine smile. "Thanks."

As she guided Venus back to the trail, the guilt inside her melted to warmth.

Hot and dusty, Francie stopped below the ridge and pulled her canteen, gesturing for Mitch to do the same. The creek's crystal water burbled over river rock in the gulch, cool and inviting. Many a time, she'd stripped to swim in the deep, placid pool around the next bend.

She rested her canteen on the pommel and pointed to the crest with its dense row of pines, dark green and brown against the blue of the sky.

"See that gap? The tree fell after ... after the figure appeared." Francie gestured at the toppled trunk, now stretched across the streambed like a bristled footbridge. "I watched it crash down into the gully."

Mitch studied the tree line. "Did you check the stump? Maybe the tree was rotten and needed to fall. Wind, storm, decay. Something ordinary. I see other trees in the creek."

"Those are all older, broken, and waterworn. This one snapped clean." Francie sighed. "I wasn't here this morning because of that tree. I saw a streak of purple light, and then, somebody, something, in a puffy white suit, helmet with a dark faceplate, impossible to make out what was inside. A—"

She hesitated. Alien, spaceman, creature— Astronaut? She didn't know what to call it, just that it was not from around here.

"Whatever it was," Francie finished, "it caused that tree to fall, not natural causes."

Mitch stared up at the gap in the tree line. "Were you seen or heard?"

"I don't think so. Orion and I were well hidden in that stand of trees over there."

He studied the dense shadows behind them and nodded. "What did you do next?"

"I tethered Orion and climbed up the ridge trail."

His eyebrows rose. "You went *toward* this unknown entity?"

Francie couldn't tell if she'd impressed him or if he thought she was an idiot.

"It might have been the pilot of some experimental aircraft out of White Sands or Roswell Army Airfield—even with the falling tree." She nodded to a large tumble of boulders downstream. "Before we head up, we need to—"

"No. Show me, step-by-step. Don't deviate from what you did this morning."

"But—"

"Step-by-step."

She hissed a sigh through clenched teeth as Mitch dismounted. Francie slid from her saddle and led him to a sun-freckled clearing where she secured the horses. Their mounts lowered their heads to the grass and cropped.

Francie jogged down a gentle slope into the creek bed and splashed across the water at a shallow section of the stream. Mitch followed, his borrowed boots clunking behind her.

The ridge trail climbed steep and narrow, switchbacks twisting through powdery dirt that filled rough depressions.

She halted at a print the likes of which she'd never seen before. Oval-shaped, the toe and heel blunted, narrower in the middle. Ridges ran across the width like ripples in sand. Mitch knelt next to the odd print.

"That wasn't there this morning." She hunched, fingers sliding over her holster, and scanned the ridge. "Stay close."

Francie didn't realize Mitch had fallen behind until a snick sounded on the trail. She whipped her head around to see him slide his hand into his shirt pocket. He hurried up to stop behind her.

"You took a picture," she said. "That's a camera, then. I saw it at the barn. What kind?"

He hesitated. "Have you heard of Minox B subminiatures?"

"Military police confiscated a couple of them at Los Alamos, but they didn't look like that." Still, in her experience, military innovation advanced rapidly. Mitch's Minox was probably cutting edge. "Good. This way, you can take the evidence to your superiors, and they'll believe me."

"Is that important? That you're believed?"

"Yes." It shouldn't matter so much, but it did.

Francie topped the ridge and moved through the trees, sticking to shadows, careful with footfalls. "There's no sign of him."

His gaze swept the gap where the fallen tree had once stood. "Is that the tree stump? It looks like lightning hit it."

"But that's not what happened. He blasted it with something."

Mitch shot her a glance and pulled the brushed-silver Minox from his pocket. As he snapped pictures, she crept to the border of a clearing covered in tall grasses burgeoning with seeds. Mitch's footsteps crunched through the pine needle carpet. He stopped behind her, the warmth of his body at her back.

"Is this where the alien landed?" he asked.

Alien. Did that mean he believed her now? She stood a little taller.

"I think so, but I didn't see a defined burned spot or any wreckage. I did find an artifact—like a spear—on the other side." Francie led him around the meadow's perimeter until she placed her palm on the rough bark of a mature pine. "It was propped here."

Mitch's hand settled beside hers as if he'd be able to divine what happened.

"This is as far as I ventured. I wanted to avoid ending up as one of his voucher specimens." She quirked her lips at the quip. He didn't smile back.

"What did you do next?"

"I grabbed the spear and left. I hid it down by the creek."

Francie led Mitch down the ridge to the pile of boulders lodged at a bend in the stream. She rounded the rocks, nerves pulled taut with every step, and pointed to a dark triangular cavity.

"The spear's in there. As far back as I could push it."

Mitch studied the hole, then her, suspicion sharpening his features. "And if nothing's inside, what will you say? That whoever fell from the sky followed you down and took it?"

Francie drew back, confused. "What?"

He pressed on, his voice turning flat. "Or maybe you never saw a purple streak or an alien or a spear. Did you and your friend Adelaide set me up? A little meet and greet for a lonely ranch girl?"

Francie's fists clenched. "You egotistical, big-headed worm!" Her voice shook. She turned her head toward the creek, the sparkles of sunlit water blurring. "I've already gotten rid of a man as arrogant and unfaithful as you. Why would I ever accept another?"

But even as the retort left her mouth, doubt shivered through her, cold and unwelcome. What had Adelaide said that morning? *Stop wallowing. It's been over a year.*

Adelaide had begged Francie to trust her. She'd sent her to Mitch. Had it been a ruse? A setup?

Francie shook her head. No. Adelaide wouldn't betray her. She'd been the one person who believed her.

Frowning, Mitch stepped closer, his hand outstretched. "Francie, I'm sor—"

"Don't." Her lips trembled as she struggled for control. "I saw something not of this world. And I found that spear."

She nodded at the hole. "It's still there. He didn't take it."

Mitch's frown softened. "How do you know?"

The same electric certainty hummed beneath her skin, just as it had that morning.

"Because I can feel its presence."

Eight

Francie's boots crushed the short grass growing close to the tumbled boulders, arms hugged around herself, bracing against the invisible pull of the alien spear. The breeze tousled her curls then died. Somewhere behind her on the mountain slope, a bird's musical trill cut short. It was as if the surrounding forest held its breath.

Her gaze slid to the dark hollow in the rocks.

"You *sense* it. What do you mean, exactly?" Mitch's tone had changed. Turned less mocking, more intense.

She searched for a way to explain. "Like a charge in the air. Or a force field pulling at me."

"A charge in the air." It was as if he tested the words for weight.

"That's how I knew the spaceman couldn't be from Earth. That he must be from some advanced culture. How can I have a physical connection with an inanimate object?" Her voice faltered. "You don't feel it in there?"

She wanted him to say yes, wanted not to feel so alone.

"No. But ..." He hesitated, his gaze focused on the hollow, and Francie caught a flicker of something in his expression—curiosity, maybe. Or calculation. She shivered, even though the sun-drenched stones radiated warmth.

He crouched by the hollow and pulled out the Minox. A beam of light, brighter than any flashlight she'd ever seen, cut through the shadows as he swept it over the rocks. "Something's off here. I'll give you that."

She shifted her weight and held her breath.

"You said your ex was unfaithful. Is that why you've been hiding out up here?" He angled the light into the hollow and bent to peer inside. "Or was there some other reason? What's your father's name, again—" He broke off, something in the hollow catching his eye. "*Holy cow.*"

Mitch switched off the light, shoved the camera into his pocket, and threaded his arm into the hollow until the boulders blocked his reach. He grunted softly, then eased back out.

Francie's gaze locked on the artifact as it threw out a surge of energy that chased over her skin, raising goose bumps along her limbs. The spear seemed to recognize her, to yearn for her. She clenched her fists, fingernails cutting into her palms, the urge to snatch it away from Mitch almost overwhelming. Yet fear of its power pinned her in place. The same fear that had driven her to stash it in the rocks instead of taking it to Roswell.

Mitch stood. He shifted the artifact across both hands, holding it parallel to the ground.

Nearly five feet long and light in her hands, the brushed, violet-tinged metal didn't resemble any alloy Francie had seen in the Los Alamos metallurgy lab. Nothing this exotic, nothing that hinted at a world beyond aluminum.

What set it apart, though, were the scrolled designs etched along the shaft—patterns that looked unearthly. A seamless blend of metal and stone capped one end and twisted into a wicked, conical point, still smeared with her blood where she'd cut herself that morning. Francie rubbed the prick on her index finger, the memory of its sting vivid.

Mitch rolled the spear in his palms. He thumbed a V-shaped chip in the smooth cylinder. "It's damaged. You didn't find this piece when you found the artifact?"

"There was nothing else on the ground." The spear's pull grew stronger. She gestured to it. "Now do you feel anything?"

"Nothing." He turned the artifact in his hands, and his brows furrowed. "Something's etched along its shaft. I can't read—"

"You think it's writing?"

Mitch's face was inscrutable. He shrugged. "Can you hold it so I can take pictures?"

She took a step back. "Why? Take it to your commanding officer as proof."

The spear's energy pressed against her skin—restless, insistent.

"What if it's dangerous?" Her voice came out thin, barely there.

"Did it hurt you before?"

The memory shimmered—euphoria, not pain. She shook her head.

He stepped closer, the heat of his body increasing, the space between them shrinking. "Francie. Take it."

Her hands opened before her mind made the conscious decision to do so. Mitch laid the artifact across her palms. She curled her fingers around the shaft.

Nothing. Just metal in her hands.

Then it came alive, light racing along the scrollwork, violet and bright, its power tingling through her skin. It hummed.

"Do you hear it?" she whispered, not sure if she meant the sound or the rush flooding her veins. Her gaze locked with Mitch's, and nothing else existed but the current running between them.

"It's ... I think so. What's happening?"

"It's drawing—I don't know—something like electricity from my body, but not draining me. Should I be afraid?"

He backed away from her, his hand falling to his sidearm. Her eyes widened in alarm before anger surged, hot and bright. The spear's tip flared, its glow intensifying in time with her heartbeat.

"Are you going to *shoot* me? You *made* me take it."

"No!" Mitch's hand hovered. "I just—"

An unnatural sizzle whipped through the air. The rock crowning the boulders exploded.

"Get down!" Mitch dove at Francie. His arms enveloped her as the shards of pulverized rocks pelted their bodies. She clutched the spear, his breath teasing her cheek. Was he *counting*?

"... eight ... nine ... ten."

Another blast shattered a tree behind them, wood splintering. Mitch leaped up, weapon drawn. He aimed over the tumble of rocks and fired, a surge of bright light swelling from the barrel.

Francie stared. That was no ordinary gun.

Mitch dropped back beside her. "Top of the ridge, using that big rock as cover." He counted again. At ten, he tensed. Another shot from above scored the dirt to their left. Mitch jumped up and fired.

"We need to get to the horses." Francie shifted the spear and pulled out her six-shooter. Both hands shook, but she tightened her grip on the gun. The spear pulsed brighter, its hum steadying her nerves.

"Wait for his next shot. We can make a run for it while his weapon recharges."

She hunkered low, every instinct screaming to flee. But this land was hers. This fight was hers. She'd worn the label of quitter for too long. Not today. She planted her boots in the dirt.

Her shoulder brushed Mitch's. She caught his eye and nodded. He nodded back with a flicker of respect. Or maybe fear. No time to wonder. She focused on the threat.

"Ready?" he said. "Seven ... eight ... nine ... *ten*."

The air sizzled, light flashed, another stone exploded.

Mitch vaulted to his feet, firing through a haze of grit and dust. Francie leaped up, pumping bullets from her revolver, the buzzing echoes of the spent lead ricocheting off rocks at the top of the ridge. Her gun kicked with each pull of the trigger—*five, four, three, two* …

Her final round. *Make it count.*

Francie twisted, bringing the barrel of her gun and glowing spear into perfect alignment. The white-suited alien rose, weapon leveled, visor a featureless black stare. Time slowed. Ozone stung her tongue, gun oil bit her nose. She set her stance. Drew a breath. Sight locked.

She squeezed—

The artifact jerked. A bolt of light shot out of the tip, pulverizing the shielding boulder. The alien reeled, his weapon firing skyward before he ducked out of sight.

She stared at the glowing spear. *How on God's green earth—?*

"Francie!"

Francie whirled to see Mitch had reached the horses. He fumbled with Venus's reins, but the young mare threw her head, tearing the leather from his hands. Venus, wild-eyed, bolted down the trail, a cloud of dust in her wake.

Orion reared. Mitch grabbed for his reins, feet skidding as he hung on. If they lost both horses, they'd be sitting ducks.

Francie holstered her gun and sprinted, catching Orion's bridle. She stroked Orion's cheek, pressed her forehead to his neck. His shivering eased. Mitch stepped back, one hand wrapped in the reins, the other holding his weapon, eyes watching the ridgeline.

"His saddle." Mitch's voice was tight.

Orion had pulled it and the blanket off, leaving a tangle beneath his feet.

She shoved the spear at Mitch. He gripped it. Its inner radiance faded. Francie threw the pad over Orion's back and cinched it, hands moving on instinct. "We ride double."

A crack split the air. Blue light scorched the treetops. Francie whirled, spotting a shadow darting along the ridge.

Mitch fired. The spaceman took cover behind a tree. "Ten seconds before he's recharged."

How does he know that?

Francie clutched Orion's mane and vaulted onto the horse. She caught Mitch's hand, dragging him up in one hard pull. He landed belly-first, clumsy, unbalanced, the spear still locked in his grip, then swung a leg over the dancing palomino. Pressing into her back, his arm clamped around her waist.

"Hold tight," Francie yelled.

She spun Orion and dug in her heels. The horse bounded away from the ridge.

"Five seconds. Four— *Whoa!*" Mitch lurched and clutched her tighter. "What the *hell*?"

The world blurred. Light warped and rippled. The spear's energy throbbed through Francie as air folded around them. The ground seemed to slip, stretch—then snap out of time.

NINE

Orion bolted, the alien spear's glow flickering at the edge of Francie's vision as they tore through mountain brush—Mitch's shout echoing behind her. Panic pressed in, but Francie kept her grip on the reins, knees tight over the horse's flanks. She couldn't let either of them fall. Mitch depended on her to get him out of this.

She dug in, released one hand from the reins to squeeze the arm around her waist. His trust steadied her—a silent anchor holding her in place when fear threatened to shake her loose.

"Don't let go," she said over her shoulder. Mitch leaned into her, his warmth a solid weight at her back. They'd survive together, and that counted for something, even if only for now.

The horse ran down the trail with purpose, as if guided by an unseen force, while Francie's sense of direction spiraled into chaos. The Capitan Mountains loomed familiar, but the trail beneath Orion's hooves vanished, swallowed by a bite of ancient glacial air. The surrounding forest transformed with dizzying speed. One moment, Orion dodged towering cedars erupting around them, their trunks so massive they blocked out the sky. The next, the trees dissolved, and he galloped through sweeping meadows of grass and sage, crisp scents she recognized in the alien landscape.

Francie swallowed a gasp as enormous, lumbering beasts materialized beside them. Elephants— No. *Mastodons.* Their rumbling calls vibrated through her body, ancient and unnerving. One beast pivoted, its eyes blazing. It charged, scimitar-curved tusks arcing through the air with lethal intent. Eyes wide and blurred with wind-driven tears, her muscles tensed until it felt like her bones would snap.

We'll be sliced in half.

Instinct took over. Francie hunched low, fingers latched into Orion's mane and Mitch heavy on her back. She squeezed her eyes shut, bracing for the impact, for the tearing of flesh and crushing of bone. A gust of hot, musty air washed over her, reeking of earth and age and wildness.

Then nothing.

She raised her head, and the mammoths were gone, replaced by a herd of burly pronghorns sporting oddly shaped horns. They darted past Orion, hooves skimming the ground. Tawny fur caught Francie's eye—a cheetah, sleek and impossible, paralleling Orion. Sweat trickled down her neck.

Francie's sense of time buckled, but she rode on, clinging to what hadn't changed—the rhythm of Orion's stride, Mitch behind her, the ridge somewhere ahead.

Tumbled rocks appeared ahead, a landmark on the trail to the ridge, yet no oaks clung to their side, and the aspen grove above had vanished.

Orion's muscles bunched beneath her.

"Hold on," she yelled. Mitch fused his body to hers.

She leaned into Orion's sudden 180-degree switchback, her knees squeezed to his sides as they navigated into a gathering storm that shouldn't exist.

The blue above them rippled and warped, and the day went black with menacing clouds torn by sheets of rain. Thunder cracked. Lightning charged the air in blinding flashes, leaving an intense smell of ozone. Temperatures plummeted, rain turning to ice that stung her cheeks, so cold it burned, yet her skin stayed dry, a phantom assault on her senses.

The ground leveled out. Orion's stride lengthened. Through the gray curtain of driving sleet, semi-circular structures sprouted from the earth. Hogans. Tanned animal skins stretched taut over woven branches, entrances covered against the storm. Smoke curled through openings in the tops, defying the deluge. Orion zigzagged, the hogans like pylons on a riding course. He shied around a smoldering firepit, red coals sizzling as the torrent fell from the clouds. Francie clung like a limpet as Mitch careened from side to side, her body the one thing keeping him in the saddle. They burst from the clustered hogans onto a flattened expanse, the distant horizon obscured by the deluge, every thumping hoofbeat their last if Orion misstepped on the treacherous terrain.

Francie unknotted trembling fingers from Orion's mane. Mitch's arm steadied her as she grasped the loop of reins she didn't remember dropping. She caught them and tugged, signaling to the horse she'd taken back control. Orion slowed.

The storm disappeared in a blink. Another blink, and the ground softened beneath Orion's hooves. The sky ahead glowed with copper-tinged lights suspended in the air until giant redwoods sprouted to hold them, their branches threading through each other like intricate biological tapestries, fusing into a single, vast organism that defied anything Francie had ever seen.

Dwellings nestled in this impossible canopy that seemed plucked from the pages of a futurist's fever dream. Soft light spilled from windows set into structures that blended organically with their living foundations. Walkways and stairs linked these homes to sidewalks meandering in the overstory. On the ground, people strolled, children played, and voices called out to neighbors, but the sounds reached Francie as if through water. No one stared or pointed at the woman riding double on a golden horse. They were invisible.

Orion's sudden shy caught Francie off guard. Her tired legs clamped to the horse's sides as a small tan dog with a piggy butt and a flat black face darted from the bushes. Its eyes, like shiny glass marbles, fixed on them with unnerving intelligence as it nipped at Orion's heels.

The dog could see them. Like the mastodons.

It barked, a muffled gruff caught inside the rounded head, before it once again dove into the brush.

She'd heard that bark before—at the crash site this morning. Familiar and alien, much like her life.

She'd had enough of this ride, enough of the dizzying dreamscape. Francie hauled back Orion's reins, bringing him to a crowhopping stop. She slid off to the ground. Her boots hit hard-packed dirt, knees buckling. Her head spun. Someone retched. Mitch doubled over near the fence, clutching the spear to steady his swaying body.

A horse whinnied. Venus. Francie leaped to her feet to find herself in the ranch yard between her home and the barn, Orion sucking water at the trough. Venus stood near the closed barn doors, sweat-streaked, ears perked, saddled, her reins still looped over her neck.

Mitch held on to a fence rail for dear life. He weakly kicked at the dirt to cover—

Francie stepped toward him, palm outstretched. "Mitch?"

He straightened with a jerk, and swung the spear toward her, leveling it at her heart. "Who the hell *are* you?"

The wildness in his eyes echoed her own turmoil after the crash that morning, and her anger and frustration when he said he didn't believe her. But after everything that happened ...

Her hand shook, but she stepped closer.

"It's me. Francie Cortez." She exhaled, searching for composure. "The same person who found you at the diner, and ..."

The dark spear hummed and lit the air, bathing her with a violet glow. Time stuttered.

A child's laughter echoed. She stilled, listening. That was *her* laughter, years ago, chasing fireflies through the orchard beside the house. A man's voice—her father's—twined with hers—her past, alive and close enough to touch. An echo of the past.

In that moment, she wanted nothing more than to slip back to that simpler world. But the present intruded. The artifact's violet glow unsettled her. She hadn't run when Mitch needed her, not when it counted. And she couldn't run now, not with her land and everything she loved at stake.

Francie drew a settling breath, and the memory faded. "Mitch. We need to take this to your superiors. Now. I don't have all the answers, but I'm not leaving this unfinished."

TEN

Francie braced, waiting for Mitch's reply, absorbing the normalcy of the ranch yard around her. A mockingbird fussed in an apricot tree. Orion stamped a hoof to dislodge buzzing flies. She pulled in the air sweet with hay and the tang of dust in the breeze. The familiar sounds and smells peeled away the worst of her nerves.

Mitch gathered himself, his shoulders loosening, his jaw unclenching. He managed a smile that held a shadow of the charm he'd shown back in Roswell, even if it didn't quite reach his eyes.

When his grip on the spear eased, Francie lowered her arm and mirrored his smile.

"We can talk about what happened on the drive," she said, and notched her chin at the artifact. "Come inside and clean up. I'll put away the horses then get us something to eat."

And reload her revolver.

Mitch glanced at the dark patch in the dirt where he'd been sick. "Sorry about that."

A pang of sympathy stirred in her, but the artifact's low hum pulled her attention. She approached Mitch slowly, her movements unthreatening, and touched the hand he'd wrapped around the spear. He stilled, his gaze tense.

"It's okay," she said, letting her fingers glide above his to encircle the shaft. The hum shifted, softer now, low and soothing. She tugged, and Mitch released the spear, but his other hand hovered near his holster and that impossible weapon he carried.

Francie willed the spear to stay quiet, and after a brief flicker, it went dark. She met his wary gaze and understood. Maybe this was how trust worked—earned again and again, in small moments like this.

She stepped around Mitch and headed for the house, pausing when he didn't follow.

"You go ahead. I need a chronon. Sorry. A second," he said.

He stood rigid and unsmiling, shaken by what had occurred. She recognized the blank, shell-shocked look—a mirror of how she'd felt herself that morning.

"Fine, but I want to leave as soon as possible. It'll be dark in a couple of hours."

Francie opened her front door and stepped into the cool quiet of her home. She turned, her eyes on Mitch. He stood, head bowed, his hands clenching and unclenching in the bright midday light.

Their frightening encounter with the alien had happened so fast, there'd been no time to think. But she could think now and replay their crazy shootout. The way he'd counted off like he knew the rhythm of the alien's attack, and now dropped a strange term, "chronon," as if he'd used it all his life.

If reality hadn't shifted enough today, she now had to contend with a mystery closer to home.

Sure, Mitch looked shaken. But with every new detail, she grew more certain he knew more about all of this—maybe even about her—than he was letting on.

Sergeant Mitchell Ward was keeping secrets.

Francie laid the spear on her bed and unbuckled her belt, dropping it and her holstered pistol on the coverlet. She dashed into her home's single bathroom, splashed water on her face, and braced her arms on the lip of the sink. Brown eyes, shadowed and strained, stared back at her from the oval mirror, Mitch's words echoing in her head.

Who the hell are *you?*

She abhorred profanity, but it certainly fit into this question. The wild ride, the shifting world, and her connection to the artifact. Though none of it made sense, yet understanding circled closer, like a word she couldn't quite recall on the verge of sliding into place.

She and Mitch would discuss this whole weird and amazing experience on their way to give evidence to his superiors at the base. That would mean the Army crawling over her land like they had last June at the Brazel ranch when they'd told the world one thing one day, then another the next. But after today's pulse of unreality—alien, artifact, echoes of long-ago voices—those crash-turned-weather-balloon stories felt like a cover-up hiding secrets too incredible to admit.

And Mitch had been brought in specifically for that incident.

She firmed her chin. She wouldn't let the Army or Mitchell Ward hide what had happened today.

Francie dried her hands and face and, with deliberate steps, walked to her bed and studied the spear. It seemed content, almost purring. Like the stray barn cat she'd sometimes allowed inside to curl up on her coverlet to sleep. It had vanished when her father had disappeared, along with all the animals that used to find their way to the ranch.

Everyone except Orion. Her father had been riding him the day he'd gone missing—and Orion was the only one who came back.

The screen door creaked and banged shut. *Mitch.* Francie hurried into the hall for clean towels and met him in the parlor, where he'd paused to study her home. Francie stopped and hugged the linens.

The tidiness, the polished floors, the scent of beeswax she'd worked into every wooden surface. The dining room table gleamed, six chairs pushed in close. No cheerful tablecloth, no place settings. A signal that she wasn't expecting guests, wasn't ready for anyone to probe or judge, even after a year.

Let Mitch look, see the boundaries she'd drawn around her life. This was all she had left from before. Her space, her rules, and her shield to keep the world at arm's length.

When she'd retreated home after her broken engagement and her father's disappearance, she neglected the house. This place, a symbol of family and love, became a daily reminder of what had been taken from her.

Don't lie, Francie. No one took anything from you. You left when the going got tough.

At first, she rode every day, from dawn to dark, searching for her father, returning home too exhausted to dream. It had taken months before she'd noticed the accumulated dust and inattention, and she'd found relief in its restoration, each sweep of the broom a quiet attempt to reclaim control of her life. For what, she still wasn't sure. She had no clear picture of her future.

Right now, she was glad she'd cleaned and tidied, eager to appear rational and sound to Sergeant Mitchell Ward.

Mitch studied her reading nook. A frilled standing lamp, a scalloped-edged table, her father's high-backed armchair, the faint scent of peppermints and coffee lingering in the fabric. As a child, she'd curled beside him, her cheek resting on his shoulder, listening to his low voice when he read her stories or the scratch of his pen as he filled a succession of green lab journals.

After he disappeared, she'd sat in that chair for weeks, seeking comfort in its familiar embrace and the single journal he'd asked her to safeguard.

"In your room, Francie. I need you to keep it safe. Do you understand?" He'd been serious, and she'd nodded. Then his eyes had twinkled. "You know how much I like puzzles. Decipher it, if you can." A challenge from him to her.

"Fresh towels." She thrust the folded stack at Mitch. "The washroom's down the hall."

But Mitch didn't take them. He stepped around her, drawn to the chair. One of her books lay cracked over a chair arm, another on the seat cushion. Books her ex and her professors told her weren't normal for a woman to read. His hand hovered before he picked up the book resting on the arm.

"*The Evolution of Physics*, by Einstein and Infeld." He canted his head to read the second title on the seat. "*The Principles of Quantum Mechanics*, by Dirac. Self-taught. Like your father."

He didn't set the Einstein book down right away. Instead, he set his finger as a bookmark, his thumb tracing the margin, slow and careful, as if holding something rare. His gaze found hers, almost searching.

He started to speak, then stopped, lips curving with something close to a smile—a little unsteady, as if surprised with what he'd found here. The question from earlier echoed in his eyes—*who* are *you?* Except now, she caught a glint of approval there, reluctant but real.

Francie pushed the towels into his arms again and tugged the book away, breathless for reasons she refused to name.

"When you're done, the kitchen is off the dining room." She pointed behind him. "There's lemonade in the refrigerator."

His mouth quirked. "Nothing stronger?"

She hesitated. "In the cupboards above the sink. I need to tend to Venus and Orion."

Francie set the book on the pie-crust table and started to head out, but paused as Mitch spoke. "Did you name your horses? I mean, you've experienced an alleged visitor not of this world, and your horses' names are not of this world, too."

And you, Mitchell Ward, knew to count to ten between each ray gun blast. Her hand tightened on the screen door latch, unpleasant prickles running up her arm.

"I named Venus. My father named Orion." She closed the door behind her and jogged to the corral.

He'd snoop, but there was no stopping that. She had to make sure her horses hadn't suffered from their adventure and get them settled, even though she hated leaving them. Since she didn't have a phone, she'd stop in the small town of Arabela and ask Betsy Sizemore to feed them and let them out into the paddock in the morning. She might even return before morning with the Army, but if not, she could count on Adelaide and Dr. Baer for a bed.

Venus and Orion, heads together, dozed by the corral fence. She picked up their dusty reins and led them into the barn, flicking on the overhead light. Venus first: unsaddled, a quick cooling wipe down and brush. Francie scooped some rolled oats, changed the water in her bucket, and secured her in her stall.

Orion next. Francie grabbed his halter and stepped in front of him, seeing her reflection in his dark, liquid eyes. Her father's horse had been as much a part of the visions as she and Mitch had, yet he appeared no worse for wear after galloping double through fantastical lands, dashing alongside mastodons and antelope. And he'd snorted his annoyance at the little tan dog barking on his heels.

He rumbled a low whinny and blinked golden lashes before bumping her chest with his head, his ask to be scratched on the diamond of white under his fetlock. He'd always been different, which she'd attributed to his circus training. But was there something more to him than she knew?

She wrapped her arms around his neck, pressing her cheek against his dusty coat. She didn't ask the question aloud this time. Instead, it hummed inside her, as strange and persistent as the artifact.

What are you, really?

~

Francie hurried inside, washed up, and changed into a clean blouse and dungarees before packing an overnight case. She picked up her Enfield revolver, ejected the spent casings, and reloaded five bullets. She paused over the sixth—the cowboy load. "Never keep a round under the hammer, so you don't shoot yourself in the foot." Her father's caution and humor wrung a smile as she left the chamber empty, wrapped the gun, and tucked it deep in her bag.

There was one more thing she should take, but she vacillated, chewing the inside of her cheek in indecision. She slid her hand under the mattress of her bed and pulled out the green, cloth-covered lab journal, *1946* stamped in gold on its spine—her father's. Part of Francie wanted to clutch it to her chest, keep it hidden. But a hunch told her the journal's importance hadn't ended with her father's disappearance.

Francie shoved the journal to the bottom of her overnight case, beneath the gun. She paused, touching the spear's shaft with her index finger. It flickered with light then darkened as she drew back. The artifact felt truly alien and held power beyond her—or anyone's—understanding. She wasn't sure she had the right to hand it over.

Was she doing the right thing? Her stomach twisted with doubt.

Francie glanced once more at the spear. The artifact pulsed faintly, almost beckoning, but she couldn't bring herself to pick it up. Not yet.

She strode through the living room and hit the swinging door into the kitchen with the flat of her palm. Her gaze traveled where it always went first—the dish rack holding her father's handmade mug, ready for his terrible coffee in case he miraculously returned.

Mitch sat at her kitchen table. He'd made the sandwiches, and coffee was percolating on the stove. He smiled up at her, hair damp and combed into a sweep across his brow. Francie took in the scene —her father's mug, the familiar kitchen, the not-quite-stranger at her table. Mitch looked for all the world like he belonged, and she almost let herself believe things could be ordinary again.

"Time to go," Francie said. "We can eat in the truck."

She hurried across the linoleum for wax paper and a thermos, ignoring the itch between her shoulder blades from Mitch's continued perusal.

He stood, and Francie thrust the thermos and wrapped sandwiches into his arms. She collected herself and gave him a small smile.

"Survival kit," she joked. "First rule of alien encounters: Don't face them on an empty stomach."

For a second, Mitch stared. Then a smile broke through his reserve, catching at the corner of his mouth. The tightness in his shoulders eased, but his gaze on her was keen.

"Duly noted, ma'am," he said, his formality softened by something a little awestruck.

Francie's cheeks burned, so she busied herself with two apples from the fruit bowl and muttered that she'd meet him at the truck.

Alone in her room, her hand hovered over the spear. This time, she didn't smother its light. The delicate scrollwork glowed, rich purple threading through the metal. Energy quivered up her arm. Familiar now, almost companionable. She closed her eyes.

A memory drifted through her bedroom door. Her parents would talk before they slept. Sometimes, she could almost believe she heard her father's deep, quiet laugh, the teasing reply of her mother in a conversation hazy with time. Her lullaby as a child.

If she kept the spear, could she relive those lost moments? It seemed to sweep her into the past in some way she didn't understand, and the thought tempted her—anything to ease the loneliness.

The truck door slammed. She opened her eyes. Mitch was

waiting for her. Duty, tugging at her. She should turn the spear over, let the Army handle it.

But the idea of handing over the artifact made her stomach knot. What if they locked it away or broke it down to nothing? Her father wouldn't have trusted them—not after Los Alamos, not after the bomb. She'd taken that secretarial position believing she could help, that she could be part of something good. Yet she'd felt the weight of his disappointment, how he'd warned her that power, once given, is rarely returned.

With a heavy sigh, she curled her fingers around the spear. The artifact's hum settled her—a pact between them, for now. Later, she promised, she'd decide what to do.

But not yet.

Francie set her jaw, marched down the hall, and pulled the front door shut behind her. Mitch sat on the passenger side of her truck, his elbow hanging out the open window. She clipped the spear in the truck bed rack that normally held a shovel or a post hole digger, then slid behind the wheel and dropped her overnight bag on the floorboard next to his pack. The cab smelled of coffee and dust. The wrapped sandwiches rested on the bench seat between them.

She twisted toward him, meeting his eyes. "Do you think that ... entity will come here?"

"Yes," he said. "You took something that belongs to him."

Her hands tightened on the wheel. "Then I have to stay and protect my horses and home."

"Francie." His tone softened, turned coaxing. "If you're worried, then we'll stay. Together." One brow lifted in quiet challenge, as if to make sure she understood the weight of being alone, isolated, *together* in a town like Roswell.

Before she could protest, he continued, "The entity's still high on the mountain with a lot of rough ground between him and us. It'll take him hours to find your ranch, if he even tries. It's already getting dark. Whether we stay or leave, I believe your horses and your land will be safe tonight."

Safe, he said. The word rang hollow, sliding over a memory she kept padlocked away. She wasn't afraid of him—he'd given her no reason to be—but the thought of being alone through the night was enough to push her to a decision.

"Then we'll leave." She turned the key in the ignition.

The engine coughed, stuttered, and went silent.

The sun was sinking past the mountains now, the air glowing gold in the last light. Shadows stretched long across the yard, and the night was coming fast.

ELEVEN

A shiver ran over Francie's arms. She checked the manual choke, depressed the clutch, turned the key again. Another growling rev, then silence.

Francie gripped the wheel, staring at the dashboard in disbelief. *This can't be happening. We have to leave—*

A sick thought hit her. She whipped her head toward Mitch, her words staccato and breathless. "You did this."

Francie halted on a flash of doubt. He'd been her anchor earlier, steady in the face of chaos. But the day's fears crowded out her better judgment. She pressed on, wanting reassurance, needing a denial.

"You told me something was wrong with the truck so you could get under the hood and sabotage—" The accusation snagged in her throat, fear choking it off.

He tipped his head back and barked a laugh, rough and bitter. The air between them crackled.

"Do you hear yourself? Why would I damage your vehicle when I didn't even believe you?"

He held her gaze, face shuttered, giving nothing away. For a breath, Francie wished she could call the accusation back, almost. But the fear wouldn't let go.

He *always* had an answer. His odd words, his impossible gun and unusual camera, the way he examined the artifact, as if it were both familiar and dangerous. And his probing questions about her father's disappearance, like he believed she knew more than she was saying.

She tried to chalk it all up to the military. Secret gadgets, code words, classified questions—she'd seen it at Los Alamos. She wanted to believe that simple explanation, wanted it so badly she could almost convince herself. But the justifications felt thin.

"How did you know the countdown for the spaceman's weapon?" she asked.

"I didn't, but I was issued a newly developed sidearm to field test, and it has a recharge interval, so I assumed ..." Mitch shrugged.

Francie's gaze fell away, the knot of suspicion still tight. Finally, she managed, "I'm sorry. It's just that ..."

"I know. It's been a rough day for both of us." He rubbed a hand over his face. "Let me take another look at the engine, okay?"

She slammed her door and joined him at the hood.

"There's the problem." He pointed at a black hose. "Fuel line's got a small crack, which means air gets in and stalls the engine. Unless you have a patch, we're not going anywhere."

Francie bit her tongue to stop herself from snapping, *"I know that."* She'd lived on the ranch almost all her life, mentored by a father who fixed what broke. Maybe the women in Roswell, simpering and batting their lashes, had let Mitch play the rescuer.

Well, she wasn't some frail damsel in distress.

That thought shook her. Since she'd scuttled back to her ranch, she'd spent a year wringing her hands instead of doing anything.

Not anymore. She needed to fix this. She couldn't stay overnight with a strange man in her house. Then again, was that her biggest worry, given that a homicidal spaceman with a ray gun that turned stone to powder could be storming her way?

Mitch's smooth, "Didn't you say your father had a workshop and a lab?" grated on her nerves. "Could he have stored extra parts there?"

Francie nodded. "I'll get the key."

"Grab the key to the lab, too. You search one, I'll search the other. Save time." He twirled the hose and flashed her a smile.

"No need. The lab's connected to the workshop. Stay here."

Francie started toward the house then doubled back for the spear. As she lifted it from the truck bed, the artifact's light flickered—restless, attuned to her agitation. She didn't question it now, and she wasn't about to leave it exposed.

"It'll be in the way," Mitch called after her.

She strode to the front door and tossed over her shoulder, "I won't make it easy for the alien to waltz in and take it."

Inside, Francie hurried down the dark hallway, the spear's purple glow lighting her way. She couldn't shake the sense that Mitch moved two steps ahead, leaving her to catch up.

Francie paused at her father's bedroom—a room she rarely entered, his presence sometimes so palpable it hurt. She set the spear against the wall, drew in a steadying breath, and opened the door. The herby sweetness of dried lavender and desert sage she kept in a bowl on the dresser mingled with the faint stuffiness of the closed-off room. Sunset smoldered burnt orange through the west-facing window. She crossed to the bed, running her hand over the colorful cotton Indian blanket, freshly laundered and free of dust. She missed the squeak of bedsprings at night, that quiet comfort of not being alone in the house.

At the tall dresser, Francie pulled the tasseled cord on the lamp. Soft light pushed back the shadows. Her father's absence and the not knowing hovered like a dark cloud in her mind. With a sigh, she opened his wooden valet box.

Inside, her mother's wedding ring gleamed on the green felt lining. Next to it lay silver cufflinks inset with bright blue turquoise, and a matching bolo tie, her mother's last gift to her husband before the cancer took her. It was so long ago, and she'd been so young, Francie's memories of her mom were hazy. A laughing face, gentle brown eyes, the scent of baking bread and apples, songs sung in a lilting Spanish accent.

Blinking back the start of tears, Francie lifted the tray of jewelry, revealing an iron ring of five keys. Four were familiar—workshop, truck, tack room, tractor. But the fifth was strange. A long, thin rectangular prism with circular divots and channels. She turned it over in her palm, the metal cold and unfamiliar. Her father's secrets—and hers—pressed in, heavy on her slim shoulders.

Francie grabbed the keys and reached to switch off the lamp. She caught a movement at the door.

Mitch stood there, arms crossed, his gaze sweeping the room.

"I asked you to stay outside." Her words came out harsher than she intended. The spear glowed in the hallway behind him.

"Why? You're only getting a key." He straightened, his eyes lingering on her father's valet box. "You said your father disappeared into the mountains about a year ago. Just the horse came back. No other trace?"

He kept circling back to her father, questions slipped in here or there. She shifted, clutching the key ring tighter. "That's right. I searched—the entire community did—for weeks."

"He didn't leave a note or anything? That maybe he was going to take his own ..." He shrugged.

For a moment, she couldn't speak.

She shut off the lamp and brushed past him to grab the spear. It shone brighter, red tinging its purple light. "He wouldn't do that," she said, voice rough with anger.

"How do you know?"

"Because I know. He wasn't that kind of man." She pivoted and hurried to the kitchen, Mitch right behind her. She propped the spear and snatched the kerosene lantern off the peg by the back door. Clanking it down on the countertop, she pulled open the drawer, hands shaking as she dug for matches.

"This ranch is hard to get to, hard to find. Was he wanted for something?" Mitch pressed.

"You mean, was he a criminal? No. He was a good man. He wasn't running from the law." Teeth clenched, Francie lit the lantern, pumping in air for brightness.

"He could still have been hiding. You said he was a physicist. Why didn't he apply for a position at Los Alamos?"

"He had his reasons."

My fingerprints on the start of the nuclear age could bring consequences I don't want to deal with. What will happen will happen whether or not I help. She hadn't understood, but after witnessing what the bomb could do, his words felt prescient—as if he'd already seen where it would all lead.

Francie grabbed the lantern handle and pulled up short. Mitch blocked the exit.

He unlatched the lock, half smiling as he swung the door open. "Ladies first."

With a jerky nod, Francie picked up the spear and skipped down the steps, the lantern carving a sphere of light in the growing darkness. She marched across the yard, Mitch at her heels.

The front of the workshop grew out of the shadowed cliff behind the house, inset with a thick wooden door. She slotted the key in the lock and snicked the bolt open.

"He wasn't hiding," she repeated. But her words sounded weaker. "And if he was, why allow me to work at Los Alamos? We have the same last name. They could've tracked him through me."

She pushed the door open, breath held, waiting for Mitch's answer.

"Maybe they did trace him through you." He paused, eyes narrowing. "That could be why he vanished."

It hit like a blow. It could be her fault he'd disappeared—all because she'd dared to leave, to make her mark. And all for nothing, now that she'd retreated home.

She was always so off-balance around Mitch, his questions pulling her in directions she hadn't expected.

"Don't blame yourself, Francie. If he was on the run, he would've been found, eventually. That he encouraged you to work and go to university places him ahead of his time. What you did was brave." His hand settled on her shoulder, his thumb stroking her back. "I'm sorry for all this. I wish it were different."

Her jaw loosened, her arms a little less tight. But she wouldn't let her guard drop for long. In a gruff voice, she said, "My dad always told me comfort makes you weak. Finding your place in this universe means leaving comfort behind and setting out into the unknown."

He chuckled, a sound that made her want to smile, a shift to something real passing between them. "Let's find a fuel hose."

Francie leaned the spear on the workbench, flipped on the overhead lights, and dimmed her lantern. Mitch handed her the cracked hose, and she moved to the shelves, eyes scanning boxes of truck and tractor parts bracketing the door to her father's lab.

She spotted a metal tin. "There. Patch kit!"

Francie pulled the tin from the shelf, waggling it in her hand with a triumphant smile, but Mitch held a framed photo, the one her father kept in the workshop. She laid the hose and tin on the bench top and stepped to his side.

"This you?" He swiped his thumb over the glass. "You still have a few of these freckles."

She touched her face, self-conscious.

"They're still cute." He smiled, and heat flared in her cheeks. She caught herself smiling back at him before she could help it.

His brows drew together, finger tracing the photo. "What's this bandage on your arm?"

"Dad gave me an injection. He worked in Spain as a scientist during the Great War. After all the deaths from disease, he wanted to protect me and my mother."

"Vaccinations?" At her nod, "Where did he get them?"

"He made them. Here. In his lab."

Mitch held her gaze, searching, but instead of speaking, he put the photograph down and gestured to a corkboard filled with snapshots, color and black and white, of animals. Dogs, cats, skunks and miner's cats, rabbits and foxes. Orion's golden coat and creamy mane and tail made him a popular color photo subject.

"What's all this?" he asked.

"My dad loved animals. He believed photos captured intelligence we couldn't always see."

A color image of a tan, bat-eared dog with a flat black face caught Francie's eye. She unpinned it, studying the details.

"This is ..." She tapped the photo. "On the ride back, I saw this dog."

The dog barking after the spaceman landed, the same bark attached to the flat-faced, bat-eared shape darting through the impossible village in the trees. And now, the same animal stared out of a photo from her father's workshop. This was the dog present at the heart of every bizarre event. And her father knew this dog.

The hair on Francie's neck prickled. Whatever connected those events, whatever plagued the ranch, her father had been at its very center.

"I saw him, too, Francie. And the elephants, and antelopes, and villages." Mitch leaned against the workbench, expression unreadable now, his warmth gone cold.

Below her ribs, a knot cinched tighter. Francie suppressed the urge to grab the spear and run.

Mitch jerked his head to the back of the room. "Is that your father's lab? What are you hiding in there?"

Francie bristled at the edge in his voice. She understood he was investigating, doing his job, but his attitude gave her whiplash. She snapped, "I'm not hiding anything."

"Then you won't mind if I look inside."

TWELVE

itch disappeared into the darkened space. Francie hurried to follow, switching on lights as she entered the room.

Her father had built his lab before Francie was born, carving it out of solid granite to penetrate deep into the mountainside, its opening concealed with his workshop's façade. He'd polished the room's walls, ceiling, and floor to a liquid shine that accentuated the richness of the stone. Might as well create in beautiful surroundings, he'd say, and swing a giggling Francie to perch on a stool beside him. She'd sit, the heels of her Cowgirl boots hooked over a metal strut, her ankle socks in a jumble, and listen while he talked, too young at first to absorb the science, later enthralled by it.

Mitch prowled through the overlapping funnels of ceiling light, surveying the shrouded benchtops. Stools were stowed into the kneeholes between the benches. A wide glass hood lay at the far end of the space. Francie shifted, biting her cheek. She'd searched the lab after her father's disappearance, uncovering nothing.

Mitch lifted drop cloths to study the instruments. "This place is set up for sterile processes," he said. "For the vaccines? I thought he was a physicist."

"Physics, chemistry, engines, radios. Whatever gadget he could get his hands on. He called himself a polymath, like da Vinci."

"For all I know, he could be da Vinci," Mitch muttered. "Did he bring any of those animals into this laboratory? Like his yellow horse? It's a big enough space."

"I can't see Orion in here, can you?" She forced a smile.

"What else did he work on?" When she didn't reply, he started opening drawers.

"What are you doing?"

"Looking for his research workbooks. Weren't you ever curious?"

"Yes, but I couldn't read them. He wrote in some kind of cipher. He didn't leave me that key. Just these." She jangled the key ring, then unlatched a cabinet and pushed the doors wide.

Dozens of lab journals, each spine dated by year and bound in plain green fabric, were shelved inside. And on top lay a first edition of *Through the Looking-Glass, and What Alice Found There*. She traced a finger over the reddish cloth, lingering on the gilded lettering and trim. She could almost hear her father's voice, and the weight of his absence settled over her.

"He read this to me as a child." She smiled up at Mitch, then froze at his pale face. "Are you okay?"

Alarmed, she laid her hand over his forearm. Beneath taut muscles, something hard and unyielding pressed against her palm.

"What's this?" Her fingers trailed over a bullet-sized lump above his wrist.

He tugged his arm away, then forced a smile.

"I'm fine. Old war wound," he said, and pulled the oldest lab journal free. "January 1920. Nothing earlier?"

"No. He bought the ranch the year before." Francie's gaze studied his stiff profile, the odd shape beneath his skin unsettling her.

"No. He bought the ranch the year before."

Mitch opened the lab book, and Francie moved beside him.

"It's written in ancient Greek. One of the dead languages of science. It shouldn't be difficult to translate." He ran a finger down her father's tight, crabbed script, turned the page, then another, until he stopped at a formula, its symbols indecipherable. He took out his Minox camera and hovered the device over the open book, scanning it inch by inch. Her jaw slackened when the camera lit up, and the handwritten Greek changed into typeset, the text scrolling like ghostly ticker tape on a tiny glass rectangle. At the top sat a single word: UNKNOWN.

"His own personal cipher," Mitch said. "We'll need the key."

"I told you that, and—and that's not merely a camera." Her voice shook, and she rubbed gooseflesh from her arms. "That's a computing machine."

Mitch glanced up, his expression flat, and pocketed the Minox. He plucked another bound lab book and perused it, then another. His hand paused over a slim gap between the final two notebooks. The dates jumped from 1945 to 1947. Francie stilled, waiting, but he didn't ask her the obvious question. Instead, he pulled the last journal off the shelf and opened it, flipping through until he found the end of her father's notes. He touched the date, the only decipherable words and numbers on the page.

"August 21, 1947."

"My father disappeared the next morning." Francie backed away from him. "I need to patch the fuel hose."

His head bowed over the open notebook, Mitch didn't reply.

Back in the workshop, Francie pried off the lid from the patch kit and reached for the hose. Her hand jerked back.

The fuel line was shredded. Sliced clean through in several places. Her hand hovered, brain refusing to catch up—until it did.

Behind her, Mitch loomed in the doorway, the spear locked in his grip.

"You did this. You want us stuck here." She stopped, hands

shaking. She didn't know him, had met him that day. But she'd wanted so badly to be wrong about him. More than anything. "You tricked me. I'm such a fool."

Mitch's jaw flexed. He dropped his gaze for a heartbeat before he fixed her with a flat stare, his expression unyielding.

"Why does this artifact respond to you, Francie?"

I don't know. She swallowed her retort and the hurt welling up inside her. She didn't owe him anything. She fumbled for the latch on the door to the outside, depressed it, and backed slowly into the night, the grass and dirt of the yard spongy under her boots.

Mitch followed, silhouetted by the workshop's light, his shadow enveloping her.

He dogged her steps, no longer feeling like an ally, his presence as unpredictable as the alien on the ridge. Francie's breathing quickened as she retreated, fear and anger shoving her toward action.

She forced her chin up. "We'll ride to Arabela. There's a phone in the general store. Call your commanding officer and tell him I— I want someone else to help me. I'm done with you."

Mitch met her eyes, letting the silence stretch until she wanted to scream. "He doesn't know I'm here. No one knows I'm here."

Of course—always a step ahead, always in control. Her gaze darted to the spear in his hand, willing it to light, to give her some advantage. But it stayed dark and lifeless. If she could take it away from him—

"Never play poker, Francie. You're too easy to read." A real smile flickered, unexpected, warm, the kind she'd started to hope for, as he hefted the spear. She almost smiled back. Almost wanted to forget the danger and the doubt and close the space between them.

His smile faltered. "I've seen what you can do with this thing, and I don't want to be on the receiving end."

A surge of anger steadied her. She needed a way to hold him off long enough to get away. Her mind raced to her gun, tucked in her overnight bag. It could buy her a chance to escape.

She needed to get to the truck.

Francie backed away from the workshop's open door so that she and Mitch were cloaked by the night. That comforted her. She had the advantage of territorial familiarity in the darkness.

"Francie, I'm not here to harm. I just want to figure out what's going on," Mitch said. "Don't you see? Everything points back to your father. Where's your father from? Where was he born?"

An innocuous question. She'd keep him talking, look for her chance to run.

"Lincoln, New Mexico. Just over the mountains. His parents died when he was young, and he traveled all over the world."

Crickets chirped all around her in the dark, and long stems of bunch grass swished against her jeans.

"Your mother?"

"A Basque region of France called Port de la Lune. It's where they met. He was in Spain during the Great War. I told you that."

She could barely see him, even as her eyes adjusted. She quickened her pace, the truck maybe a hundred feet from her now.

"Why is your horse a shift animal?"

She checked, brows furrowing. "A what?"

"As we rode him from the ridge, away from the spaceman, we were riding through time."

"Are you out of your mind?"

Mitchell Ward was officially a lunatic. She was in much greater danger than she'd thought.

But she'd felt the rain, smelled the smoke. Had tasted the bitter air of winter and the heavy musk of the mastodon.

"This is some kind of psyop to steal my land, isn't it?"

"Francie? In Roswell, why did you come to me?" Mitch asked. "Me specifically, if you didn't know what was going on?"

"I don't know what's going on. And Adelaide Baer gave me your name."

"Someone I've never met." He sighed. "It'll make my investigation so much easier if you'd tell me the tru—"

Francie rushed him, slammed both palms into his chest. Mitch staggered back. Satisfaction surged at the thud of his fall. She twirled and bolted, pounding through the sparse grass, dodging fruit trees in her small orchard. Her boots hit the hard-packed earth of the driveway. Ahead, the corral's pole lamp blurred the darkness, throwing enough glow to smudge her truck's outline, a hulking mass in front of her. A mastodon, poised in the haze, waiting for her escape. She nearly laughed at the thought.

Francie skidded to a stop at the truck, gravel crunching underfoot. Her hands, slick with sweat, fumbled with the handle. She yanked the door open. Mitch's footsteps thundered behind her, the sound filling her head.

She threw herself onto the driver's seat, pulling the door most of the way shut and wedging her heels against it. When Mitch's shadow darkened the window, Francie kicked the door with all her might. It crashed into him with a thump. He vanished from sight.

She twisted on the seat, hands fumbling through the overnight bag, every second stretching. Her fingers closed over the gun—cold, solid, a lifeline.

Got it. She slid from the truck, boots hitting the dirt, hope flaring. She'd run into the trees, escape, then—

Arms locked around her waist and slung her clear of the truck. The world spun. She and Mitch tumbled to the ground. Francie hit hard, the air knocked from her lungs. She gasped, panic spiking as she struggled to breathe.

She still held the gun.

Mitch straddled her, pinning her down. Francie's vision blurred at the edges. She raised her gun, back bowed, her arm shaking, desperate for space, for control. Her finger on the trigger ...

She couldn't do it. Couldn't shoot him. Her hand went slack. She flung the gun away.

"*Dammit*, Francie—" Mitch grabbed her wrist with crushing force.

They lay tangled on the ground, the world narrowing to the press of their bodies and the grit of dust on their skin. Tears stung her eyes. Her chest heaved. His forehead pressed against hers, but she jammed her arms between them, refusing to let him see her fall apart. The gun sat forgotten in the dirt, her escape plan gone with it.

Finally, Mitch's voice broke the silence. "Oh, God, Francie, I'm sorry ... I thought you'd back down if I pushed. I should've known better."

She glared up at him, voice choking. "Don't try to charm your way out of this. It won't work."

He let out an odd, high chuckle. "I've messed up everything, haven't I? If I let you up, will you promise—"

"No."

He laughed again, this time with genuine humor. "Fair enough."

In one swift motion, he sprang to his feet and snagged her gun. He tugged the Minox out of his pocket, switched on its light, and clipped it to his shirt. She watched him from where she lay, dull-eyed and motionless, as he rolled out the pistol's cylinder.

His eyes narrowed. "Even if you'd pulled the trigger, you wouldn't have shot me. There's no bullet in the chamber."

"I know."

Frowning, he dumped the shells into his palm and slid them into his trouser pocket, then shoved the gun into the waistband at the small of his back. He held out his hand to Francie.

She turned her face away and steeled herself against another false reassurance. Like the one he murmured now.

"It's okay, Francie. I'm not going to hurt you."

Funny. Because he already had.

She wished for her father to appear and rescue her from this mess, but she pushed the thought away. He'd left her. She had no one else to rely on but herself. That meant she would have to uncover the mysteries surrounding her—including what Sergeant Mitchell Ward really wanted and what he knew about the crash landing and the spaceman.

Francie looked up into Mitch's shadowed face before taking his hand and letting him tug her to her feet. When his arms went around her, she allowed herself to feel the solid warmth of him, the scent of dust and pine.

When she pulled back, heat prickled under her skin, thoughts in a tangle.

Mitch's hands remained on her upper arms, steadying her, unwelcome and electric, a reminder of everything she wanted to resist but couldn't ignore.

Francie lifted her chin, meeting his gaze. A tremor shook her, but steel edged her voice. "Who the h-hell are you?"

The Minox clipped to Mitch's pocket switched on, bright light pulsing. Francie narrowed her eyes as an image appeared on the small computing surface. She went still, heart slamming as if jolted by an unseen current. Her hand crept to her throat.

There, on the glass display, was the sleek helmet and impenetrable black faceplate of the spaceman on the ridge. A voice burst from the silvery metal rectangle.

"Mitchell Ward, you son of a gun. What the hell, man? You almost killed me."

Thirteen

Francie knocked Mitch's hands from her arms, her eyes so wide open they stung. She couldn't tear her gaze away from the image on the Minox, a moving picture broadcast in real time and color. Like television, but in miniature.

The spaceman continued talking. In *English*.

"That woman took my periapt. I want it back. And have you seen that damn dog—"

Mitch tapped the Minox, and the voice went silent. But the screen remained on, the spaceman still gesticulating with his puffy white gloves.

Gloves with four fingers and a thumb.

Francie lifted her hand. She stared at her palm, strong and callused from working the ranch. *Four fingers and a thumb.* The same as the spaceman.

"Not an alien," she said. "Did you know that?"

"No." Mitch grimaced. "And yes. Look. If you want to save your ranch and maybe find out what happened to your father, we need to talk."

Francie's jaw tightened. Her father. Again. He knew exactly what he was doing.

Fine. She'd stay for answers, but ...

"You get one hour," she said. "Then I'm riding to call the sheriff."

Francie stared from under lowered brows at the sandwich on her plate. Mitch had cut it crossways, given her half an apple, and poured her a cup of coffee from the thermos.

He sat down, holding a kitchen towel her mother had stitched when she could no longer leave her bed. He folded and laid it next to his plate, his fingers running over colorful threads that spelled out her full name, lingering over the elegant cursive "F."

"Francisca—not Francine or Frances—Pearl Cortez. Eat, then I'll answer your questions." He picked up his sandwich.

She bit into her food, surprised when her hunger kicked. She took a second bite, and they ate in silence, Francie marshaling her thoughts.

The coffee warmed her inside, loosening the tight set of her shoulders. Over breadcrumbs and the apple core, she eyed Mitchell Ward. He'd polished off his first sandwich, made another, and gave her half. All without a word. Was he stalling? Thinking up more lies?

"You've wasted ten minutes of your hour, so if this is some kind of delay tactic, it won't work. Start with how the spaceman knows you." She thunked her coffee cup on the table and leaned forward. "Because if this is some military scheme to take my ranch, and you and that spaceman are working together—"

"Francie, please. There's no scheme to seize your property. But if we report this, it'll be out of my hands."

"What do you mean?"

"I'm not working with the spaceman. And I don't know who he is or how he knows my name. I can guess, though."

She straightened in her chair and eyed him over the rim of her cup. "How?"

"The Minox. It can act like a two-way walkie-talkie. He must have picked up the frequency and listened in on us."

She swirled the dregs of her coffee, assessing his explanation. If the spaceman invaded the Minox with his image and voice, he *could* be spying on them. Or Mitchell Ward could be lying.

"Why are you in Roswell?" Francie asked.

"Because of the V2 rocket program at the White Sands Proving Ground. I'm part of the recovery crew—photography documentation, among other things." He lifted the Minox. "My appointment to the recruiting office allows me to be called at any time for cleanup duty."

The truth, maybe. But the whole truth? Francie dug deeper.

"You were in Roswell for the inaugural V2 rocket launch? March 1946?" At his raised brows, she shrugged one shoulder. "Everyone knew about it, even if it was a secret."

"I wasn't assigned here until mid-July of '47."

"Right before my father vanished. Then how is it you didn't hear about his disappearance? It was in all the papers."

"I might have. I don't remember." Mitch mirrored her shrug and sat back in his chair, arms crossed. "I was investigating the Brazel ranch crash during that time."

"That's why Adelaide gave me your name. She said that your presence in Roswell stemmed from the crash and that you'd help me."

"I don't know how she came up with that. With her past top secret clearance—" He halted, a flicker of alarm passing over his face, and whispered, "She knows who I am."

"Why wouldn't she?"

He held up a hand to halt her words, then stared into the cup. When he lifted his head, his studied casualness put Francie on alert.

"Let me get the timeline straight. Your father disappeared a few weeks after the Brazel ranch incident. Your father knew about that crash?"

"The whole world did." Mitch's question made no sense, which meant another layer lurked beneath this conversation, one she didn't grasp. "He called me in Socorro after the second press release—the weather balloon correction."

Mitch hesitated. "It wasn't a weather balloon. The crash debris came from a secret listening project, meant to spy on the Soviets' atomic weapons tests."

Francie's stomach dropped. "They have atomic weapons?"

"Not yet, but acquisition was inevitable." He paused. "How long have your father and Adelaide known each other?"

"Forever, I guess. She's like a surrogate mother to me. I came to you about this because she sent me, but ..." Francie lifted her chin. "You didn't believe me."

He barked a laugh, but it sounded more weary than amused. "Okay. Fine. I believe you."

"And you know what's going on now, but you're not being truthful to me. It's a top secret military mission, isn't it? Because that spaceman is human." Francie ran a trembling hand through her curls. "And that thing he called a periapt—my spear—and your gun. They're some kind of self-contained lasers."

He topped off his mug with fresh coffee. "Probably. How do you know about lasers?"

Something sparked inside her. She was done pretending she didn't know things. No more sitting at the back of the classroom, letting the other students fumble when she had the answer.

"Einstein, 1917, and the principle of stimulated emission. I guess the military has moved them along further than I thought."

Mitch started to answer, but his gaze slid away, as if caught off guard. He huffed a laugh, rubbing the back of his neck. "Yeah. You guessed right."

"But my father told me they'd never be as on-demand as gunpowder. You had to count to ten before recharge."

"Your father said that?" His smile grew, slow and genuine. "Your father was familiar with lasers."

Francie shrugged, a small, secret thrill warming her. For once, she wasn't behind the curve. She started to ask another question, but he raised his hand.

"As far as I know, that spaceman is not part of a military mission." He paused, frowning. "But after seeing your father's lab, I wonder if there's something important in his journals. And whoever is out there wants the contents."

"*I* don't know what's in them. How would they?"

Mitch frowned. "He disappeared with no trace. That sounds like an abduction."

"*What?* But it's been a year."

"They may have extracted as much as he could give them. Francie, what's his secret code? You've accused me of keeping the truth hidden, but I have that same feeling about you. You must have some idea."

"I—I don't." She lurched to her feet, the blood rushing from her head. "We have to report this now. We can ride to Arabela, borrow a truck. We'll take the journals, show ... Oh, Mitch, what if they hurt him? What if he's already ..."

Mitch stood, too, something almost like regret passing over his face as his hand settled on his sidearm.

"I'm sorry, Francie. None of this can leave your ranch."

She gaped at him. "You're going to *shoot me*?"

"No!" He gaped right back. "I want this ready in case—"

A flash outside the kitchen window snapped Francie around. The hair on her arms rose, the air sizzling and sharp.

The pane of glass shattered in a dazzling blast of light and sound.

FOURTEEN

Erie green light split the air between Francie and Mitch. The dish rack with her father's mug flew off the counter. She lunged to save it, but a powerful blow toppled her backward. She hit the floor, Mitch's forearm cushioning her head before it slammed against the linoleum, his body a shield against falling crockery and raining glass. The mug—one she'd made her father in high school—hit the ground with a crash.

Francie lay there, stunned, Mitch's weight crushing as the last tinkle of sound faded. For a fleeting moment, she let herself sink into the comfort and safety of his closeness. She stared up into his eyes in the growing silence as he gazed back, and his expression softened.

"You okay?" he asked.

She nodded. "It must be—"

The spaceman's voice broke their fragile spell, blaring like thunder from Mitch's front pocket.

"You turned me off, Mitch, right in the middle of my dramatic, threatening declaration. So, I thought I'd get your attention another way. I want the periapt. Now. Bring it to me or I'll take that house apart piece by piece, then start on the barn."

Francie's shock snapped into hard, hot anger. Orion and Venus. She tugged the Minox from Mitch's pocket and spoke into the front screen like it was a microphone.

"If you touch my home or any part of my ranch, I will come after you and shoot you, you son-of-a—" She halted and gritted her teeth. She refused to curse out loud again, no matter how good it felt. *Get a grip. Grip. Grip strength of pliers is force applied to handle, F-h, times effective length of handle, L-h, equals—*

The spaceman burst out laughing. "She's a feisty one, Mitch, I'll give you that. Is she your target? Or is it her fa—"

Mitch yelled, "Mute, code-ax," and grabbed the Minox from Francie. He pulled her up and flashed a glance around the shattered kitchen—chairs toppled, china smashed.

"We can't stay here—he'll keep hitting us. We've got to leave, draw him away. Where's the spear?" Mitch's voice was low and intense.

She stared into his face, mouth open. "*You* had it last."

But something flared beneath her skin—faint, electric. An unseen thread winding straight to—

"The truck," they said in unison. Side by side, they dashed to the front door, and with a fierce clarity, she knew she didn't have to do this by herself, but she didn't have to lean on him, either. For now, they'd face what was coming side by side.

But before Francie could bolt outside, Mitch grabbed her again.

"No. The porch and truck could be in his field of vision, and there's too much light. Where's it coming from?"

Above the red-checked curtains, a diffuse glow streamed inside through the multipaned windows.

"Solar lamps on poles. They sense when it's dark and turn on. Dad wired them to recharge automatically."

"You have solar-powered lights?" His voice rose. "Your father invented something that no one else had?"

"In 1883, Charles Fritts invented the first solar-powered light. In 1905, Albert Einstein proposed the photoelectric theory. My father was always tinkering, finding ways to make work on the ranch easier. He said in the future, electricity created from the sun would be everywhere." Francie held out her hand, palm up, demanding. "Give me back my gun."

"No. Is there a way to turn those lights off?"

"There's a switch in one of the barn's tack rooms, but it's a long walk without cover." She paused. "Why not?"

Mitch lifted the curtains and peeked outside. "Why not what?"

"Why can't I have my gun?"

A slow smile touched his lips, and Francie's pulse leaped. "Because I don't trust you not to shoot me."

"Right now, I'm your only ally. Besides, I always leave that chamber empty."

"I know that now." He released the curtain and eased back into the door's interior shadow. "From the angle of the kitchen shot, I'd say he's up high on the east side of the mountain. That means the front door is a no-go. Even if we make it and shut the lights off, he'll have thermal imaging, a range finder, and a hundred other detection methods to find us."

"Infrared sight capability? A night vision scope?"

"You've heard of ...?" He shook his head, his smile lopsided. "Another Los Alamos gadget?"

"The Battle of Okinawa. Night vision scopes turned the tide for the Americans," Francie said. "There are no lights outside Dad's bedroom on the west side of the house. He left the trees and understory, and booby trapped it instead."

"That didn't make you suspicious that your father had something to hide?"

She shrugged. "I dismantled everything months ago. We can climb out his window, and then what?"

"Drive back to Roswell, and you take me to your friend Adelaide. I need to speak to her."

"You disabled the truck, remember? Besides, I can't abandon the horses if he targets them as leverage to get the ... What did he call it? The periapt."

Mitch narrowed his eyes. "Right. Orion."

"And Venus. If he hits the barn with one of those ray gun beams, they'll go crazy. They could hurt themselves. I won't leave them. That means we ride."

Another sizzle erupted, followed by a muffled explosion lighting up the kitchen doorway. Francie grabbed his hand and pulled him down the hallway into her father's bedroom, unlatched one of the windows, and flung up the sash. Mitch climbed out first, his ray gun in hand, and Francie scrambled down beside him. The trees blocked the lights from the ranch yard, cloaking them in darkness. The truck stood thirty yards away, the hood and windshield bathed in weak yellow light, the passenger side swallowed in shadows that fused with the thick shrubbery fronting the house.

"Stay low," Mitch said, and darted behind a fir tree, luxuriant branches sweeping the ground. Francie followed, her gaze combing the east side of the mountain for movement. If they kept the bulk of the truck between them and the spaceman's night vision, maybe he wouldn't be able to track them.

Mitch ran again, his body bent double, following the long shadow of the truck to its passenger side. Francie leaped up from her position, boots pounding dirt. She slid beside him, her back pressed against the metal of the fender flare.

"I dropped the periapt when you slammed me with the driver's side door." He slanted her a glance and slipped to the end of the truck bed. Mitch peeked around the tailgate, his black hair glossed with light from the corral. "I don't see it."

But Francie saw it—a dark shape lying still beneath the carriage, the periapt's power drained. She sank to her stomach, arm stretching out, fingers scrambling across the dirt. Not close enough. She edged herself under the truck... *More* ... Inched farther underneath ... Her fingers brushed the shaft.

Almost...

The spear flared. Bright purple light coursed along the scrollwork, illuminating the metal ribs and undersides of the truck. *The spaceman will see it. No, no, no.*

Her hair prickled, static crackling in the air. *Hurry, get out, hurry.*

With a desperate lunge that left her deep under the truck, she grabbed the spear and reversed. Her skull connected hard against the metal underbelly. Sparks marred her vision. A wave of sound crackled in her eardrums. Green light swelled, washing away the shadows beneath the truck.

Time seemed to slow. Every breath elongated, every heartbeat echoed. Francie clenched the spear tight, her mind screaming she wouldn't make it. Wouldn't—

Strong hands yanked her ankles. Mitch hauled her through the dirt, his arms locked around her waist. He hauled her upright and dragged her behind the cover of a fir's sweeping branches.

Francie caught a flash—a glowing ball of energy hurtled toward them.

BOOM.

The explosion lifted the truck a foot off the ground. Windows shattered. Sparkling glass showered to earth. The truck's chassis crunched down on the hard-packed gravel, its tires erupting in fiery bursts.

She would've been killed. Mitch had dragged her clear of the blast.

He still held her close. "I thought I was too late," he whispered, voice raw.

Francie blinked, startled by the crack in his composure, his vulnerability ... *over her.* An unexpected warmth uncurled, threading deep inside.

A loud thump yanked her attention behind them. The truck's

roof had been blown off and sat upside-down, bent and scorched in the bunch grass yard, rocking back and forth. The acrid scent of smoke stung her nose.

Francie stared, speechless. When her eyes met Mitch's, she was sure hers were as wide and startled as his. Bug-eyed and open-mouthed, they probably looked ridiculous, but the first time in years, she didn't care what other people thought of her.

Except maybe for the man who'd saved her life.

"Great. Just great," Francie said, voice trembling, eyes rolling as she flung out a hand toward the flaming wreckage. "Now I have a convertible."

Mitch choked and dropped his head. His shoulders shook, a laugh breaking free.

He was laughing. *Laughing*. And her own laugh burst out of her, wild and shaky.

Francie slapped her dusty palm over her mouth, the spear running its light up and down the shaft and sending a pleasant tingle through her fingers and up her arm.

Still chuckling, Mitch raised his head, his eyes brimming with something like wonder.

"Every other person in this situation would run for the hills," he said. "And then there's Francisca Pearl Cortez." He smiled at her, and her heart stuttered.

Oh, that smile.

This time it felt real. Not the practiced charm he used to manipulate, but as if he was finally seeing her clearly. And in that moment, Francie saw past the polish to the man underneath.

Sound crackled from his pocket, and his face fell into a scowl.

"He broke the code-ax." Mitch yanked out the Minox, and Francie crawled next to him to stare at the screen and the image of the spaceman's helmet-covered head.

"Code what?"

"An encryption program. It's supposed to block hostiles from commandeering the Minox."

"Olly olly oxen free! Come on, Mitch. You didn't think you'd get away with—"

Mitch touched the glass. The spaceman's voice cut off, even though his helmet stayed on screen. "He's tracking us."

"Codes and ciphers, like during the war?" Prickles chased down her arms. "Is it thermal? Or—radio waves?" She glanced at the Minox. "Can he see us now?"

Mitch grimaced. "Not thermal—the flash burned that out. He's tracking us through the Minox itself. There's a kind of signal beacon inside, far more advanced than anything we have now. It should be impossible to break, but somehow he's cracked it and is stingraying us."

Her mouth went dry as he spoke what was technical gibberish to her but held great meaning to him. The warmth created by Mitch's smile leached away, flinty cold taking its place. They needed to get to safety, but she had questions screaming to be answered.

"So, he's following us by radio waves? Or radar? Or ...?"

He smiled faintly. "Think of it as a supercharged signal finder, a beacon catching a far-off distress call—except the encryption is supposed to block it. And it's not. It's showing him where we are."

"Can you turn it off?"

"That's the trouble—it's a failsafe. Since I elected not to be transposed, the locator is the only thing that can guide my retrieval if the mission goes south."

Transposed? Retrieval? What did it all mean? Francie swallowed down her questions before glancing at the screen. The spaceman was still talking, his face shield lit up by whatever he spoke into. Wherever he was, tree trunks and low-hanging pine boughs wrapped him like a blanket.

"Even if I could disable the location beacon, your father's solar lights will give us away when we run to the barn to turn them off. A nice logic loop." He peered at Francie. "Or I can shoot them out with my, uh, ray gun."

"But you can't! I'll need those when everything returns to ..." *Normal* was the last word she'd use after all that had happened. "If he knows where the Minox is with his ... stingraying, do you see him on your ... box? Stingray him back. Ping him like radar or sonar on a ship or submarine. Then cover me with your ray gun so I can turn the lights off and get the horses out. I won't let him harm Orion and Venus."

"I don't think he will. He's desperate. He's lost his shift animal and, if I've read the situation correctly, he needs Orion—" Mitch bit off the rest of his sentence. "What will we do once you get the horses?"

"You said we should draw him away from my home." Francie slid a glance to the man whose arm pressed into hers. "But if he follows us to Arabela, we'd put others in danger."

"Didn't your father camp out at a hidden canyon? Let's go there and regroup."

"But he'll still be able to follow the Minox signal."

"Which is what we want. Besides, he's on foot and we'll be on horseback. The canyon walls will block his location tracker. We'll lose him in the wilderness." Mitch put a hand on her shoulder. "Your horses will be safe. You'll be safe."

The periapt dimmed to a dark, foreboding plum. *I'm missing something important.* Exhaustion and agitation clouded her mind. If they could get to her dad's hideout, she could rest and think.

"Okay," she said. "We'll ride to the canyon. You distract him with your ray gun so I can get to the barn."

"Yes, ma'am." He hunkered low and crept toward the damaged truck, Francie close behind. The explosion had blown both doors open, but their bags were still in the passenger footwell. She tugged her Samsonite overnight case free. The handle hung twisted and broken, but the latches and hard shell had protected its contents. Her arm snaked inside again to grab the rucksack's strap, bumping it to the dirt.

Mitch looked up from the Minox and took the backpack. He unzipped a panel and tucked her empty gun inside, then slid the bullets from his trousers into a pocket. He shouldered the pack and moved around the tailgate.

"I've located him and code-axed—"

"*Mitch.*" Frustration rang in Francie's voice.

"Sorry. I've blocked our signal, so he doesn't know where we are—for now," Mitch said, his smile grim. "It's cat and mouse as we break each other's encryptions."

"He's been awfully quiet. Why hasn't he shot at us again?" she asked.

"Because he's on the move." He held up the Minox.

A smaller black rectangle winked, coordinates shifting next to it, while a larger section of the screen still showed the spaceman muted and stationary, framed by pine boughs.

"He's streaming a vid loop to trick us into thinking he's static. But he'll know by my first shot that we weren't fooled. He's about a quarter of a kilometer away as the crow flies."

"He can't fly, can he? I mean, I saw his descent from the sky this morning—"

"If he could fly, he would've met us at the house. Either his suit can't, or it was damaged in the shift." Mitch pulled his ray gun.

In the shift.

On an impulse, Francie reached out, brushing her fingers against his cheek. The rough stubble sent a shiver through her. Their eyes locked, and the world narrowed.

Francie let her hand linger, then pulled back, clearing her throat. She wasn't ready to name the pull building between them, but she was glad he was here.

Mitch's lips quirked as if he'd say something, but he just nodded, the moment suspended between them. Then, businesslike, he adjusted his pack and pointed his weapon at the mountainside.

"Ready?" he asked.

Francie tucked her overnight case under her arm and moved to his side, her grip tight on the periapt.

"Once I'm in the barn," she told him, "get out of here. I'll meet you at my father's workshop."

Fifteen

Francie bumped open the hook latch on the barn doors, slipped inside, and pulled it closed behind her. She leaned against it, breathing hard, shedding the gut-churning dread of a laser strike during her dash across the yard. The earthy-sweet scent of hay and horses calmed her. Mitch's covering fire had kept her safe.

Their sleep interrupted, Orion and Venus stuck their heads over their stalls, ears perked, shadowy in the glow of the solar lights that seeped through the eaves. Francie ran past the horses and dropped her case at her feet, propping the spear over it. She flipped off the large switch to the outside lights. The periapt's purple radiance replaced the yellow light of the solar lamps, only to be smothered by flashes of the brilliant white and green of Mitch's and the spaceman's ray guns.

With swift efficiency, she saddled both horses and stuffed her saddlebags with a change of clothes from her case, along with her dad's lab book. She added C-rations stored in the barn for emergencies and tied bedrolls to the back of the saddles before rummaging through a second cabinet for mess kits and canteens.

Another bright sizzle of shots lit the barn, but the light had shifted. Mitch must be on the move. Francie's blood drummed in her ears, and she closed her eyes tightly. *Please let him stay safe.* The canteens clattered in her grip as she veered around Venus, who danced skittishly. She grabbed the periapt, its purple glow bleeding into the dark corner that housed the freshwater spigot. The water gurgled in the canteens as she filled them.

Her restless eyes landed on a door by the spigot, secured with a padlock forged from a metal she couldn't name. It wasn't brass or steel—its color hovered somewhere between gunmetal and burnished silver, with hints of an odd iridescence. A lock that felt out of place ... until now.

The keys in her pocket pressed heavily against her leg, the odd rectangular one nagging at her. And her father's message—his last to her—lurked at the edge of her thoughts.

She'd told no one about the note she found wrapped around her father's keys after he disappeared. The wording had struck her as final. She'd memorized and destroyed it, the message too much like goodbye for comfort.

Francie,

I must leave you. I'm sorry. The ranch is yours, and there is enough money in the bank for your independence. I'm proud you decided to pursue a degree. It won't be easy in this era, but comfort makes you weak. The only way to find your place in this universe is to venture from the known into the unknown. Remember, who you were yesterday won't lead you where you must go tomorrow.

Four keys open all my doors and will give you access to all I have. But the fifth key is special. The fifth key will allow you access to all I know. Use that key when it's time.

Love,

Dad

She shoved her hand deep in her dungarees' hip pocket and pulled out the jangling iron ring. Using the periapt's purple light, she isolated the fifth key and turned it in her fingers. With its odd shape, its circular divots, and etched lines, it resembled nothing she'd ever seen—much like the padlock.

She smothered a hysterical laugh. Her whole *day* had resembled nothing she'd ever seen. Like she was caught in some twisted scavenger hunt following Alice through the Looking-Glass.

Use the fifth key when it's time. If ever there was a time, it was now.

Francie lifted the padlock and found a small rectangular hole. Breath held, she inserted the key into the slot. The lock buzzed, and the curved shackle popped open. She hadn't even needed to turn it. She muscled the heavy metal bar up and pushed the door ajar. Grasping the periapt for light, she stepped inside.

Her shoulders wilted. Broken-down tools and farm implements filled the room. Piled wooden boxes, worn-out household items. Nothing that promised revelation or answers.

Then the periapt's glow intensified to a focused purple beam that cut through the dust motes to rest on a wooden jewelry box. Her mother's, the match to the one in her father's bedroom, packed away at her death. At age seven, Francie hadn't understood any of it. She'd just absorbed his devastation.

"I could have saved her, but she wouldn't let me," his tear-filled voice echoed in her memory. "She understood. I was too afraid I'd lose her. Too selfish, too arrogant. I thought I could control—"

He'd broken down, clasping Francie against his chest, where she'd cried until she'd fallen asleep.

His words made no sense then. They still didn't. He could have saved her, but was too afraid? And she'd died of cancer, anyway.

Francie stood over the jewelry box. Her tears blurred her vision as she wiped away the dust, her fingertip tracing the carved rose on top. The periapt's glow lightened to a shimmering violet, steady and warm. With a deep breath, Francie opened the box.

She blinked in shock. In the velvet-lined tray lay a V-shaped wedge. It was the missing piece of the artifact, spear, periapt—whatever it was—she'd taken from the ridge, and now held at her side.

She scooped up the piece, the metal warm and satiny, and cradled it in her palm. A tingle shot up her arm, hair rising, her skin prickling with goose bumps. Turning the periapt in her hands, she angled the wedge toward the shaft's dark notch. With every millimeter closer, its glow brightened—first a soft violet, then a searing, blinding purple-white that scorched her vision, painting eerie afterimages behind her eyelids.

Her fingers trembled as she slotted the wedge into place. The barn's interior plunged into absolute darkness. In the hush, Venus snorted, her hooves thudding in hesitant rhythm on the wooden planks.

Francie's pulse hammered all the way to the tips of her fingers. The spear's energy didn't fade—it coiled, condensed ... and then surged.

A thin ring of purple light flickered at the base, pulsing with a low electric hum. The glow crept upward, casting wild shadows that danced across the storage room. As it reached the tip, the metal vibrated in her grip, heat radiating into her palm.

The scrollwork along the shaft writhed, the etched lines sparking to life, sizzling with energy. Glyphs—letters? symbols?—spilled from the shaft in a shower of light, casting fractured projections across metal, wood, dust. Francie squinted against the glare, trying to make sense of it. Writing? A message? But she couldn't read it, not the way it lay broken and stretched over the jumble of stacked junk.

Francie ran into the open barn and into an empty stall, closing the door behind her. Knees shaking, she turned and read the periapt's message, projected as light on the wooden walls surrounding her.

Francisca Pearl Cortez

Below her name were numbers corresponding to the letters: 1 for F, 2 for R, running to 14 for Z, the last letter in Cortez. Below that, each number was given a Greek letter designation.

Greek letters. Like those that filled her father's lab books. The cipher she hadn't cracked.

She'd found his secret code.

And she—*Francisca Pearl Cortez*—was the key.

Sixteen

A flash of light through the eaves jolted Francie. The periapt dimmed, and the scrawled symbols and numbers disappeared from the stall's wooden sides.

Mitch. Time to get out of the barn and to her father's workshop.

She buckled the rifle scabbard's latigos through D-rings on Venus's saddle, then slid the spear into it. It protruded awkwardly over the horse's hindquarters, but that couldn't be helped. The periapt's glow simmered to a deep purple. Good. She didn't want the spaceman to see its light and track them again.

Francie rested her hand on Venus's saddle. She'd tell Mitch about the periapt wedge and her findings after they were safely away. She had the 1946 journal in her saddlebag and could picture the two of them bent over the journal, deciphering her father's work together. Trusting him—with the code, with whatever came next.

Except she knew the pattern now. Every time she decided he was an ally, he pivoted, or withdrew, or hid behind his orders. The back-and-forth left her off-balance.

Still, when the chips were down, he'd circle back, say the right things, and stand beside her when it counted. That teamwork, that cooperation, felt good. It felt real.

Plus, he'd just saved her life. He was in just as much danger as she was, and it was her problems that had placed him in that danger.

Like it or not, she needed his help. For now, they were tied together.

Another flash, sickly green this time, brightened the barn's interior, dragging her back. *Ten ... nine ... eight ...*

Whatever he was hiding, whatever doubts she held, it would have to wait. She needed to go.

Francie untied Venus and Orion and tugged the barn doors open. The cold night air rushed in. Stars scattered above the ranch yard, which was still flickering with the glow of smoldering truck wreckage.

Two ... one ... A green light burst above her like a flare, illuminating the ranch yard. Was he looking for them? At least he wasn't targeting her home.

She counted down again—another burst of green light. When it receded, she jogged the horses across the open space, Venus skittering as they passed the smoking truck. Her breath steadied despite the pounding in her ears when she made it into the trees before the next flash rose in the sky. She mounted and strong-armed Venus around the house, keeping tight to the cliff wall behind her home as she trotted to the workshop, Orion on his lead behind them.

Mitch stepped out of the shadows as the sky brightened again. "What took you so long?"

She opened her mouth to tell him about the cipher ... then stopped. *Not yet.* "I had to dig out an old saddle for Orion. Remember? We left the other one at the ridge. Can you get on Orion by yourself? Left side."

He stepped into the stirrup and swung his leg over the saddle, but caught the cantle, pitching forward onto Orion's neck. The horse pinned back his ears but stayed quiet.

Once settled in the saddle, Mitch tugged the Minox out of his shirt pocket and stared at the screen, his face painted with its glow.

She leaned over his shoulder. The blinking dot had stopped. "Can we go? Is it safe?"

"Yeah. He's above us on the mountain, but farther south."

Francie waited until the next flare had burned out before she backtracked along the rocky wall, Mitch and Orion next to her.

"There's a trail up the mountain. Once we're past him, could you ease up on the code-axing? Let him catch our signal so he'll follow us."

Mitch gave a faint smile. "Good plan, Francie. It's the safest move for us and keeps others out of danger."

Another flash of green split the darkness, casting long shadows among the trees. She spotted the break in the underbrush and nudged Venus forward. The trail closed in as they climbed, branches from the trees lining either side of the track brushing her sleeves. The fading odor of burning rubber from the truck mingled with the scent of turpentine sap and loam. Venus's and Orion's hooves clicked on rocks, sending pebbles skittering down the slope. Mitch's fatigues whispered against the foliage. Another burst of light lit the black night sky.

"Does he ever run out of rounds?" Francie asked, her tone dry and edged in irony, breaking the heavy silence. The question was rhetorical. At least, it should have been.

But Mitch answered without hesitation, his tone distracted and flat. "Never. The ray gun's power is infinite—" He caught himself. "I mean, yes. Eventually. He's moving again."

She twisted in her saddle to stare at him. His eyes were locked on the Minox screen, his face lit from below by its light. He flashed her a look before dropping his gaze once again, his jaw tight.

Infinite. That one word slammed into her, rewinding everything she thought she understood. Infinite power? That defied the first law of thermodynamics. No perpetual motion machine had ever worked—not without drawing more energy in than it gave out. Not without a cost.

Yet Mitch spoke with offhand certainty, as if it were proven technology. Then he backed off, quick and smooth, changing the subject. Again. Francie turned, gaze on the trail.

He was back to hiding things, shifting from ally to stranger with practiced ease. Cagey, even calculated, and now that they'd be buried in the wilderness all night, frightening.

A sharp reminder that he knew more than he admitted. Way more.

"The angle of his flares isn't over the ranch now," Mitch said. "He must realize we're gone. We need to get ahead of him, so I can ping him to follow. Otherwise, he might double back to your home. That's still the idea, right? Draw him clear of the house and barn while we shelter and regroup in the canyon. Your plan."

Your plan.

It wasn't. Hiding in the canyon had been *his* idea all along. Now he was planting it like it came from her. Classic manipulation. Soft tactics for someone hungry, sleep-deprived, and worn thin.

But Francie wasn't stupid.

The puzzle pieces piled up—the spaceman, the periapt, the cipher key. Her father. All of it twisted together. Somehow.

And even though it was in Mitch's sights, the canyon wasn't just a place to hide. It was a place where she could *think.*

For now, she'd keep the cipher and what she'd unearthed from her father's journal close. Not tell him anything, because two could play that game. When Mitch slept, she'd use the periapt to crack the code herself. Maybe finally understand what her father hid in his journals, and its value.

Mitch's insistence that they go to the canyon didn't make sense unless this wasn't about saving the ranch from the spaceman. Or it was about her father. Mitch was after something. She just didn't know what yet. A slow prickle crawled along her arms.

Fine. Let him push them there. Let him think she was following.

He didn't know the half of it.

She'd ridden every cutbank and draw on her land. Knew every dead end, every escape route. If he wanted to maneuver her, she'd maneuver right back.

Francie brushed her fingers across the smooth leather scabbard holding the periapt, the metal beneath warm to the touch.

One way or another, she'd get her answers.

And maybe take back an advantage.

SEVENTEEN

The light of a half-moon threw dim shadows down the tree-lined trail Francie followed. Most people missed the canyon's narrow entrance, but she'd found it during the days and nights she'd combed the ranch for her father. Not on Venus, whose coat was slick with nervous sweat, her muscles trembling and ears perked for any threat of danger. During her searches, she'd ridden Orion, and Orion's presence tonight kept the skittish mare from bolting every time a branch bobbed in the breeze.

The horse's calm allowed Mitch to focus on tracking the spaceman. The flares had finally stopped. Francie glanced back. Mitch cupped the Minox in his hand, the bright screen illuminating his frown, while his mount's reins fell in deep loops, providing no guidance. Orion, his eyes half closed to catch snatches of sleep, ambled behind Venus. No circus tricks now.

Mitch broke the silence. "How much longer?"

"Close." Francie nudged Venus through a stream, water splashing softly. "Is the spaceman still following? Is the ranch safe?"

"He was an hour ago before I code-axed him. This one stuck. He hasn't managed to break it, and we pulled him miles away from your home. He's stuck out in the wild and if he does break the code-axe, he'll be blocked from tracking us once we're in the canyon."

"Except it works both ways, right? We won't be able to track him, either."

"But we'll be safe." Mitch lurched and grabbed the saddle horn as Orion scrambled up the stream bank. "We can rest and regroup and figure out what to do next."

Francie urged Venus into an almost invisible slot in the mountainside. "Another half mile to the campsite."

"This is the entrance to your dad's hideout? No wonder it's hard to find. These canyon walls go straight up. I can't tell where they end and where the sky begins." Mitch's voice was hushed.

"They rise a couple hundred feet." Francie's gaze traced them until the cliffs dissolved into the void of dark sky, their boundaries barely indistinguishable from the blackness adorned with tiny pinpricks of light.

"How can you be certain your father came here before he vanished?" he asked, tone cautious.

"I never said that. The searchers thought he might have fallen or taken ill on the trail and collapsed. No one imagined ... abduction." Her fingers tightened on the reins. "By the time the sheriff called me in Socorro, dozens of people had searched for days and found nothing."

"So, you came back to help search, then chose to take over the ranch instead of finishing college."

"I'd already made that decision. My car was packed."

Mitch hesitated, then said, "Because of your ex, right?"

His question stole her breath. A breeze brushed past her, rattling dried leaves at Venus's feet. Francie struggled to swallow, let alone speak.

Her public breakup with Maury had spread across campus like fire through dried tinder. How she'd gotten through the end-of-term exams was still a mystery. She'd stayed, though, chin high, because of her summer clerical job in Socorro, but retreated to her apartment after work, rarely stepping outside unless it was necessary. Even her roommates avoided her, like a broken engagement was some kind of disease they didn't want to catch.

That evening, two students from her former fiancé's physics-engineering cohort, Ray and Jack, knocked at her door in Socorro. She knew them, had even tutored them. They were sympathetic about her broken engagement. She'd teared up. But then, they asked if she missed Maury, if she was ready to move on, and their faces had changed, turning predatory and ugly. In low, rough voices, they told her they knew what she liked because Maury had given them intimate, personal details about her ... needs.

Her tears had burned out in a heartbeat. Her body had frozen.

Ray grabbed her hand, crushing it, and pressed her palm to his crotch. Panic gripped her, stealing her breath. "Girls like you come to college for one thing," he said, his breath sour with stale tobacco and beer. "And we can give it to you."

Jack's hand yanked her collar. The front of her dress tore. The sound snapped her out of shock. She'd ripped away, slammed the door on his hand. His howls cut through the jeers. "*Tease. Hussy.*" Worse.

She'd stared at her pale, aching fingers, the shredded fabric they clutched. Shame gnawed her gut like acid. How many others had Maury lied to? Were rumors and gossip about her swirling at the college? The courage she'd bolstered, hoping the humiliation of her broken engagement would fade with time, melted away. She couldn't face it.

The next morning, she reported the attack to the dean's office and was told that pursuing charges against these young men could ruin their lives. She returned to her apartment to pack her car, only to field the phone call from the sheriff about her father's disappearance. It was the final wave that broke the dam. She left.

Venus's hoof slipped on gravel, jolting Francie back to the

present. She kept her eyes ahead, but the memory gnawed at the edges of her thoughts.

Maybe she hadn't outrun the girl who'd left everything behind. But sometimes, running meant survival. And this time, she wasn't running blind. Tonight, she'd made her choice. To fight for her home, to draw the danger away, to face this threat with her eyes open. Strategy, not surrender.

Francie couldn't say yet if resolve would hold if something worse came. But she kept moving forward, the future she wanted feeling a little closer. Close enough to reach for when the time was right.

The creak of leather and the muffled shush of hooves in sand filled the narrow space around them. The slot opened, the walls falling away into darkness. She wove Venus along a pine- and scrub oak–forested trail. Mitch stayed silent when she didn't answer, but she braced for another probing question about why she'd left school.

"They searched this canyon?" he asked.

The knot between her shoulder blades eased as he steered the conversation back to her father's search. "I don't think the searchers ever found it. The opening's well hidden, even during the day. It was his best hideout, and he never brought me up here. Just Mom." She released a long sigh. "The last few years, Dad came here often, sometimes disappearing for two, three days at a stretch."

"Who reported him missing?"

"Adelaide and Dr. Baer. They had dinner together once a month, either in town or at the ranch house. It was Dad's turn, so they drove up. When they arrived, they found Orion saddled and bridled, standing outside the corral. I know Dad left that morning because we spoke over the telephone the night before. August 22, 1947."

The click of hooves turned into splashes.

"Hey. The water's back," Mitch said.

"The creek we've been crossing originates in the canyon. There are lots of seeps and springs in the mountains."

"Why doesn't it flow out the same way we came in? Water obviously cut the walls."

"Waterways shift in time." Francie guided Venus along one side of the stream. "These canyons are riddled with water-carved caves and passages."

She waited for his next question. He'd settled into a rhythm—almost casual now that they weren't being shot at.

"When he called that last time, your father didn't sound any different?"

"I've thought about it a hundred times, but nothing seemed off. We talked about the Brazel crash and a new critter that had shown up at the house. Other goings on in Roswell." And her father had always been kind enough not to say anything about her broken engagement or the town's gossip mill.

"A new critter? Like those animals in the workshop photos? What was it?"

"A red fox," she said. "He was excited about it because red foxes aren't native to this region. But I never saw him. He disappeared like the rest of the animals."

"Her," Mitch muttered.

Francie twisted in the saddle to stare at Mitch. Starlight fell over his frowning face. "What?"

He waved a hand dismissively. "If you'd never been to this canyon, how did you find it?"

"Orion. I would've ridden right past otherwise. I've explored it dozens of times since then and found nothing." She sighed. "To be truthful, this wasn't the first time he'd left."

"When was that?"

"One time before Mom got sick, he was gone more than a month. He came back with three trucks stacked with crates. That's when he started staying late in his workshop and lab. He put up solar lights and water filters for the wells and made the vaccines.

He'd gone to get the tools he needed for his little projects." Francie smiled. She could hear his voice saying that exact phrase in her head. "Maybe that's what he wrote about in his lab journals."

"Then why the cipher?" Mitch said. "Seems strange to keep it locked away. You never asked for the key?"

"I did. He challenged me to figure it out myself." She stopped there and snuck a quick, guarded glance at Mitch. She'd found the key. With any luck, she'd crack the code tonight. Francie touched the periapt.

Francisca Pearl Cortez.

The half-moon had risen until it seemed hooked on the lip of the rocky rim above them, its silver cast crystalline in the waterfall at the canyon's end.

"We're here," she said and dismounted. "Dump your gear by that boulder. I'll take care of the horses. Can you gather some wood? There's a fire ring behind those rocks. Are you hungry?"

"Not really. But coffee would be great."

Mitch groaned as he swung his leg over Orion's side, steadied himself, and stretched as Francie offloaded her gear. He clipped the Minox onto his front pocket to provide light before he untied his pack and dropped it by the boulder.

Francie led their mounts to the stream and let them drink before splashing them across. She highlined the horses, plucked the periapt from the scabbard, and propped it against an alligator juniper, its split and gnarled trunk cradling the spear. The periapt woke up and glowed a faint purple, which seemed to soothe Venus. Francie pulled off saddles and blankets and hung them over a log set up for the purpose, keeping an eye on Mitch, following his bright progress through the pines and scrub. She settled both horses for the night. They'd had a long day.

As had she. Exhaustion pulled at her, but while Mitch was busy ...

Francie ambled to the piled gear. She dug out the tin of coffee, unfastened a pouch in Mitch's backpack, dipped her hand inside—

Blinding light hit her face. Her arm shot up to shield her eyes, blinking against the afterimage that danced in front of her.

"You won't find your gun in my pack." Mitch rolled an armload of wood next to the fire ring.

Francie stood her ground. "Can't fault a girl for trying."

"Maybe you could trust me."

Irritation flared beneath her skin. How many times had she heard that from her ex-fiancé? Her arms flew out wide, defensive.

"I'm alone with you—a stranger—in the wilderness, running from ..." She let her sentence drop. "We're right where you wanted us, not where I ever meant to be. No matter how you tried to put it in my head that this was my notion, it never was. But I'm here. You need to start treating me like a partner."

His face, scowling and lit from below by the Minox, hardened. He stomped back into the trees.

By the time he'd returned with a second armful of wood, she'd started the fire. Coffee percolated over its flames, its rich aroma scenting the chill air. Francie filled two cups, passing one to a still-scowling Mitch.

"You didn't tell me about the cave behind the waterfall," he said. "I saw it while gathering the firewood."

"I'm not trying to keep it from you. You want to see it now? Fine." Francie clattered her cup on top of the boulder and pushed to her feet. "Bring the Minox. We'll need the light."

Eighteen

Francie strode along a wide ledge behind the waterfall, Mitch following. Mist rose around her, dampening her anger as the Minox's light sparkled in the spray. She stepped into a shadow and entered the cave, its walls worn smooth by time and its floor leveled by countless feet over millennia.

"This is it?" His tone was flat, disappointed.

"Dad used to say this was William Bonney country—Billy the Kid. That he and the Regulators might have hidden from pursuers in this canyon and cave. It's big enough to conceal half a dozen horses and men. And before him, others." She touched a rock-chipped petroglyph of a tight spiral. "Stay close."

Francie headed for the back of the cave to where the stony walls folded into a handful of shadowed niches. She stepped through one of them and into a long mining tunnel. With each step, the temperature dropped.

"Dad told me he followed some kind of vein, maybe silver, maybe gold. And that's why he'd stay up here for days," she said.

"It's too straight," Mitch said. "He lied to you."

Francie bristled but bit off her retort. The passage stretched too precise, too purposeful. Her father's guileless looks and persuasive story didn't match the glaring facts before her eyes. And when she'd first seen the tunnel, that left her off-kilter.

The tunnel ran about twenty feet into the last section of the hideout, opening into a spacious cube-shaped chamber. Stark and silent, its back wall gleamed like black glass polished to mirror-smooth granite, like the walls of her father's lab. She shivered from the chill.

Mitch stepped to the center of the room, touched the Minox, and filled the space with light. Circling slowly, he stopped before the wall, placing a palm against its cold surface.

"This is it," he breathed, fingers spread wide. "It has to be."

"I don't know if it has to be anything, but it's all I found. I've explored every foot of this canyon, every inch of this hideout. Satisfied now?"

She led him back outside, shivering against the damp and disappointment, and checked on the horses. When she returned to camp, Mitch had already laid out their blankets on opposite sides of the fire's smoldering coals, saddlebags as pillows. He'd refilled Francie's coffee, steam rising thick in the cold air. He topped off his own cup, and Francie settled onto her bedroll, shoulders propped against the boulder.

Night sounds blanketed them, a chorus of crickets accompanying the splash and gurgle of the waterfall and stream. Bone-tired, Francie wanted nothing more than to fall asleep and wake as if the day were only a half-remembered nightmare.

Mitch stretched out on his blankets, propped on an elbow. The flickering firelight revealed deep lines bracketing his stubbled cheeks. He looked wrung out. She suspected she did, too.

She sipped the hot coffee, grimaced at its bitterness, but was grateful for the heat.

He slumped, his face drooping, eyes on the Minox, thumb swiping the glass surface back and forth. "We need to talk," he said. "You need to know what's really going on."

Francie straightened. Anticipation tightened her stomach.

"Before I say anything, I want to apologize for how I've treated you. For my distrust." He paused, his jaw tight. "We've had our problems, but you've been pretty straight with me and with everything that's happened. I'm not sure if I deserve it."

"You don't."

Rising smoke shadowed an odd bleakness in his expression. She frowned and searched his eyes.

He looked away.

"I can't tell you everything, but I'll give you what information I can. You'll understand. You worked under top secret conditions." Mitch scruffed his palm over his chin, gaze dropping to the Minox again. "My recruiting job's a ploy. A cover. My superiors at the base know that, but not much else. I'm in Roswell on a mission from a division the government created to confront and mitigate potential threats arising from the war."

Francie nodded slowly. Scientists at Los Alamos worked in siloed isolation, given only the information necessary to their specific work. But whispers of security and warnings against "loose talk" never ceased. It made perfect sense that new agencies would be created to curb fresh dangers.

"Potential threats. Like the spy balloon crash last year at the Brazel ranch?" she asked.

"I was mobilized because of that. Sure, the war's over. We won. But the danger is worse than you think. We've already spoken about the possibility of kidnappers." A chill crept through Francie as Mitch tipped his face to the stars on a long, slow exhale. "Spies. Infiltrators. Even assassins are deployed across the US to sow chaos and strife. Like the Nazis did in 1944 with Germany's Operation Greif, or the Soviet NKGB safe house in Santa Fe."

"Communists? *Here?*"

"New Mexico's far from safe. Los Alamos, the V2 rocket program at White Sands, Operation Overcast. Clandestine presence of Nazi scientists in West Texas. Ongoing nuclear weapons research. These programs draw dangerous people. This spaceman must be one of them." He stopped, thumb resting on the Minox screen. "I'm saying too much."

Francie swallowed the flood of names and dates, mind whirling between the weight of those historical details and a creeping unease. He met her gaze as if measuring her acceptance of his confession. Spies? That made sense. But assassins? Kidnappers? Her *father*? She struggled to wrap her head around it. It all seemed plausible and explained Mitch's technologically advanced equipment, his suspicions about the spaceman's purpose on her ranch. But what about the facts he hadn't listed?

"The spaceman knew you," Francie said. She pushed. "How did he survive that fall without a parachute, or rocket, or airplane? What is the periapt? And why does he keep asking about a dog?"

Mitch shifted, lips tightening as he fixed her with a look that had lost any trace of warmth. Then he turned abruptly, seized a handful of dry twigs, and flung them onto the coals with more force than necessary. The tinder caught fire swiftly, crackling and popping, the smoke racing into the night as if escaping their strained conversation.

His reply was measured, but each word carried veiled frustration seeping through the calm. Francie registered the shift immediately. He didn't like being challenged. But she didn't like his partial truths wrapped in facts.

"He might know me, but I don't know him. That puts my mission at risk. The technology I'm assigned is classified, which means it's almost certainly been stolen, possibly to sell to the Soviets. He could be a double agent or a mercenary out for what he can get." Mitch shook his head. "Look. It's not like the advanced technology your father engineered was a secret. You had visitors. Your fiancé, your friends, or even the Baers could have reported your father to someone at the base, and word got out about who he was. If an enemy government kidnapped him and made him talk, the spaceman might be here for cleanup."

"I—I don't understand."

"The laboratory, its equipment. You. You could be in danger."

Her pulse jumped but settled quickly. How much more danger than what she was in right now? She sipped her coffee, mind racing.

Mitch rubbed fingers against his temple, the skin around his eyes pinched with worry. "If we only knew what was in those journals."

This was her cue. She could—*should*—confess she'd found the missing piece of the periapt, give Mitch the link implicating her father in everything going on.

She carried one of the journals with her. The one he'd said to keep. She had the means to check now. She could get answers to all the questions that danced in her—

Dizziness spun her vision. Francie squeezed her eyes shut, then blinked them open. She was so tired. A headache pressed in, dull and persistent.

"We left them at the ranch. His journals. What if he ..." The heat and smoke were affecting her. She rolled her neck. "What if the spaceman, if he didn't follow us. Turned back."

"The journals aren't all at the ranch, are they, Francie? You have the missing year in your saddlebags. Is that one important?"

The trees behind Mitch swam in swirls of gray smoke. "Yes. He told me to ... I have to keep it safe." With hands clumsy with fatigue, she set her cup on the boulder. It teetered and fell. She watched it dully, heard the sizzle as liquid splashed into the glowing coals. "The journal. I have ..."

Mitch spoke, but his voice faded in and out.

A blur of movement. His arm around her shoulder, supporting her melting muscles. A bark of shocked laughter threatened to escape, but fear took over. *Danger.*

"We must go back. We need to—" Her tongue felt thick. She grabbed Mitch's biceps, thoughts scattering. The Minox. He'd clipped it back to his pocket. Eyes narrowed against its light, she read the screen.

Soviet NKGB safe house in Santa Fe ... Operation Overcast ... Did the Minox record their conversation? And teletype it?

"If he wants the journals maybe he tricked us into leaving." Her voice slurred. "We need to go back."

"We're safe, for now." He lowered and released her. "It's the periapt he wants."

"No. It was broken. I fixed it ..." Her head was full of cotton, her speech slurred. She melted onto the bedroll, eyelids heavy. "Found it. The key ..."

"Where is it, Francie? Where's the periapt?"

"I can feel it. The periapt. It's mine. I'm the key. Me. Francisca Pearl ..." His face hovered above hers. She fought the bone-melting lassitude, forcing focus. The world tilted around her. "Mitch? What did you do?"

Strong hands tucked the bedroll blanket around her, then stilled. "God, I'm sorry, Francie."

She dissolved into darkness with a sigh, warm lips pressed against her forehead.

School of Mines

Socorro, New Mexico
One year, three months, and eleven days ago

The cafeteria was packed with lunchtime students wearing suits and ties, or military uniforms on men who'd remained in the service. The cavernous space mixed their voices to an indistinguishable masculine rumble. But it didn't drown out Francie's fiancé hectoring her with the same argument they'd had since she'd enrolled in the physics degree last fall.

"This is a waste of your time and your father's money." Maury elbowed his crumb-scattered plate to one side. He stretched an arm across the table, picking up her hand, his fingers playing with the diamond solitaire engagement ring. "When we're married, I don't want my wife working, especially not with a bunch of horny men."

"Maury! Language." Francie frowned. "I worked with men at Los Alamos."

"But those were old duffers too deep in their heads to

notice a dish like you. Besides, that Baer fellow promised he'd keep you safe for me."

Maury had changed since he'd given her the ring back before the war, before his service and return to New Mexico. He was impatient now. Driven. Lately, his impatience carried an edge that felt like desperation. But she'd loved him since she'd been a sophomore in high school, thrilled that the handsome senior with the shy smile had asked her to prom. Adapting to these changes in his personality was proving difficult.

She squeezed his hand, determined to make him understand. "But that will change in time. More women—"

"Hon, let's get out of here. Go back to your apartment. Your roommates are at work, right? We can be alone and ... discuss this and our future together." His eyes heated as he slid the ring slowly, suggestively, back and forth on her finger.

Francie pulled her hand away and tucked it on her lap, face hot.

"We have class in thirty minutes, and I've already told you I won't have relations with you until after we're married."

Patricia James had dropped out last semester to snide remarks about getting her M-R-S instead of a degree after she got pregnant. She would not make that mistake.

Still, she tempered her refusal with a smile. "I'm good at physics, at math. I tutor you, don't I?"

He sat back and crossed his arms, digging in.

"I'm not leaving school," she said. "This degree is important—"

"Yeah, more important than me."

"Don't be childish."

His cheeks flamed brick red.

"I'm sorry. I shouldn't have said that." She leaned forward and softened her expression in an attempt to coax him back to good humor. "You are important to me, but I believe I have a contribution to make. We can do this together."

"Excuse me."

A pretty young woman with dark hair in a smart gray suit and stylish hat stood next to Maury, one hand latched to an adorable little girl wearing a pink polka dot dress, sweet lacey socks, and Mary Janes. She smiled shyly up at Francie, a smile so much like Maury's.

Francie's stomach lurched. The room tilted beneath her. Her eyes flew to the woman's left hand, curled tightly around the strap of her handbag. A gold wedding ring glinted in the overhead lights.

"Hello, Maury," the woman said. She turned to Francie. "I'm Maury's wife. We got married in Hawaii. And this is our daughter."

Maury's face went from dark red to stark white.

Nineteen

The periapt needled Francie, breaking her out of a disjointed, uneasy sleep. Campfire smoke teased her nose. A small, sharp rock dug into her shoulder through her bedroll, and she groaned and extended her arm to the space next to her.

She startled upright, the coldness of the night snapping her awake and crowding out the scent of worn leather and the feel of scratchy wool. Her head swam. She pressed her palm to her temple, but the urgency inside her only intensified.

She kicked free of the bedroll. Boots scraped the ground as she staggered to her feet. The darkness clung to her. Her legs buckled before she caught herself. A wave of nausea swept over her, threatening to pull her back to the ground.

She blinked hard, willing her mind to clear, and turned in a circle, squinting at the ground around her bedroll.

It's gone.

Moonlight spilled across the camp. The fire was a scatter of ash and a few stubborn coals, barely enough to see by. Francie staggered to Mitch's bedroll.

"Mitch. Something's—"

He wasn't there.

The echo of his voice flitted through her mind. *Maybe you could trust me.*

She scanned the trees, searching for the faint glow of the Minox, half hoping he was out of sight. If he needed privacy, she'd turn away. But no light was visible. He must have ventured farther afield.

"Mitch?" she called. Her head pounded, mouth dry as sand, but a gnawing pressure grew. The periapt called. She had to find the periapt.

The horses.

That's right. She'd left it with the horses. Venus had seemed calmed by its light and hum. She'd propped it against a tree to retrieve later. She frowned. Except she'd fallen asleep.

Francie stumbled down the bank and splashed through the stream. Venus snorted, restless hooves muffled by a layer of fallen leaves. She rocked to a stop.

Orion was gone.

Francie grabbed his highline, her knot still intact. He must be nearby. Orion wouldn't leave Venus. He wouldn't leave Francie. She'd grab the periapt, use its light to search—

The gnarled juniper loomed out of the darkness, but no periapt leaned against the trunk. Nor had it fallen to the ground.

Francie bolted back to camp. She fell to her knees by the saddlebags, hands shaking as she unlatched the first bag. Nothing. The second one was empty, too.

The journal was gone. Mitch must have taken it.

I'm sorry, Francie.

She stood slowly, stepped into the fading moonlight, and stared at the cliff face. The cave behind the falls yawned dark and wide, large enough to swallow horses and men.

And secrets. Her father's and, it seemed, Mitchell Ward's.

She crossed her arms tightly, as if holding herself together. Her father's hideout had been Mitch's objective since she'd told him about it. That was why he'd sabotaged her truck, made sure they'd stayed on the ranch after their encounters with the spaceman. Why he kept her isolated, and why he drugged her coffee?

She wiped at her eyes, smearing hot tears with the heel of her hand.

He was still in the canyon, in the cave. She could run. Take Venus and ride to Arabela, get the local authorities involved. Let them figure everything out. It would be the easy thing to do.

Francie stepped toward the waterfall, the periapt's pull a pulse beneath her skin.

She didn't want easy, and she didn't want to run anymore.

She wanted answers.

Twenty

The cave beyond the waterfall was black as tar, stopping Francie short when her outstretched hand found stone, slick with mist. The chill air wrapped around her, dampening her skin as she waited, shivering in the darkness. Slowly, the gloom yielded to a faint gray suggestion of light deep in the tunnel. The periapt tugged at her, an insistent pressure she couldn't ignore. She stepped forward, boots scraping the floor, and caught the earthy scent of horse. A little of her worry ebbed. Orion was somewhere ahead, although why was still a mystery. The roar of falling water muffled all other sound, but as she moved deeper and her eyes adjusted, an echo emerged—Mitch's voice drifting from the back of the hideout.

"Okay, horsey. Steady ..." Mitch grunted, then released an exasperated grumble. "Nothing. Damn."

Francie pressed her lips into a thin line. *That man and his damn mouth.* She paused at the chamber's threshold and took in the scene. A wobbly Mitch straddled Orion, one hand holding the dark periapt, her father's 1946 green lab book clamped under his arm. His other hand clutched a fistful of golden mane, his reflection a blur on the polished wall. He'd propped the Minox in a niche near the entrance. Its light had been Francie's breadcrumbs to follow and find her horse, her spear, and her—

Her Mitch. That slip caught somewhere deep inside before she stepped into the room. Orion swung his head in her direction, nostrils flaring in recognition, hooves clattering as he shifted.

"Whoa! *Stop.*" Mitch slid to one side, and her father's lab journal thudded to the cave floor.

"I told you to clamp your knees around his barrel," Francie said.

Mitch lurched before swerving toward her, his jaw slack. "Francie! You should still be ..."

"Passed out? You slipped me a Mickey." The tears she'd suppressed burned again. "You drugged me."

She wanted Mitch to deny it, to scoff at her accusation. Yet as she waited, his gaze turned grim, and the truth pressed in. Awkwardly, he swung his leg over Orion and slid to the ground.

"It was for your own protection," he said.

He protected her by drugging her. That was funny. But instead of laughing, she wanted to scream. *Stupid, stupid girl.* How many times would she let herself be fooled? Was there something broken in her? Some flaw that made her an easy mark for men who thought they knew best? She forced her lips into a brittle grin.

"Like my father protected me from deciphering a dangerous code, then disappeared?"

"I don't think he's dead. I think he ran because his crimes caught up with him. Because he found out about me and the reason I was stationed in Roswell and thought I was here to arrest him. Maybe by vanishing, he believed he was protecting you."

"Oh, that makes it *much* better. He abandoned me and ran when things got tough. I guess the apple doesn't fall far from the tree." She flung out her arms as if to embrace the echoes of her words.

"Except it's not just you and my father *protecting* me. Dr. Baer protected me from my female *hysterics* and the crash I saw by refusing to help. My ex-fiancé stood between me and ruin when the woman *he'd married* in Hawaii turned up in Socorro last year with their child in tow. The college protected me when I was cornered by two of my fellow students."

The tears she'd banked breached her lashes and fell, but they didn't stem from self-pity. Not this time. This time, they were backed by fiery anger that she'd repressed for too long. "Why is it that I attract such men who are so bound and determined to shield poor little ol' me?"

"Cornered ..." Mitch's face paled. "That's why you left college."

His words left her raw. He had her spear, so she grabbed his Minox off the rock shelf. The light swung crazily, moving shadows into the squared-off corners of the rock-carved room. She waved to the spear, now glowing with a dark purple light. The periapt glowed a dark, wounded purple, but its gentle hum took the edge off her temper. "Does this ... Minox only respond to you like the periapt does to me?"

The Minox's glare softened. A single word appeared.

No

Her mouth opened. Closed. She shot a wide-eyed glance at Mitch. Had it answered her?

But her question dissolved as her gaze met his. He'd used her. Like her fiancé. And her father.

She swallowed. "Care to explain who you really are?"

The light of the Minox flickered again, and Francie glanced down. The words on its screen staggered her back a step, one heel skidding in the dirt as though the words themselves had shoved her backward.

Certainly! What I Am:
    I am an Artificial Intelligence assistant designed to

provide immediate information, answer questions, and assist with an almost limitless variety of topics. My primary goal is to help users by delivering accurate and insightful responses.

She gave a short, incredulous laugh and pressed her palm to her middle, half expecting to find her stomach had plummeted clear through to her boots.

The Minox had heard her. It had responded to her question. She touched the smooth surface but yanked her hand away as a fresh block of type spilled across the screen, dense and urgent, as if the little spy camera had been dying to unburden itself.

—assassins deployed across the US and the world to sow chaos and strife. Like an extension of the German Operation Greif and the Soviets' GRU and NKGB safe house in Santa Fe. New Mexico may seem isolated and secure, but the Los Alamos Laboratory and the dispersal of scientists after the project was complete attracted—

She continued to read silently until ... until...

"The V2 rocket program, 1946 to ..." Her voice faltered. "To 1952. Operation Overcast. See also Operation Paperclip, 1945 to ... 1959. And the top secret presence of Nazi scientists, at Fort Bliss ..."

Francie lifted her head, tears drying with shock, her feet rooted to the damp stone. Mitch's face was wiped of all expression, but the whiteness of his knuckles around the spear's shaft was answer enough.

"I thought it was recording us. But it's ... it's information stored as computational memory." She rushed at him, stopping so close that she could pick out the gold flecks in his deep green eyes and the spray of laugh lines.

"1952. 1959. That's the future. How can you have information about the future in this thing? It's August 1948. *1948.*" Her voice rose, each word pitching closer to a churning internal panic, enough to startle Orion, who tossed his head, eyes rimmed in white.

"Francie. *Please.* I'll tell you if you'll give me back the Minox." He spoke as if to a child—a *girl*—and raised his palm in supplication. "Please."

She slapped the Minox in Mitch's extended hand and grabbed the periapt. He refused to let it go.

"I'm sorry, Francie, I can't let you have it back."

He yanked back, hauling her forward. Purple lightning arced from the shaft's scrollwork, searing her vision. A shock coursed down her arm, but she hung on to the periapt. Mitch cried out, his hand thrown from its grip.

His abrupt release of the spear pitched her off-balance. Her boots skidded, and she flung out an arm to catch herself. Her palm slammed against the wall—and the polished granite flexed and stretched beneath her hand, concentric rings spreading outward like a stone had been dropped in dark water. Everything around Francie seemed to mute, as if she'd plunged into the deep end of a pool. Then, impossibly, the wall turned liquid and clear as glass. Through it, Francie saw into another world.

Or, technically, into another room.

Twenty-One

The otherworldly chamber mirrored the one Francie stood in now, except every wall gleamed like oiled obsidian. Golden light pooled from fixtures overhead, warming the room's smooth tiled floor that mimicked her home's kitchen linoleum.

Francie stood rigid, hand still pressed into the transparent wall, her mind struggling with the impossibility.

A table stood in the center, an uncanny twin to the one she'd sat at a few hours ago with Mitch, eating sandwiches and apple slices, one of its chairs pushed askew as if its occupant had fled midmeal. A blue-speckled coffee pot rested on the counter by the sink. Beside it, a ceramic mug hung upside-down in a drying rack. It was the broken cup from her kitchen, shattered in the spaceman's attack. Francie's gaze followed the gleaming gold lines that fused the jigsawed shards back together. Nearby, a faded flour-sack towel, decorated with her mother's cross-stitch Xs in soft pink thread, hung over the sink's rim. Strange as it was, each piece seemed to link this place back to her life.

A metal cot lined one wall, draped with a sunset-hued Indian blanket like the one in her father's bedroom. Francie peered beneath the bed, her astonished gaze touching on a fuzzy tennis ball and a rumpled scrap of tan cloth. Dog toys. She didn't have a dog, but the barking on the ridge, the photo in the workshop, all implied the tan dog with the black face was an occupant of the room, although why she knew that with such certainty escaped her.

Her eyes drifted to the opposite wall, where a skeletal desk loomed in sharp contrast to the homey touches, its curves foreign and eccentric, a towering grid of black glass on top. A doorway beside the desk yawned wide, swallowing the warm light.

The surreal fusion tightened something deep inside her. It felt like a monk's cell inhabited by a thief, every piece stolen from her life to make this alien space his own.

Then her eyes landed on the hat rack.

Wooden, simple, mounted on the other side of the dark opening. A well-worn cowboy hat hung from one peg, its crown marked by the same thumb-pressed dent he'd made adjusting it each morning, a silent signature of a daily ritual. In that moment, every familiar thing in the room made the missing piece of this astounding puzzle seem within reach.

Somehow, some way, *her father lived there.*

The chamber tilted with that certainty. She pressed her palm to the clear wall, seeking a solid anchor for her spiraling thoughts. But instead, her hand slipped past the rippling surface, submerging into warm, dry air that washed away the damp chill clinging to her skin.

A shadow pooled at her feet, cast by the glow behind her. Her own.

She could step through. She could find him.

Without warning, a siren pierced the stillness. The wall stuttered, the scene beyond jerking and doubling. Pain clamped her wrist, an electric surge searing the skin submerged inside the clear barrier to the other room. Heat burned along her forearm. Muscles cramped. Her hand curled hard, and a cry escaped before she could stop it.

An arm caught her waist, hauling her back into a solid chest. *Mitch*. She'd forgotten he was even there.

"Are you okay?" he yelled over the blaring siren. Then, "*Cut the alarm!*"

The sound stopped. The chamber—her father's room—vanished in a blink beneath solid granite.

He caught her wrist, swearing under his breath, his thumb trembling as he traced the angry welt on her forearm. "That's on me. I shouldn't have let you—"

"*What just happened?*" The pain was intense, but the periapt resumed its low healing hum, grounding her.

Mitch hesitated, then turned her to face him, his hands tight on her shoulders. "He's figured it out." His eyes were bright, searching. "It's *you*, Francie. He transposed *you*, not Orion. You're part of the shift. He'd only transposed animals, I thought—"

Transposed. Part of the shift. The words meant nothing, just more proof he was three steps ahead in a game she didn't understand.

She wrenched away, any leftover wonder curdled into suspicion. "Where is Orion? What's that place?"

"Orion's in the tunnel, and that—" Mitch jabbed a finger at the polished wall. "That's an anchor portal. *Alice Through the Looking-Glass*, but this one isn't theoretical. It's real. Is this what's in the journals? How to create it?"

Francie pressed her back against the rough rock. "Wh-what are you talking about?"

He ran a shaking hand through his hair and muttered, "No wonder they're after him."

Her gaze darted from the solid granite to Mitch, the sudden feverish light in his expression setting off a warning inside her.

"Glimmer portals open wherever, whenever. All it takes is a qubix, and a shift animal. They're never fixed to one place. This portal is fixed. An anchor portal." His words tumbled over her, too fast, too strange.

Then his gaze flicked to her, acute, calculating ... and frightening. "But this one's anchored. He's used it. Repeatedly. Why else dig out this cave? Did he create the portal, or was there already a portal here? Is that why he settled here in these mountains, on this property?"

"You're saying my father did this?"

"Your father must have used it to disappear with my shift animal. But the portal's unstable because the glimmer's almost dead. It'll collapse in a day or two."

Francie's mind tripped on words she barely understood. They tumbled through her thoughts without settling. Her mouth went dry. "What's almost dead?"

"The glimmer." Mitch held out his hand, not quite touching her. "It's important I get back before I'm phase-locked here. Trapped, stuck in this timeline."

Francie sidled away from him, the artifact held tight to her body, her shoulders scraping the cave wall. "Get back where? Where are you from?"

"Not just where. When." Mitch lowered his outstretched hand. His fingers drifted to the inside of his forearm, rubbing there as if to ease a lingering ache.

"I'm not from here. Not from this time. I traveled here from the year 2557. My mission was to cover up an unauthorized probe from—" He swallowed. "From the future that crashed last year in the desert north of here. The Roswell incident. It wasn't a weather balloon or a secret project. I was to turn the crash into a conspiracy, keep time travel secret. I didn't— Nobody expected to find your father. He broke the rules, and ..." Lips pressed tight, Mitch shook his head. "He's an outlaw. He's ... he's wanted for crimes against humanity."

"Stop. You don't get to rewrite my father's life. Or mine." The periapt hummed, its vibration almost nauseating.

Then the numbers clicked. *2557.* Almost six hundred years in the future. Her father's two- or three-day trips to his hideout suddenly stretched into centuries. "You're saying my father isn't gone. He's ... he's alive in another time?"

Mitch hesitated. "Possibly. But time can be an odd construct."

A sound escaped her—a strangled laugh. Mitch's secrets, his half-truths and lies, the artifact's glow, her father's hat on that impossible rack. Her skin tingled with cold, but her mind was burning with questions.

Not just where. *When.*

She circled away from Mitch, edging toward the slick granite wall. She wanted to see inside again, find proof. Something that anchored her back in her world.

"I'm so sorry, Francie. You weren't supposed to find out. Your knowledge creates ... problems." Mitch shifted to block her, but she met his eyes and held her ground.

"Then arrest me or move. I'm done asking permission to exist in my own life."

"Francie. Please. Listen to me. When the glimmer closes, I'll be stuck here. I lost my shift animal. The red fox. I can't return without her, without a shift animal. But you've been transposed. You can take me back. *You're* the key."

She changed direction, the periapt in her grip glowing a deep, stormy purple, and pointed the spear at Mitch. He winced but didn't back away, shadowing her as she edged past the corner, her back now against the polished stone.

"Let's step through the looking glass together," Mitch said.

Her gaze snapped to his. He smiled, but she saw the strain in it.

"That's what it's called—the looking glass. Like Alice in Wonderland. Like the book we found in your father's laboratory. We can go through and find your father. You can ask him why he left, or why he stayed in this time—*here*—for so many years. Aren't you curious about that?"

She kept the spear between them, her back to the wall. "You

said he's wanted for crimes ... like the Nuremberg trials. They *hung* the men they convicted. My father is not like those ... monsters. I refuse to believe you. How do you even know he's—"

"Because you pricked your finger on the periapt and left blood. I checked your DNA against my criminal database. You're a fifty percent match. You're his daughter."

"You checked my blood against some ... future criminal registry?"

"In my time, people can tell who's related to who by blood. It's like fingerprints, but a hundred times more precise."

Francie frowned, struggling to grasp the idea. "I don't understand."

"And you won't for another forty years."

"Stop making me feel stupid!"

His voice grew rough, the words rasping. "I know you're not stupid! It would be easier if you were."

He unclipped the Minox from his pocket and touched its glass face. "I have pictures of your father, except younger. Would you like to see one?"

"I'm not coming any closer."

"I promise I won't touch you or the periapt." He held the Minox out toward her. "Tell me if this is your father."

She stayed fixed in place, turned her head away. She didn't want to see, didn't want to ... confirm. Finally, she whispered, "What ... what did he do?"

He exhaled slowly. "He and the people in this picture shifted back to a time after the Great War to kill someone close to the man who started the Second Great War."

Francie stared at Mitch in confusion. "But it didn't work. I lived through it, and it ended in 1945 with Japan's surrender after ... after they dropped the atomic bombs. So why—"

"It *did* work. But time can resist change. The unexpended energy left behind from the collapse of the war they stopped created a vacuum," Mitch said. "That vacuum allowed something far worse to rise in its place. That's the theory of how Hitler came into power. And what he destroyed—cultures, countries, lives—was a thousand times worse than the war they'd stopped."

Mitch's expression was bleak, and the sight of it made her flinch. "Your father and his group tried to rewrite history, but their actions are responsible for the deaths of millions because they murdered Arrosa Bitxilore."

Francie pressed a hand against her mouth to suppress a cry. "He couldn't have killed Arrosa Bitxilore. He would never—"

"All but your father and one other were captured and confessed to the murder."

"No." She couldn't stop her tears. "You don't understand. Arrosa Bitxilore was my grandmother. Bitxilore means 'pearl.' I was named after her." Francie choked on a sob. "She died before I was born."

"Francie." His voice was gentle but insistent. "Take the Minox. Look at the screen."

She shuddered in a breath and wiped away blurring tears with her sleeve before she stepped closer, hesitated and took the Minox into her hand.

"It's black. The picture's gone."

"Sorry. It's keyed to me." He reached for the camera, but Francie shrank back. "It's okay. Let me—"

He pressed one side of the Minox, and a picture appeared in the glass.

Her father, younger even than in his and her mother's wedding photos, grinned, eyes sparkling with excitement, his arm slung around the neck of a woman in profile. She stared up at him, her face glowing with adoration. Behind him and the woman, others smiled and laughed.

"Who's the woman he's hugging?"

"An accomplice. One that was never caught. Delinae Leonides, a nuclear phase-shift expert. His fiancée."

Francie's heart skipped, knees turning watery.

"No." She shook her head violently, the room lighting up with bloodred light strobing from the periapt. "No. This is all a trick. Time travel is impossible. You're lying!"

"You think I want this? By telling you, I'm violating a dozen regulations. If I—" He stopped, a muscle twitching in his cheek. "My directives require that I silence you. Eliminate you. I ... can't. I won't. If you come with me to the future ..."

His expression softened, his tone almost pleading. "You could attend whatever university you want. No one would question you or bully you. They wouldn't demean or ignore you. It would be so much easier for you in the future. Men and women have equality you won't see in your lifetime."

Easier. The word echoed inside her, hovering over an abyss of regret and fear. What did she have ahead of her? No college degree, no fiancé, nothing but the weight of small-town gossip and pity.

"Don't you want that? Not having to fight for every inch of progress? Having the freedom and ability to learn and grow, and make the best of your mind?" Mitch's brows knotted, lips pressed tight with worry. "You're still in danger. If the spaceman—the time traveler—knows who you are, he could use you to get to your father. I can protect you if you shift with me to the future. Francie, please. Let's go through together."

Mitch could protect her by offering her a shortcut, a way out. Like her father. Like every man who'd tried to "protect" her. And she'd let them—because it was easier.

Her voice trembled with a mix of defiance and desperation. "Which one is real, Mitch? You say you need me to leave, then you promise the future is wonderful. Now you say it's about saving me from the spaceman when at first, you didn't even believe me." She straightened, blazing with an unexpected ferocity, shocked by her own boldness. But this time, she refused to be anyone's pawn. "It all feels like manipulation. No more. If I go through that wall, it'll be because I choose to, not because you tricked me into it."

Mitch began to circle her, but she raised the periapt again, her hand now steady.

"Was the mammoth a trick? Or the villages we rode through? We saw them together. That's why I thought Orion was a shift. But it's you." He gestured to the periapt. "I see you found the missing chip. What does it do, Francie?"

Before she could stop herself, her eyes flitted to the journal on the cave floor. He followed her glance.

"It holds the cipher, doesn't it? Is that why you brought the journal?" A spark flared in his eyes. "That means I—*we*—could—"

Without warning, he lunged.

Twenty-Two

Mitch grabbed the periapt and torqued it sideways as a bolt of blazing purple light shot out, hitting the anchor portal. A surge of power ran through Francie, straight to her bones. She wrenched the spear—

But Mitch had already collapsed, his hands sliding away as the Looking Glass swallowed the periapt's lightning. The black stone flickered, transparent for an instant, her father's hat dangling from the rack like his ghost, then gone again.

Mitch hit the ground at Francie's feet, unmoving.

Knees buckling, she flung herself beside him. His eyes were closed. Was he breathing? Was he dead?

She cast the periapt away and heaved him onto her folded knees, cradling his head, brushing hair from his forehead. Everything—her father's absence, the exhaustion, shock—crashed over her. *I've killed him.* The thought looped, punishing and relentless, until she released in a whisper, *"I've killed him, I've killed him."*

~

"He's not dead."

A voice near the tunnel entrance startled Francie. She straightened, blinking away blurred tears, but kept Mitch's limp head cradled in her lap. The Minox lay near the tunnel's opening. Its screen sliced a brilliant wedge of light through the misty air.

"Who's there?" Her arms tightened around Mitch's shoulders. She peered into the stark shadows of the passage, following the line of light along the floor, and spotted the periapt, well out of reach.

Francie eased Mitch's ray gun from its holster. It felt heavier than she expected. She forced her hand steady and raised the weapon toward the tunnel's mouth, every muscle tight.

"Show yourself."

She strained to hear a footfall, a slither of material against rock, but the echoing rush of water smothered the silence. It had to be the spaceman. He'd found them. Her grip tightened, finger brushing the trigger. She scanned the dark passage—waiting. Watching. Any moment now, a figure would emerge. *Any moment …*

But no shadow shifted, no footsteps broke the hush. Nothing but an oppressive, watchful quiet. Until a voice, clipped and calm, cut through it.

"It's genefixed. It won't work in your hands, just like your qubix didn't respond to Mitchell. And Mitchell isn't dead. You sedation-stunned him. Honestly, it's poetic justice. He did put you out first."

The voice had a faint British accent. So, not the spaceman.

Francie adjusted her grip on the ray gun, slid Mitch's shoulders and head to rest on the cave floor, and stood. She ached all over but refused to show weakness. With wary steps, she edged closer to the tunnel's mouth, the Minox inches from her boot.

Its light flickered, but its screen stared back blankly. There was no image like when the spaceman had first hailed Mitch. Typeface words were etched across its face.

She hesitated, studying the dark shadows in front of her for a figure, a trick. Slowly, gun still raised, she picked up the Minox ...

And almost dropped it when words spilled across its screen:

NEW USER: FRANCIE CORTEZ AUTHORIZED BY PRIMARY HANDLER.

It *recognized* her? Mitch must have done something ....

Heart pounding, she bent over and spoke into it.

"Uh, is someone there? Can you ..." Francie choked, holding back tears. "Can you help him?"

"I cannot rouse him the way your qubix woke you up. We don't have such a connection. But don't worry. His biomonitor shows strong life signs, and he'll awake refreshed."

"His bio ..."

"The implant in his arm."

"Who are you?"

As the Minox answered, the screen rolled with typed characters.

"What I Am:

"I am an Artificial Intelligence assistant designed to provide immediate information, answer questions, and assist with an almost limitless variety of topics. My primary goal is to help users by delivering accurate and insightful responses."

"You're not real?"

"If you mean, do I have a pulse, then no. I'm operational and active. I respond to your input, assist with answering questions, and provide advice on problems within defined parameters."

"Well, I've got problems." Francie gave a watery chuckle. "What's gen-a-fixed?"

The scrolls of text that ran over the screen had Francie shaking her head. "Could you just tell me?"

"Of course. "Genefixed" means that a biometrically authenticated device is secured to respond to its owner's unique biological signature. My function is similar to your periapt's, but unlike it, I can't respond to your thoughts or emotions. I work strictly by the book: programmed input, programmed response."

Francie eyed the periapt. It had rolled onto the open lab journal and lit the pages with light strokes of purple.

"It responds to me. Almost like it's alive. But I—I don't know how to use it. I'm lost."

"I can assist."

Francie squeezed her eyes shut, jaw flexing at the utter surrealness of asking a machine for help. But she had little choice. "All right. Before I ... shot Mitch—"

The Minox corrected her.

"Sedated Mitchell."

"He said he could prove something by deciphering the journal. Do you understand what he meant?"

"No. Nor can I decipher that journal. Mitchell tried that earlier."

She bit her lip. "Okay. Can you tell me about Mitch's mission?"

"I'm restricted from disclosing specific details about Mitchell Ward's mission."

It had been worth a shot. Francie stared at the screen, the weight of dead ends pressing down harder than ever. She needed real answers about the spaceman, about what had happened to her father—and what Mitch was still hiding. She was done waiting for someone else to decide what she was allowed to know. If the journal held any part of that truth, she'd dig it out herself, even if it meant taking risks.

"I have the key," she said. "If I give it to you, could you try?"

"Of course."

Francie hesitated, her gaze gliding to the sleeping Mitch, before moving across the cave to pick up the periapt. It winked merrily, and she brightened, but butterflies fluttered in her stomach. She planted the butt of the periapt in the dirt, closed her eyes, and wished for the artifact in her hand to display her father's cipher.

Which was a bit ridiculous. It wasn't a magic lamp or genie, no matter how much she wished it could be.

A soothing warmth seeped into her palm, and when she opened her eyes, her name and the Greek code glowed on the wall.

"It worked. What do I do now?" she asked the Minox.

"Hold my screen to face the cipher and walk in a circle around the qubix."

She completed the turn, tracing the glowing symbols, as a tentative hope took root.

"I have deciphered the pages Mitchell scanned in at your father's laboratory, even though the cipher provided is not a complete match. This translation uses logical inferences to decode the Greek text, prioritizing narrative coherence where conflicts arose."

Francie stared at the Minox screen and gasped.

January 13, 1920

We are here and safely hidden from my pursuers. Chessy has once again sent me out of the house to the workshop and is singing as she cleans and arranges every glass, plate, and spoon in the kitchen. How have I deserved such a woman as my wife? The sink has a hand pump for well water, but I'll change it for a touch system, install an on-demand water heater, and a reverse osmosis system.

Anything to make her life easier after what I've done.

A list of equipment and parts followed, but Francie remained caught on her father's final words.

After what I've done. After he'd murdered her grandmother? The Minox voice broke into her thoughts.

"There's another page comprising mathematics, but the numbering system in the periapt's cipher and my ability to infer specific numerals based on the equations are limited. The translation will not be completely correct. However, they appear to be a fragment of a larger equation—far more advanced than those for which I am familiar."

Francie frowned, pushing a curl back over her ear. "What are they for?"

"Calculations for time travel. Although I've never seen calculations written out in this format before. Yet the existing anchor portal in this cavern verifies the concept."

Francie's gaze dropped to the time stamp—1920. She hadn't even been born yet. The cipher couldn't be her name. At least, not yet.

But the 1946 journal her father had insisted she keep safe might use her specific cipher.

She swept the green notebook off the cave floor, brushing it clean. "Can you decode this journal if I help you scan it?"

"I can try."

Francie settled in the dirt, the book resting in her lap, Mitch's silent form warm against her leg. She flipped the pages to exhortations of *faster* from the Minox.

When she scanned the final page, she asked, "What does it say? Uh, summarize."

"The universe is permeated with glimmers, which the writer quaintly describes as, and I quote, *"like tiny bubbles in soda pop."* Transient Glimmer Phenomena—TGP—which scientists have theorized but have never proven. The work in this notebook details confirmation that shifts, and therefore shifting by humans to the past, are no longer restricted."

"I'm sorry. I don't understand. Could you simplify and elaborate?"

"Currently, time travel is limited to glimmers detectable at durations of one Earth calendar year or longer, each anchored to fixed spatial coordinates, or pockets of time and space, not tiny bubbles. The calculations in this journal predict glimmers down to the nanosecond, unlocking more times and locations across the universe exponentially."

"This—" Francie weighed her words. "This would allow time travel—shifts—freed from constraints that bind missions like Mitch's. He said he came here last summer, 1947, and must return before this glimmer collapses—1948."

"Correct."

Francie swallowed, the implications sinking in. "That's ... all?"

"Not remotely. Currently, travel from the present to the past and back is possible via glimmers, or temporal portals. The present is considered the farthest point in the timeline—the edge of known time. Not your present, of course. Your present is the past. However, the calculations in this journal predict glimmers extending into the future, enabling travel beyond this edge."

"What does that mean?"

"Whoever wrote this can control the past, present, and future because he can control time."

"That's a little dramatic, isn't it?" Francie said, then rolled her eyes. Now she was talking to this thing like it was alive. "What about free will?"

The Minox paused, the silence as crisp as a raised eyebrow.

"I do not *do* drama. Humans do drama. Free will is the ability to make choices independent of external constraints. This includes freedom from causes linked to one's past, present, and future. To move through time without restriction is to reclaim a measure of that freedom. Therefore, time travel unencumbered by limits would be the definition of free will."

She bit the inside of her cheek, unease growing. "Is the journal valuable because of these calculations?"

"I can't assign a precise value to this discovery as nothing comparable exists in my records. However, I can confirm that access to time travel is regulated by governments and military authorities. Given this, the information in these journals reveals more than theory. It offers a way to loosen the hold of those who have long controlled passage through time. What was once reserved for a select few would be opened to something broader, to the many. It's a shift not just of power, but of possibility."

Her fingers tightened on the canvas cover as the Minox's words sank in.

Over two dozen notebooks, each a possible key to that incredible power, sat unguarded in her father's laboratory. If what Mitch said was true and the spaceman was hunting the journals and their content, then the reward was more than secret knowledge.

Whoever held this knowledge could rewrite everything. Could change everything.

Could access almost unlimited power.

And if the journals fell into the wrong hands ...

"Where was the spaceman when you could no longer detect him? Was he close to the canyon?"

"Ah. Mitchell might not have been completely truthful about my ability to track the spaceman and the spaceman's ability to track us."

Francie shot a glare at Mitch before she brushed her fingers through his hair. "Figures. Do you know where the spaceman is now?"

"I've measured his pace and calculated that he is one hour and seventeen minutes from your ranch house. If you leave on your horse and travel swiftly, you will arrive at your home at about the same time."

"How long before Mitch wakes up?" she asked the Minox.

"Based on his biomonitor output, I calculate he will remain sedated for one hour."

Francie stood, the journal heavy in her hand. Mitch lay motionless on the cold floor of the cave, and a loneliness she hadn't felt since this began closed in around her. The thought twisted in her stomach. She glanced toward the cave's mouth, the faint light outside, the Minox's screen glowing with impossible knowledge.

She'd always had someone to lean on—her father, Maury, even Mitch. But now, if she didn't act, those journals could fall into the wrong hands.

Before, when life got to be too much, Francie ran. This time was different. The nights she'd ridden out alone to find a lost calf, before he'd sold the cows, storms she'd faced head-on, fences patched against wind, and coyotes outsmarted. She'd been alone then, too. And her stubborn grit—not perfection, not fearlessness —had seen her through the worst.

She could do this.

Francie pressed the journal tight to her chest, feeling the

weight of her father's legacy mixed with a deepening resolve. She wasn't just protecting her ranch anymore.

Francie glanced down at Mitch. "Will he be okay if I leave?"

"He'll be fine as long as the glimmer remains open. However, he is phase-locked in this timeline as part of his shift contract. If the glimmer closes while he remains in this space-time, his biomonitor will initiate his termination."

"What?"

"To prevent damaging the present and affecting the future, he's agreed that if he doesn't return to *his* future, his life will end."

Save Mitch. Or protect the journals and save the world.

A heavy silence settled over her as the impossible choice rang in her head.

Twenty-Three

Francie did everything she could to make sure Mitch could make it back when he woke up.

She bent over the Minox. "I have no choice but to leave him here, you understand that, right?"

"Hair splitting. You possess many choices. This choice to leave is us here—alone—is one of them. But I don't make moral judgments."

The Minox could be a real thorn. "If you say so. You have the coordinates. You can guide him to the ranch?"

"Of course I can. Coordinates and route are stored. Path replication will follow."

"I'll leave Orion saddled and give Mitch back his gun. It should take you a little more than an hour."

"One hour and nineteen minutes."

"If he doesn't show by then, I'll come back here. We'll shift—both of us—wherever he needs to be safe. Please tell him that."

"Of course."

"Where is he? The spaceman?"
The Minox didn't reply right away. Seconds dragged, Francie itching to leave.

"Apologies. Extraction of that data is impossible. Space-man's coordinates are blocked."

Her nod was jerky and final. There was no more time left. She fell to her knees beside Mitch and laid the Minox on his chest. She hesitated, sighed, then pressed a kiss to his forehead.

"Like Sleeping Beauty. How sweet."

She ran from the cave, scowling.
A real thorn

Francie wheeled Venus around a switchback, the guilt for leaving Mitch alone and vulnerable her constant companion. She'd always counted on the ranch as her refuge, but the danger now stretched far beyond downed fences or washed-out trails, and time was running out.

This felt like Los Alamos all over. The hush, the coded conversations, world-changing knowledge twisting itself toward something monstrous. She'd known the burden of such weight—Trinity. And now the journals.

If her father's work fell into the wrong hands, the consequences would be catastrophic. And she was one woman, armed with her empty six-shooter reclaimed from Mitch and the periapt slack in its scabbard.

Doubt tore at her resolve. She'd barely kept her life together, and now the world seemed to be asking for even more.

She would do what she could with what she had.

Ahead, the ranch awaited. She was afraid, but she was moving forward.

The dawning sun slanted peach and pink through glittering dust as the road leveled. Francie slowed the horse, pausing on the mountainside to scan the ranch yard below. All was quiet, but that offered no guarantees. She might not have beaten the spaceman here. She grimaced, regretting leaving the Minox with Mitch. It was his qubix, and she couldn't in good conscience take it when she had her own. Her gaze dropped to the periapt tucked in the leather scabbard. Maybe it held clues to the spaceman's location. She gripped its shaft and asked if it could detect the spaceman nearby, but it remained mute.

Francie nudged Venus down the road toward the water trough. Stomach jumping, she slid from the saddle and let the mare drink as she fished her pistol from the saddlebag, tucked it into the waistband of her jeans, then tugged out the 1946 journal. So many tasks to complete. Take care of Venus. Get ammunition from the barn. Hide the journals in her father's lab. Get back to Mitch, and ... disappear, like her father. Maybe never come ba—

Her horses. She couldn't leave them behind. She had to shift Venus and Orion with her. But how would she ...?

"Francie."

She spun toward the house. Adelaide Baer, leaning heavily on a black cane, emerged from the shadows of the veranda, the red geraniums making her pale face seem ghostly. How had Francie missed Adelaide's car parked behind her wrecked pickup?

She slid the periapt from its scabbard and rushed to Adelaide, propping the spear against a pillar before gathering her friend into a quick embrace. The frailty beneath her hands was startling, but relief flooded her at the familiar presence. Even so, unease was already pushing its way in.

Adelaide frowned at the book tucked under Francie's arm before her hand stretched out to touch Francie's pistol. "Is this the Wild West? What happened here? Your kitchen, the truck?"

Keeping a steady grip on Adelaide's shoulders, Francie searched her friend's face—and, unbidden, pictured again the profile of the woman gazing up at her father.

"What is it, Francie?" Adelaide asked.

"Nothing. I'm glad to see you." But she found her own anxiety mirrored in Adelaide's faded blue eyes. "But why are you here?"

"I hadn't heard from you and was worried. You went riding this morning?"

"I was out all night and got back a few minutes ago. Have you seen anyone on the ranch? Anything odd or out of place?"

"No one. Francie—"

"I need your help." Francie glanced over her shoulder at Venus, the idea half-formed, but it would keep her horses safe. "I need you to drive to Arabela for me. It's about the horses. Ask Betsy Size-more—" She pressed a hand to her brow. "I'll write a note to explain."

Her friend shook her head. "I don't understand."

"I don't have the time— I have to take care of—Adelaide, you need to leave."

But Adelaide ignored her. She pulled away, her hand flicking toward the periapt. "That is the artifact you found. And you have one of your father's journals."

"Is Dr. Baer with you? That artifact's my proof that what I told him is true. There was a landing, a—a spaceman."

Not an alien as she'd originally believed. A time traveler. A human from the future.

"I'll show him this spear. He'll have to believe me." The urge to see his face, to watch disbelief dissolve into wonder and excitement, sent a brief surge of triumph through her, tempering her urgency.

And yet if the crash at Roswell had excited a hysteria, what would this revelation bring?

"Then you can prove yourself to me," Adelaide said. "I am also Dr. Baer."

"What? I know. It's just that he—"

"Matters more because he's a man?" Adelaide cut her off, voice sharp, but hurt and anger simmered behind her glare. "Must a man stamp his approval on everything you see and do?"

Adelaide's words stung because they were true. Dr. Baer, her father, her professors—she always wanted men standing behind her, backing her up, as if her own words were never quite enough —even to herself. Heat rushed to her cheeks, part embarrassment, part recognition.

"Eitan is not here. And neither am I leaving." Adelaide turned her back on Francie and walked through the front door, her cane tapping the patio tiles. "Bring the periapt and come inside. We'll sort everything out over coffee."

Twenty-Four

Francie swept up the periapt and followed. The living and dining areas were dark, and the bitter hint of coffee permeated the air. Adelaide tucked herself into a chair at the far end of the table, a delicate cup steaming at her elbow, a bone china plate at her elbow holding two apricot thumbprint cookies. Sunlight sliced across the room from a narrow gap in the curtains. It reflected off the closed cake tin and scattered into a distorted rainbow on the kitchen door.

Her patience frayed, nerves stretched to breaking. "Adelaide, *please*—"

"I am at my strength's end." Adelaide's voice was final. "Cancer, I'm afraid."

The word struck Francie hard—a fresh echo of her mother's illness.

"Don't despair, my dear. I still have a chance." White knuckles gripping the head of her cane, she closed her eyes. "Get a cup, Francie, and sit with me."

Her chest and gut tight, her mind screaming at her to *go*, Francie stood and stared at Adelaide. Time slipped away, but compassion nudged her to stay a few moments more.

She breathed deep, to dispel some of her disquiet, before she laid the gun and journal on the table. The periapt she kept close because it held the cipher.

Except it didn't. The wedge held the cipher.

She hurried into the kitchen, fingers playing over the small piece on the periapt's shaft, her boots crunching glass and crockery, and reached for a second cup—

Her father's mug. It lay broken on the floor, its jagged edges mirroring her own sense of uncertainty about Adelaide, her father, herself.

But disorder ruled. In the end, no matter how you tried to mend what was lost, everything seemed to break apart again. The entropy of the system always won.

She picked up the pieces and laid them on a cross-stitched dish towel by the stovetop before she poured herself coffee and stared out the destroyed window, her hand slipping into her dungarees' front pocket.

"Come sit, Francie." Adelaide patted the table in front of the closest chair, and Francie sat, itching to leave. "I know you are in a hurry, my dear, but tell me what has happened since I last saw you. Did you find Sergeant Ward?"

Francie weighed her words carefully. Her mind still rang with the shock that time travel was possible, but she wasn't sure how Adelaide would react to her revelations.

"I found him and told him about the spaceman and the artifact. He came back with me, and—"

Adelaide held up a hand. "He has already left? To report your story to his superiors?"

"He's still on the ranch. Investigating." Half-truths and lies. Francie's eyes stared at her fingers fidgeting around the coffee cup. "He didn't tell anyone he was coming because he didn't believe me at first."

"Good, good." Adelaide nodded, a small smile curving her lips. "Did he say why he was sent to Roswell?"

Francie hesitated. "Because of last year's weather balloon crash and clean up, the V2 rocket project. But that's not—"

"The Roswell crash." Her expression thoughtful, Adelaide sipped her coffee as if they had all morning to waste.

Francie sprang from her seat, movements jerky. "I have chores to do, and then you need to leave."

"Sit down, Francie. Stop acting like a child."

Adelaide's reprimand stung, but this time Francie saw the rebuke for what it was. Manipulation. And it wasn't new. Adelaide had shaped their conversations this way for as long as Francie could remember, and now the truth slid into place. She'd accepted it, again and again, letting others guide her choices because she believed they wanted what was best for her. And because she'd never fully trusted herself.

She leaned back in her chair.

"Shaming me into obedience won't work anymore, Adelaide."

Adelaide's expression hardened, her eyes like ice chips. "I see you've finally grown a spine. Your timing is unfortunate."

Francie bristled. "Finish your coffee. I need to settle Venus."

Adelaide added milk to her cup and lifted it to her lips. Rising steam veiled her expression. "Ah, the horse tied at the corral. Your animals are so important to you." She sighed softly. "I'm sorry, Francie. My cancer, my fear. They sometimes make me act ... unpleasant. Please. A few more questions. The sergeant didn't believe you at first. What changed his mind?"

"I took him to the spaceman's crash site. I showed him where I found the spear and where I hid it. That's when the spaceman shot at us. But he isn't an alien. He's hu—"

"This ... spaceman attacked you? You are not injured." Adelaide nibbled a cookie.

"He uses this strange gun. Nothing like the ones we see around here. It reminds me of those illustrations in *Amazing Stories* or *Weird Tales* magazines—silver, curved. Impossible. But aside from the kitchen window and the truck, he never hit us."

Francie frowned. Each shot came close—warning, not wounding. The spaceman had been herding them, and the thought sent a chill slipping up her neck.

"My worry is that the spaceman might be watching us now. He wants the periapt back, and ..." Francie stopped.

"He also wants your father's journals."

"How did you ...?" Francie's throat dried. "Do you know what's in them?"

"A little. When Eitan and I first arrived in Roswell, your father and I worked together on a few projects—the solar lights, the water purification. Yet, he encoded them in that bedeviling cipher to conceal the rest of his work from me."

Francie leaned forward, searching Adelaide's face. "Why?"

"After we went to Los Alamos, he didn't trust me anymore."

Adelaide's gaze fell, her shoulders slumped and desolate. But her gentle sadness seemed deliberate. They were both circling, both holding back.

Francie's chest tightened. Her father's warning about her decision to work at Los Alamos lingered in her mind. Maybe what she'd done then or afterward had affected their relationship, too. Maybe that was why he hadn't told her why he'd needed to leave. He hadn't trusted her, either.

Now, with him gone, possibly trapped in the future, she would never know.

She didn't want that with Adelaide. Not to lose her completely. What she wanted, maybe needed, was one honest moment to rebuild the truth that had been a part of their lives. Even if telling Adelaide her plan felt risky, if she was going to move forward, she had to confess.

"I, uh, came back here to hide my father's journals and keep them out of the wrong hands. But if the spaceman is willing to use violence, then what's inside them is too dangerous." She hesitated. "I'm going to destroy them. Once they're gone, maybe things can go back to how they were."

Except, she knew that wasn't true. She'd go with Mitch to a future beyond her imagination. Part of her ached for what she was leaving behind—home, horses, small ordinary things, suddenly precious.

But Mitch needed her. If she didn't cross into his time before the glimmer closed, he'd die, erased by a cold contract she alone could defy.

Mitch, his eyes bright and green and so alive, his foolish, irresistible grin smeared with chocolate pie. The sense of safety when his arm had locked around her waist as they'd torn through time. He'd built and broken her trust a hundred times, but he'd brought her back to life when she'd almost forgotten how to live.

"After I burn my father's journals, I'll write that note about my horses. Then I'm going to find Mitch." Goodbye trembled on her tongue. Francie clutched the periapt, stood, and strode toward the front door.

"Wait, Francie! Before you go." Adelaide gave her a pained smile. "Could you please get me a wrap for my shoulders? Or one of your sweaters? I am find I am chilled."

She hesitated, but Adelaide had wrapped her arms around her middle. Her friend looked so ill. Like her mother at the end, five years old and watching cancer gnaw her away.

Francie pivoted on the ball of her foot and hurried down the hallway to her bedroom. Her father had begged her mother to let him take her to a place that could cure her. But ... he hadn't said place.

He'd said *time* ...

The memory was sudden, jarring. But *now*, she understood. Her mother had refused the future. Refused the cure. She'd chosen to stay and die and leave Francie ... behind.

The pain of her mother's decision took her breath, but she shoved it aside. She didn't have the luxury, the—the *time* to fall apart—not with the spaceman's possible arrival and Mitch's existence on the line.

She swung open the door, and glass crunched underfoot. Shock rocked her back on her heels. Her mother's photos had been smashed and ripped to shreds, littered like snow across the torn-apart room. Drawers yanked out, clothes scattered everywhere. She couldn't move. Another refuge violated. She forced herself to check her father's bedroom. It was worse.

"The spaceman," she whispered, panic rising. "He's been here. Adelaide!"

Francie bolted back to the dining room, but her step faltered. Why would her mother's pictures evoke such violence?

They wouldn't.

The spaceman hadn't destroyed them.

Francie stopped at the hallway's end, staring across the living room to the dining table. Adelaide sat upright, a bright red flush flagging her cheeks, chin lifted, her eye shining with triumph. A smirk twitched at the corner of her lips.

It was the small silver ray gun—so similar to Mitch's—in Adelaide's hand, aimed at Francie with deadly intent. Her heart slammed against her ribs.

"Not Adelaide Baer," Francie said. She'd known deep down but had refused to face it. "You're Delinae Leonides."

So much for truth and trust.

Twenty-Five

Francie's hand brushed a stray curl behind her ear, trembling fingers catching in her dark hair. She scanned the dining table. Her pistol was gone. The journal lay before Adelaide.

Adelaide pinned Francie with a wintry smile. "I haven't heard my real name in such a long time. Mitchell Ward must have been very forthcoming. That will get him into trouble, I'm afraid. You know he is from the future."

"So are you," Francie said. "And neither my father nor you ever told—"

Adelaide rolled her eyes. "Enough! Dear Lord, does your endless drama never cease? I can't let you destroy your father's scientific notebooks. They are too valuable. I need them and your periapt. Hand it over."

Francie hesitated, fingers tightening around the periapt until it bit into her palm. Her jaw clenched, uncertainty holding her still. What had happened in the cave to Mitch had been as much an accident as a wish. She didn't know how to wield it, and if she tried, she might harm or kill Adelaide instead of—

Adelaide hissed and leveled her gun at the reading chair. With a crack and flash of brilliant white light, the chair dissolved into a shower of tiny gray particles. A sharp breath escaped her as the periapt flared purple, then darkened.

"Bring it to me, Francie." The ray gun was pointed at her chest once more. "You do not dare to use it against me anyway. I won't kill you, because I need you alive, but my weapon has many ... painful settings. I will have no reluctance if I need to use it against you."

Francie edged forward and propped the periapt against the chair nearest Adelaide. She backed away, shame prickling beneath her skin.

Adelaide's smile was triumphant. "That's right. You're all talk and no courage."

Anger flared in Francie's chest. Whatever Adelaide thought, the fight wasn't over.

The drapes fluttered to allow in a strip of sunlight that highlighted the silvery shaft of the spear. Adelaide settled back, extracting a gold compact from her pocketbook, the mirror catching the light as she scanned the journal.

The aroma of coffee and cookies clashed with the deadly technology in Adelaide's hand, its muzzle never wavering.

"It cannot decipher this ... this gibberish. Damn your father." Adelaide's soft jowls quivered as she turned the page of the notebook, hovered her compact, then checked the mirror.

"That's your qubix," Francie said.

Adelaide snapped the compact shut and laid it next to the journal. She motioned with her silver gun. "Sit. No. At the other end of the table. That way, you will try nothing stupid with your newly found backbone."

Francie slipped into the seat, clenched fists tucked in her lap.

"The periapt responds to you. Do you know why?" Adelaide asked. Behind her, it glowed with a restless purple light. "It is gene-fixed, is it not? And programmed with the journal cipher?"

Francie's pulse jumped, and the periapt flashed. She turned away, refusing to answer.

Adelaide tut-tutted in the silence. "So childish and so easy to read. It recognizes you *and* your emotions, which is confirmation of what I suspected. *And* it holds the cipher! Wonderful. Then there is no doubt. The artifact is from your father."

"How can it be from my father? The spaceman brought it when he ... shifted to this time."

"Your father is an expert. A pioneer of time travel mathematics. He must have wanted you to have it. To follow him into the future? No, he could have taken you when he left last year." Adelaide tapped her lips. "Could he have sent it back as a message for me?"

"Why would he do that?"

"Because we *loved* each other," Adelaide snapped. "Your father only married your mother out of pity."

Francie surged to her feet. "I don't believe you! My father loved my mother, not you."

Adelaide pulled the trigger.

This time, there was no flash or crackle. Just a sudden, unseen strike to her chest. Pain slammed into her, stealing her breath. The edges of her vision darkened. She wheezed, struggled for air, but her lungs seized and stuttered, her knees buckled. She crashed back into the chair.

"He left me for her because he got her pregnant," Adelaide said, her voice cold. "The same reason your Maury abandoned you. We're not so different, you and I."

"*You're lying.*" Francie gasped, the pain draining away. "I'm not like you."

"No, you are not. You would never dare to change history as we did. As *I* did." Adelaide cracked a dry laugh, but her expression was bleak.

"I know what you did. I know who you *murdered.*"

"We did what we had to do. Stupid girl." Adelaide's gaze turned distant. "So short-sighted. All of you."

Francie darted a glance at the front door. If she could—

"Do not even try because the next shot will be worse." Adelaide switched the gun to her other hand, shaking out her right wrist before picking up her qubix. Her face glowed blue from the screen's light. "He must have solved it. Why else would he have layered on such encryption?"

"I don't understand." But she did. Adelaide knew that her father's calculations predicted glimmers everywhere.

"Of course you don't. He was adamant about hiding our past from you. He told your mother. She was brilliant, born in a time blind to her talents." Her voice cracked. She snapped her compact closed.

"I would have followed him to the ends of time. In a way, I did. He let me stay in your life to guide you after your mother died." Her eyes held disappointment and pity. "We did the best we could with such inferior material."

Francie felt the words like a slap.

"You both think I'm a failure." The periapt painted the wall a deep purple tinged with red.

"It's not completely your fault. Part was the culture, this era, part your personality. Nurture and nature." Adelaide sipped her coffee. "He hated that you worked at Los Alamos but hoped it would lead to something bigger. When you chose college, he was relieved. And when you broke your engagement, he was ecstatic. Then you turned coward when life became difficult."

Coward. The word cut deep. The men from her classes returned from war, eyes determined, voices certain. Forged by fire and ready to carve out a new world. And her? She'd retreated, hidden, let herself drown in doubt.

But that *girl* was gone, wasn't the same person who'd ridden up to the ridge to investigate that crash. She no longer needed or expected the world to accommodate her. A spark of anger flared in her chest—first at herself, then at all those who'd tried to shield her. Adelaide, Eitan Baer, her professors, and even her father. They'd built the walls around her, but she'd stayed inside them, thinking they were protection. Instead, they'd been barriers.

In the past day—heck, the past year—she'd been forced to act, to make choice after choice, whether she felt ready or not. She'd stitched herself back together, piece by piece, the scars still tender but holding.

"You're judging me by standards that don't apply," Francie said. "It was easier for you. Your future was shaped by women who came before you. Women who had the courage, the grit. Women—"

"Women who clearly are not you." Adelaide's mouth curled in a mocking smile.

The periapt's light dimmed, but Francie refused to let this barb sting.

"You don't understand what your father and I sacrificed for you, for your mother. We face execution for subverting history. Yet your father—where is he? He ran and left me here to die. His bounty will be high. Understandable. But mine will be equal to his when you factor in …" Her voice faded, but not before Francie heard the unmistakable note of pride.

"I already know what you did. How you murdered an innocent woman to stop a war, and time gave rise to Hitler." Francie's eyes stung. "Fifteen million soldiers dead, millions of civilians, millions of horses—Europe left in ruins. Hiroshima, Nagasaki."

Adelaide chuckled, but her expression was tortured. Francie didn't understand the joke until Adelaide said, "You are so naïve. What we did resulted in destruction far worse."

Francie clutched the chair arms. "Worse?"

"Time used to be simple. Once something happened, it was unchangeable. Einstein shattered that. He postulated that time was slippery, relative to the viewer's placement and speed. That skewed into Eternalism where all moments—past, present, future—exist at once, making free will questionable."

"I believe in free will," Francie said.

"Belief isn't knowledge." Adelaide's gaze was disdainful. "We tested it. If time were fixed, travelers would vanish, eliminated because they did not—could not—belong. Some did vanish, but some ... did not. Some returned, which meant they had traveled to times that were not fixed. The entropy surrounding those unfixed moments allowed for change. That's when we found glimmers. Brief windows in space-time where change was possible."

"Then free will exists."

"Perhaps. But only within glimmers. Your father developed models to pinpoint them. And we used them to rewrite history."

Francie sat still, the gravity of that plan settling between them.

"Something went wrong."

"We modeled every possibility." Adelaide's gaze darkened. "But it never worked. Stop one plague, and another arose. Save one life, and another is lost."

"And yet you kept going."

"Our ... target built a movement among Europe's poor, erasing traditions, destroying art and universities, outlawing religion. His armies invaded France, sparking war. Over a million dead. We decided to cut him off at the root. We killed his mother before he could rise."

"Arrosa Bitxilore. My grandmother." The words tasted like iron.

"For humanity's sake." Adelaide sniffed. "Without his mother as an anchor, he never rose to power. His name was erased from the history books."

"But another monster appeared." Francie's mind sprinted to the equations governing the universe. "You don't erase chaos. Each attempt to stop a war or a death shifts the disorder elsewhere. The system resists change. You know that."

"Time abhors a vacuum. When we cut off one head, it resulted in the Third Reich and ..." Adelaide's next words came out rough. "We thought we were heroes. Instead, we became outlaws. We had to disappear."

"My father?"

"He came back before the glimmer closed, knowing he'd be trapped here. He'd fallen in love with your mother—the daughter of the woman we killed, and sister to the first monster." Adelaide looked up. "He took her father's family name, moved here. The rest, as they say, is history."

"Don't you see your arrogance?"

Adelaide's voice was weary. "We derailed a tyrant. Yes, there were repercussions. But I was willing to sacrifice myself for what we'd done. And I did."

Francie frowned.

"I also shifted back, knowing I might never return to my time. I had to make sure the Allies developed atomic weapons, because ..." Adelaide drew in a breath, yet remained silent.

Francie waited, her fists knotting, staring at the bleached face across the table.

"Why, Adelaide? Why did you help create the most destructive power ever seen?"

Adelaide lifted her chin and met her gaze with defiance.

"Because in the alternative history we'd spawned, Hitler won the war. He developed and dropped his atomic bomb on London first."

Horror permeated Francie's body, twisting her stomach. "Dear God ..."

"I had to join the Manhattan Project, help the Allies win the race your father and I started. I found the right man to use—Eitan Baer." Adelaide's voice turned cold. "He was a means to an end. Our bomb ended the war. Hitler died. I corrected my mistakes."

Francie went still. Her mouth opened, then closed again, her voice strangled by the sheer magnitude of Adelaide's resolve.

"And I knew I was meant to be here, in New Mexico, at exactly the right place and time, for my plan to succeed." Adelaide's voice softened. "Your father sent me another message long ago. A wedding gift. He told me about a safe place to hide. Eitan and I moved here, and I made sure he was called to Los Alamos. Perhaps the gift of this periapt closes the loop. Perhaps he wants me back."

She lifted her gaze to Francie, eyes shining. "Until your visit yesterday, I was determined to both live and die in a time not my own. But your visit changed everything. I do not have the strength to run and hide anymore. Therefore, since this glimmer remains open, I will take my chances and shift back using—"

Francie cut her off. "Then why hasn't my father returned?"

Adelaide released an exasperated sigh. "You have not figured it out? The genefixed periapt, the journals, the landing site. They are all clues."

The periapt flared, flooding the room with an eerie light as Adelaide locked eyes with her.

"Francie, he has returned." She spoke gently, but her voice carried a hard certainty. "The spaceman is your father."

Twenty-Six

Through a gap in the curtain, bright morning sunlight cut a crisp stripe across the table between Francie and Adelaide. The lingering scent of coffee and the tin of apricot cookies mocked a tableau that had played out a hundred times during Francie's life. Adelaide's familiar presence, her cup at her elbow, was twisted now by her ray gun and the promise of violence. The line of light marked a chasm that grew wider with every revelation.

"You're lying." Francie steadied the waver in her voice, a trace of uncertainty she quickly covered. She glanced away, steadying herself. "The spaceman tried to kill me. He threatened to destroy this house. My father would never—"

"Think, Francie. He shifted to this ranch, he left the periapt for you, it recognized *you*."

Adelaide's words sank in, and Francie furrowed her brows. The dog in the workshop pictures, the cipher wedge that fit into the periapt. Her father's cryptic note. *When the time is right ...*

Could everything she'd struggled to believe be true?

Her eyes flew to Adelaide's "Then I have an ally, someone on my si—"

"No. The spaceman is your father, but he has not revealed himself to you. He has even attacked you. The logical explanation is that he is not as you knew him. Which means he has experienced temporal revision." Adelaide's face brightened as if she'd fit the final piece into a puzzle. "Yes. He is your father as a young man, before you were born. You are still unknown to him. And if you become a threat to him, he will kill you, like he did your grandmother.

"When he came through the glimmer yesterday, he must have shifted through a time-fold," Adelaide tapped the cover of the notebook, eyes narrowed in contemplation. "Interesting. He may not recognize me, either. I will have aged to him as if I have shifted through a time-fold, too."

"A time what?"

Adelaide waved an impatient hand. "Time-fold. Space-time waves that are more prominent at the leading and lagging edges of glimmers. The result is chronoshift. Age alteration in human travelers. That means the glimmer is closing."

Her father, but not her father. A stranger with his face, none of his memories.

Could that happen to her or Mitch when they shifted to the future? Francie pressed a hand to her forehead. She whispered, "We would be at risk—"

"Of course, we'll be at risk. If I shift back younger, my cancer will be cured. And if I chrono-drift forward, I will die like I would if I stayed here. As for you? Do not worry, dear. If you once again become a child, I will take care of you." Adelaide smiled, but it was more threat than reassurance.

"You want *me* to take you back to your time?"

"Of course! Why else do you think I came today? Now, if what you said was true, your father and Sergeant Ward will be here soon," Adelaide said, glancing at the window. "We have very little time to gather what I need and shift."

Adelaide pinned her in place with a glare.

"You will retrieve your father's journals and bring them here. I will have everything I need—my qubix, the shift equations, the periapt containing the cipher ... and you. My qubix will provide the origin anchor, but that is but half the equation for transport. I needed a shift animal."

"You mean you need me."

Adelaide's gaze snapped to hers. "You know?"

"Mitch figured it out."

"My goodness. That young man has been busy," Adelaide said. "At the time, I was so furious when your father confessed he'd transposed his own daughter. But now his actions seem almost ... prescient."

"What does it mean? To be transposed?" She kept her expression and tone impassive and was pleased that the periapt didn't respond.

"Shift animals are transposed with transposons—DNA that jumps and switches genes on and off. It's what makes chrono-genetic tunneling—time travel—possible. Using ancient DNA in the chromosomes of living creatures was your father's invention, and it was brilliant."

The science blurred past her, but the meaning was clear. Like Eitan Baer was to Adelaide, so was she. A means to an end, a tool.

She closed her eyes, resisting the label Adelaide gave her. A small flame of defiance lit inside her—a vow unspoken but fierce. *No.* She would not be used. Not anymore.

Her father had called her *the key*. It was time she took control.

"Why can't you use the shift animal that brought you here?" she asked.

"I lost her years ago. A lovely calico cat. Another gift from your father."

A calico cat had been an animal in her father's backyard menagerie and had disappeared when he'd vanished last year. Yet another piece of the puzzle clipped into place.

"And since you will be shifting with me, perhaps I will add you to my stack of bargaining chips. Something more to trade for a cure and my freedom. The authorities will want to question you about your father. If you help them find him, you will get the reward for his capture and conviction. I will make him regret he left me behind." Adelaide's voice trembled. "No more wasting time with questions. Bring me the rest of your father's lab books, or ..."

She lifted the muzzle of her ray gun.

A spark of triumph flared to life inside Francie. Adelaide had overplayed her hand. "You're bluffing. You need me to get to the future. Without me, you're trapped."

The barrel of Adelaide's gun tracked past Francie and settled on the corral, on Venus dozing in the sun.

"You are right. I have no other choice, but neither do you. If you do not cooperate, your horse will suffer the consequences."

A chill struck through to her core, but Francie met Adelaide's gaze, refusing to flinch. She was ready to do whatever was necessary to protect what she loved.

One way or another, she'd still find a way to set things right.

But with every minute that slipped past, Mitch's chance of survival faded.

Twenty-Seven

Francie slid through the door into her father's work shed and froze. Inside the rock-hewn laboratory, the spaceman sat hunched over one of her father's lab books—or, if he *was* a younger version of her father, over a journal of discoveries he had yet to make. His dark, curved faceplate was raised, revealing a profile bent in concentration as he scanned the page with an open pocket watch. Its silver case caught the glow from the overhead light.

She inched forward, wincing at a creaking floorboard. The spaceman lifted his head, his gaze assessing. Her eyes fell on lean cheeks, taut with youth and bristly with golden-brown stubble. He was a twin to the man in her parents' wedding photo. His face blurred behind her welling tears.

Her father had returned.

But I'm a stranger to him. He's from a time before I was born. If she told him she was his future daughter, would he believe her, or would he see her as a threat, as Adelaide warned?

"I like this space. Clean, efficient, with some very interesting equipment." Her father spoke with a vibrant ring bereft of the gruffness he'd developed with age. "But it's not in use. How long?"

Francie hesitated, surprised by his curiosity. Still, his future lab was unknown to him, as much as she was. "About a year."

He hefted a book covered in reddish cloth, his smile quizzical. "*Through the Looking-Glass*? An odd addition to a science lab."

"The man who built this space ..." Memory pressed against her heart. "He used to read it to me when I was a little girl."

Her father nodded and placed the book back on the shelf. "You took the qubix—your periapt. Why?"

"You left it propped against a tree, and I needed proof of ... an alien landing."

"But I'm human. Just not from this place or time."

"I know that now. Yesterday, I didn't. I took your periapt to show to the military. That's why Sergeant Ward came to my ranch," Francie said, her stare unblinking. "Mitchell Ward. You know him. He denied it, but I heard you. Saw you in his Minox."

"I'm acquainted with him." The man who would be her father smiled. "But not by listening in on his, er, Minox."

Francie frowned. "Then how?"

"Think about it." He snapped the lab book shut and stood to face her. "I've been, for lack of a better word, chasing you around for the last twenty-four hours. Why have you suddenly decided to approach me?"

"I didn't. Adelai—Delinae Leonides forced me out here to get those notebooks."

He shifted to face her, the metal stool creaking under him. "Delinae's here. Did she tell you about her relationship with me?"

"She told me that you traveled together into the past to stop a war. But instead of making the world better, you made it worse. And that you were engaged once. She's a lot older now than when you knew her before."

He nodded, lips pursed, gaze dissecting. "Did she say anything else?"

"That you were both outlaws in the future." Francie gestured to the journals. "She wants to go back and trade those lab books for absolution. Can she do that?"

"Possibly, depending on their contents." He shrugged. "She's arrogant enough to presume she can manipulate others to get what she wants, no matter the cost. These entries are coded. My qubix can't decipher them, and it's quite advanced. Does she have the key?"

Her father didn't know what was in the journals? Maybe it wasn't surprising. He hadn't written them yet.

But the whole situation confused and unsettled her. It was strange, almost cruel, to see him so close and yet so far removed from the shared memories she cherished.

"She thinks she does." Her fingers brushed the hard shape of the periapt's wedge hidden in her pocket.

"Delinae always overestimated her own intelligence. But you've found the cipher. It's in your pocket."

Francie stared at him. She'd taken it without thought, her mind clouded by grief over her father's broken cup and the chaos of the past day. When Adelaide finally turned on her, she realized what she'd done—and how it might be her only leverage.

"How did you know?"

"You're easy to read. But don't be ashamed of that. It's quite refreshing and honest." He held out a strong, ungloved hand, a half smile on his lips. "Give me your key."

How many times had he smiled the same smile, teased Francie out of worry or frustration with that same look? It tugged at Francie's heart, made her want to please him. Her hand slid into her pocket, fingers curling around the cipher key. She stopped.

For years, she'd lived trying to please others, following their wishes with the quiet hope of safety and approval. But she didn't know this younger man. Not really. And she wasn't the same Francie who'd folded beneath the weight of others' expectations.

A breath steadied her, calm and deliberate. She raised her chin, meeting his gaze without shrinking.

"I don't have to give it to you. Or anyone."

The words weren't a refusal born of anger or rebellion, but out of the strength to protect herself on her own terms.

A smile broke the planes of her father's face. "Honest and refreshing." He dropped his hand and winked at her.

"I have to get back." Francie pointed to the stack of lab books. "I need to take these to Adelaide."

"I'll come with you. Surprise her." He grabbed half a dozen notebooks and handed them to Francie, then scooped up the rest. "Lead the way."

Francie retreated into the backyard of her house, her father beside her.

"You don't want these journals for yourself?" she asked.

"I do. That's why I'm here."

Francie tightened her arms around the books. "I was going to destroy them."

"You were? Why?"

"Because these journals ... They're the source of everything bad that's happened here since—"

She paused and chose her words deliberately. "Because of them, I've been manipulated, tricked, and even forced to put my ranch, my animals, and everyone around it in danger. I thought destroying the journals might stop it all. I don't want to reset the past or rewind history or anything like that. I just want to make sure no one else gets hurt because of them."

The spaceman stopped in his tracks. Francie turned and frowned at his expression, which looked something like shock mixed with dawning understanding.

"Are you okay? Because this is taking too long. We need to hurry, or Adelaide will ..."

He jogged to her side and fell into step. "Will what?"

Francie rounded the kitchen corner, the leafy trees to her small orchard blocking her view of Venus, the scent of windfall fruit pungent in the warming air.

"I tied my mare to the corral fence. Adelaide—Delinae—has a gun like yours and a direct line of sight to the corral. She threatened to harm her."

The spaceman peered around a plum tree and frowned. "What horse?"

Francie dashed from the orchard. She stopped dead, the world falling away beneath her feet.

Venus was gone.

Twenty-Eight

Lab books tumbled from Francie's arms as she ran toward the corral, each step echoing in the quiet morning air. Her heart pounded, not just from the rush but from a deep, tightening horror. Empty rails met her gaze. No reins tied to the wood, no hackamore cast loose in panic. Hoofprints, scattered across the sand, were all that remained.

A sob rose inside her. She blinked hard, fighting to hold back tears, disbelief and loss bowing her head and shoulders.

Then her eyes caught something she'd missed in her panic.

Boot prints. Not just hers, but from her father's boots, the ones she'd loaned to Mitch.

Mitch. He'd come back.

She wiped her eyes with a shaking hand and forced herself to focus. The boot prints layered over all others—hers, the horses'—trailing to the barn. And flanking his steps were twin sets of horse tracks. Mitch had taken both Orion and Venus into the barn.

Relief warred with dread.

She had to warn him. About Adelaide. About the spaceman.

Francie whipped her head toward the orchard. He was gone. The lab books she'd dropped, gone, too. Her breath thinned, a cold prickle running down her spine. The spaceman had the journals. What would he do with them? Would he leave? Had he already shifted back?

She couldn't think about that now. She had to make sure Mitch and the horses were safe.

Francie sprinted to the barn, slowing as she reached the doors. A glance at the house confirmed she was hidden from Adelaide's view. Why hadn't the woman fired on her or Mitch or—

A gruff bark snapped her attention to the barn. Inside, Venus snorted, and Orion rumbled with a contented nicker. Another bark, followed by a scratching that rattled the wood under Francie's hand. Mitch's voice, low and steady, murmured soothingly before a stall door clipped shut.

The scratching came again, more insistent. The thud of footsteps drew nearer.

"Come on, boy. I'm not letting you get away this time—"

Francie yanked open the barn door and stepped inside.

Mitch snapped upright, the tan dog with a smashed black face and bat ears wriggling in his arms. For a breathless pause, they both stared at her. Then the dog gave a harsh, almost scolding bark.

Mitch's shoulders eased, and a smile, brilliant, genuine, broke across his face, striking her heart with unexpected force. "Thank God."

A powerful longing rooted her to the spot. She wanted nothing more than to stand there and soak in the proof that Mitch was safe. To hold him, to say she was sorry for everything in the cave, to explain what she understood now. Except ...

"Why did you try to take the periapt from me?"

He shook his head. "Not the periapt. The cipher. If your father's journals hold looking glass calculations, they're priceless. We could use them to bargain for his life, bring him out of hiding."

She searched his face. "You were thinking about *me*? But you grabbed—"

He held up a hand, brows raised over laughing eyes. "I know it seems like all my moves are choreographed perfection"—Francie rolled her eyes—"but honestly? I didn't mean for it to come off like I was going to harm you. I acted in the moment, and yeah ... I understand why you, um, sedated me." He gave a low chuckle. "Best sleep I've had in months."

"You're impossible," she murmured, unable to stop the smile tugging at her lips. Something in his gentle humor, the warmth in his eyes, made her want to pull him close and forget the world.

She leaned in, ready to give in to the impulse—

Then her eyes went wide. "Venus."

She raced past Mitch to Venus's stall. Her mare had her nose buried in a measure of grain ladled into a bucket. Her saddle was draped over its stand, her bridle hanging next to Orion's.

Francie shifted, peering into Orion's stall. He stood dozing, hind leg cocked. And in the corner, curled up on a bale of straw, lay a sleeping red fox.

The warm barn was alive with the scent of hay and the soft rustling of horses. Orion's steady breathing, Venus's contented chewing, even the fox's sleepy presence, soothed Francie. Here was a brief sanctuary in an unraveling world.

"That's your shift animal."

"Yeah. Tina." Mitch's voice came from behind her, closer than she expected. "She shadowed me and Orion through the forest and into the barn. I'm glad she's okay."

"And the dog?"

"I think he belongs to the spaceman. The one he's been searching for. His shift animal."

"So, he can't leave yet. But you can." Francie's hands clenched the stall door, rough wood biting into her palms. "The Minox told me about your contract. That you'd die if the glimmer closed. Your shift animal returned. Why didn't you leave? You don't need me anymore."

The words caught, jagged. She stared at Orion without seeing him. Mitch had his Minox. His shift animal. He'd leave, the glimmer would collapse ... She'd never see him again.

It was fine. It had to be fine. Life would go on as if none of this had ever happened.

Then why did her heart feel like it was being torn apart? She didn't even know him well, but the logic didn't matter. Longing rose, wordless and sharp. Tears stung, but then something warm pressed against her boot.

The little dog settled there, black marble eyes locking onto hers, steady, unblinking. Before she could draw breath, a heavier warmth settled on her shoulder. Mitch, the heat of his body against her back.

"I don't need you to take me back to my time," he said. "But if you think that means I don't want you with me ..."

The dog rose and padded away as Mitch turned her toward him. His green eyes held hers—open, unguarded, shining with an impossible promise. "That's wrong."

Francie's breath caught. "Why?"

He exhaled and ran a shaking hand through his hair. A strand fell forward, and without thinking, she brushed it back and let her fingertips trail down his cheek.

"Why am I wrong, Mitch?"

His Adam's apple bobbed. "Look. Yeah, sure, we only met yesterday. But it feels like I've known you forever. Like you've always been in my life."

His palms slid down her arms, gaze burning into hers.

"You'd love my future. And I'd never pressure you." His lips curved in a wry, almost shy smile. "But if there's even a chance you might choose me ... as part of your future ..."

An electric charge hummed beneath her skin as his voice dropped, rougher, more intense.

"Francie. I think I ..." He exhaled, shaking his head. "Hell. I want you in my life. It's crazy, and maybe too soon. But it's how I feel. And I know, I've messed up at least a hundred times—

"A thousand," she cut in with a shaky smile.

He laughed softly. "Yeah. But when you walked into that diner, I knew. I hadn't realized what I was missing."

She wanted to believe, but the whirlwind of events left her off balance. "How can you be so sure?"

His expression softened, earnest and vulnerable. "I can't. Not really. But I'm willing to risk it if you are."

He pulled her closer, tilting her chin up until his lips hovered over hers. "Didn't you feel it, too?"

She did. But after so long letting others decide for her, a quiet certainty settled. Here, in this barn, on this ranch she'd fought to protect, whatever came next would be her choice.

Francie rose onto her toes, closing the last distance.

Mitch groaned against her mouth, taking his time—teasing, lingering, exploring. His hands curled into her hair, tilting her head.

She matched him measure for measure, arms wrapping around his neck, pressing close. His fingers traced light, deliberate paths down her back.

When he finally pulled away, breath ragged, he whispered, "Come with me, Francie."

She searched his face—not just for sincerity but recognition. He offered her a new life, but he didn't seem to realize she'd already begun to build one for herself, in her world, in her time. She wanted him to see her not as someone to save, but as a woman who could stand on her own.

Her voice was steady. "I'm not running away. I won't hide from my life anymore."

Admiration flickered in his eyes, touched by a shadow of reluctant acceptance.

He cupped her jaw, thumb brushing her cheek. "I'm not asking you to escape. You're already strong. But what we have—it's real. You feel it, too, don't you?"

A voice, dry and unimpressed, cut through the moment like a blade. The spaceman had returned.

"You should feel it," her father's younger self remarked. "By my count, you two have met five thousand three hundred and fifty-six times. Or is it fifty-seven? Damn these time loops."

His eyes bore into Mitch. "Young man, take your hands off my future daughter before I shoot you."

Mitch stiffened in her arms.

Her father sighed. "Believe me when I say I've done it before."

TWENTY-NINE

Sunlight shot through gaps in the barn's weathered boards, highlighting a storm of glittering dust motes above Mitch's rigid shoulders. The light struck Francie's eyes like a shock of cold water. Mitch pushed her behind him, his body coiled, ray gun drawn.

Across the breezeway, the spaceman—her father—stood with his weapon raised, mirroring Mitch's stance. In his other hand, he held Francie's periapt, its purple glow off. His voice carried a strange, almost amused resignation. "Of course, sometimes you shoot me instead of me shooting you. I'm eager to see what happens this time."

Francie refused to hide behind Mitch. When she stepped beside him, the little tan dog dashed through the breezeway, bouncing around the spaceman's oversized boots. She blinked as his words sank in.

"You know who I am?"

"Of course, although it was a bit of a shock the first few times we met. Who knew I'd be blessed with a daughter? But I'd recognize you anywhere and in any time. You're as lovely as your mother." Her father glanced down as he pulled the barn door closed behind him. "Yes, yes. I see you, William."

Francie inched forward. "You named the dog William?"

"His full name is William Tell, like the apple-arrow guy. I call him William because he doesn't like Will or Willy or Billy or W-T or ..." He jerked a quick shrug and cleared his throat.

"Are you nervous?" Francie asked.

Her father smiled, revealing a shallow fan of laugh lines around his eyes, so familiar, so dear, even in this younger man. "A little. Besides being weird meeting my future child, this is about the time when everything goes to sh—uh, everything falls apart and starts all over again. It gets old."

"You're looping," Mitch said, surprise layered in his voice.

"As are you and Francie. It's part of why you two have this connection, why places on this ranch and around town make you feel you've been there before. Time-loop déjà vu. I, on the other hand, have the dubious privilege of reliving and remembering every chronon. It will continue until ..." Eyes narrowed, he studied the interior of the barn, his face like a picture in the window of his open helmet. "Until something different happens."

William Tell gave up bouncing and plopped onto the spaceman's boot, though he kept sliding off its curved surface. The hay behind Francie rustled, and the dog tilted his smashed black muzzle to focus on the sound, eyes shiny with attention. The fox peeked her head out from the back of the stall door. Her father smiled.

"Ah! There's your shift animal, Sergeant."

"She's not alone," Mitch replied. "A few animals followed me out of that hideout canyon as if I were the damn— Sorry. Dang Pied Piper."

Her father chuckled. "I'm sure whoever contracted you claimed your shift animal would stick with you no matter what. Sorry to break it to you, but that's a lie. They can shift when they want, follow their instincts, or ditch travelers they don't fancy. And I know that because I developed the transposons and genetic protocol. They respond to a special quantum acoustic. Fun fact. I never told the authorities that, so I'm the only one who can control them. Except for William Tell. He's got a mind of his own."

Francie placed her hand over Mitch's. "Could you two put the guns away? I have a few questions and prefer that neither of you die."

Her father's eyebrows rose as he holstered his weapon. Mitch hesitated and then did the same.

"What is it, Francie?" her father asked.

"Do I respond to the acoustic, too?" She clenched her fists. "Because you transposed me, didn't you?"

"I was a bit surprised that future me would do that." He waved a hand as if to brush away the idea. "But yes, you hear it, although you don't realize it. Why else do you think you were in the right place at the right time when I, uh, landed yesterday morning, and a thousand times before that during my loops?"

"Then untranspose me. I've had my fill of being told where I belong and what I'm supposed to want. I'm done being pulled by anyone else's strings."

Her father's shoulders loosened. He grinned. "*Finally.*"

Francie lifted her chin. "Then you understand?"

"I do, but my answer won't satisfy you. I can't justify or excuse any of my future ... actions because technically, I've done none of it yet, nor do I understand my possible motives. I know what comes before this time in my life, and that this ranch and you and your mother will be a part of it. I'm sorry. I can only hope that what I've done will keep you safe."

"There's not a pill or cure? Something? Like the vaccines you injected me with when I was young."

She stepped closer to her father. Mitch touched her shoulder and said, "Careful."

"I did that for you? That's new," he murmured thoughtfully,

like he was tucking that information away. "Makes sense since in my future, most disease-causing organisms are eradicated except for the occasional cancer."

"Like Adelaide's cancer?" Francie asked. "You didn't harm her, did you? When you went into the house to get back the periapt?"

"I didn't find her. Mm, and I'm sorry about the kitchen. I saw the periapt leaning against the wall, so I ate a cookie and took it. I also took—" His eyes widened, and he grimaced. "Adelaide has cancer. That's new, too."

"She said she lost her shift animal, and you disappeared and left her. She's furious with you—the *future* you. That's why she's at the ranch. She wants to use me to shift back and the journals to bargain for a cure."

Francie hesitated, her stomach twisting with what she was about to offer. She dug into her pocket, holding out her hand, the periapt's wedge nestled in her palm. "You were right. I had the cipher. You left me a note before you vanished last year.

"If I give it to you, you can use it and the journals to bargain with the authorities. I know Adelaide's done terrible things, but she's desperate. Take her with you. Maybe it's not too late to help her. And maybe she deserves the chance."

"I loved her once." Her father's face softened. "But then your mother came along, and I ... It wouldn't have been fair to any of us if I'd stayed with Delinae ... Adelaide."

Francie nodded with understanding. The sting of her broken engagement had faded over the past year and disappeared during the last day. The hurt was gone, and Maury's betrayal was behind her.

Standing there in her barn, in her world, she let go of old regrets and was ready to face what came next.

She gestured for the periapt, and, with a smile, her father handed it to her. The moment she touched it, the artifact blazed to life, bathing the barn in pulsing purple light so bright that William Tell leaped up and barked. Francie let out a startled laugh and glanced at Mitch before she fitted the cipher into the periapt's slot.

The purple light winked off. Then her name and the cipher's encryption ringed the barn's wooden walls in sizzling script.

"Francisca Pearl Cortez." Her father's eyes were wide with wonder.

"I think you used Mom's name for the first few journal years. Then you changed to mine because ..." Her fingers tightened around the periapt. Did he know about her mother's death? That he would have so little time with her?

"This damn looping ..." he whispered, tears glistening in his eyes, "has taken me away from her for so long."

He knew.

"Then let's stop this looping thing, or at least try. Take the journals. Use what's inside to bargain with your authorities for freedom."

"That was my plan, but something bad always happened. I've never even made it this far. All of this is new. This conversation, the revelation of the cipher. Maybe this time—"

A harsh laugh echoed behind her. Francie tore herself away from Mitch and her father, spinning around to face the back of the barn.

"And you won't go any farther. This is where your journey ends."

The words lashed through the barn, final and unforgiving. In Francie's hand, the periapt's light died.

Adelaide stood in the shadowed gloom, her ray gun steady, aimed straight at Francie's heart.

"You will shift with me, not him." Her eyes drilled into Francie, ice chips in her lined face. "If you do not, I will make sure your life ends here."

THIRTY

Without thinking, Francie trained the periapt on Adelaide, every sense drawn taut as a wire. Mitch and her father stepped to her side, ray guns in their hands, the brandished weapons a terrible promise of violence. William Tell's rolling growls reverberated off the wooden walls as the fox slunk to Mitch's boots, lips curled in a silent snarl. They formed a wall, a united front.

Adelaide stepped into a shaft of light. Desperation haunted her eyes, her illness etched across her face. She was nearing the end of her strength, yet the gun in her hand didn't waver.

"When the Red Queen shouts, time unravels and fates twist," her father muttered. "Here we go again."

"Then let's change things." Francie stepped forward, breaking the fragile line her father and Mitch had formed. The men reached for her, voices urgent, but she shook them off. "I'll handle this," she said, voice low and firm.

Adelaide's lips bent into a mocking smile. "You? Do you imagine you can talk me out of this? You are hiding behind men again, Francie. I have already demonstrated you lack the courage to stop me. You always have."

The words struck deep, echoing doubts she'd carried for years. Her step faltered, her grip on the periapt loosening.

Then, unexpected and brash, Mitch laughed. "Are you kidding me?" he said, shaking his head. "Francie, don't listen to her. That woman hasn't seen you in action. I have. You've got more grit than anyone else in this barn, especially her."

Mitch believed in her. Had seen her at her best and worst. Maybe she could believe in herself, too. Francie exhaled, the fear and doubt lifting. A flame of resolve ignited inside her.

She took another step toward Adelaide. "We've come up with a plan. You'll shift to the future, and Mitch and my father will bargain for your freedom and a cure using the journals."

Adelaide stared at Francie, eyes narrow and assessing.

"*Please*, Adelaide. I've seen the contents, and you were right. Their value is immense."

"Um, about the journals," her father said. His voice was rueful, with a thread of dry humor Francie couldn't quite read. "After you dropped them in the orchard, I, uh ..."

He met Adelaide's gaze. "Adelaide. Delinae. You've got to understand. I've been running since we changed history. That's turned out to be a bad habit and worse for everyone around me. Funny how decisions ripple out if you don't think them through."

He shrugged, a crooked smile twisting his mouth, bravado and regret all tangled together. "Anyway, I won't use them as a bargaining chip, even though that was why I shifted here in the first place."

"Then give them to me!" Adelaide demanded. "I have no such qualms."

"There's a problem." He winced. "I, uh ... sort of destroyed them."

Francie swiveled her head to stare at her father. "What?"

"You destroyed—" Mitch exchanged a wide-eyed glance with Francie.

"We were fools, Adelaide, to think we could shape anyone's future. No one knows what tomorrow brings. I know that sounds hokey, but it's the only promise I can make. I'm done running. I'll face justice."

"Then you have murdered me, too." Adelaide's face twisted with pain and fury. She swung her gun past Francie to her father.

"No!" Francie whipped up the periapt and shot a stream of purple light into Adelaide's chest. Adelaide's ray gun's beam arced to the barn's roof, dissolving a huge section into a drift of gray dust. Adelaide crumpled to the floor, and silence crashed around them. Francie's breath came fast and shallow. Mitch stared, mouth hanging open in disbelief. Her father had frozen in place. When he finally moved, it was to holster his gun with an unsteady hand.

"Is she dead?" her father asked, his voice low and strained.

Mitch jumped into motion and ran to the body. He kicked the gun away from Adelaide's limp hand and pressed his fingers into her neck. "She's alive. Just stunned."

Francie melted with relief.

"You did good, Francie."

Her heart warmed at Mitch's smile, but when she faced her father, confusion roiled inside her. "Why did you destroy the lab books when they could've saved you?"

"Because you said you were going to burn the journals and stop whatever was happening. Every time I've shifted with the journals, I loop right back again. I knew they were the key, and prayed the outcome would somehow change, but it never did."

He took Francie's hand in his. "You've told me in a thousand loops you wanted to destroy the journals. But this time ... it's different. I realize now that these loops were never about me. They're about *you*. Who you're meant to be, Francie."

The loops had a purpose, and it was hers—not his—to fulfill.

Francie squeezed his hand, a quiet swell of hope rising inside her.

A shrill alarm filled the barn, followed by a second screeching pulse of sound. Francie's father let go of her hand and staggered back.

THIRTY-ONE

"What's going on?" Francie spun in a circle, wincing at the noise, searching for the threat. The shrill alarm pierced her nerves, adrenaline spiking as the barn seemed to close in.

Mitch dug a hand into his breast pocket and tugged out the blaring Minox. Her father pulled the gold watch—his qubix—from a pouch hidden in his spacesuit. The shrieking diminished but didn't stop. The dog and fox stared at each other, lips curled, and milled around their feet. Adelaide didn't move.

"The glimmer's spiraling," Mitch yelled, frowning down at the Minox screen. "We have a few minutes before it collapses to a point that won't allow us to return."

Francie glanced back and forth between her father and Mitch. "But what about time-folds? Chronoshifting?"

"Temporal shear is always a risk, but there are ways to mitigate it. Once I form a glimmer portal from this side, my colleagues will do their best to stabilize it," Mitch said.

"I'll get Adelaide." Her father strode across the barn and scooped up her limp body like she weighed no more than a winter coat.

Francie gripped the periapt. "You can shift here?"

Mitch touched her arm, his gaze softening. "Don't be afraid. We'll be with you. And the chance of temporal shear is a long shot—"

"I'm not going with you. But not for that reason."

Mitch paled but didn't argue. Instead, he took her hand, his grip warm and steady. "Then I'll stay."

She shook her head, her fingertips sliding up his forearm to press against the capsule under his skin. "I know about this, too. You must shift or you'll die."

"Francie, I told you I won't push—"

"I know. But I'm still figuring out who I am, as corny as that sounds. And you're a big part of that. If I don't stay here, if I take the easy path, I'm afraid I'll revert to that girl who ran and hid. Besides, I can't leave the horses and the ranch and disappear." She faced him, gazed up into his eyes. "I know it's a lot to ask, but I need you to help my father and Adelaide back ... there."

"Without the journals, there's—" He stopped, frustration growing on his face. "Francie, there's no certainty another glimmer will open during your lifetime. We might never meet again."

"Even if we do, there's never any guarantee when it comes to the future," she replied.

"Or perhaps this isn't the end to my time loops, and I'll be back." Her father adjusted Adelaide in his arms, tucking her cheek against his grubby, puffy spacesuit. He smiled at her, pride in his eyes. "You're so much like your mother. I knew you wouldn't leave this time and place."

"I've spent too long retreating when my life got hard." She took a steadying breath. "No more running."

Mitch's eyes searched hers, and for a moment, the barn, the noise, and everything else faded. He leaned in, pressed a kiss to her cheek, the softness of his lips lingering. "Next time, I'll find you."

Tears burned at the back of her throat. She smiled up at him, unable to speak.

He stepped away from her and bent down to scoop up the fox, who snuggled into the crook of his arm. Her head tucked under his neck, Mitch spoke into the Minox. "Shift."

The rough wood of the barn wall rippled, then disappeared to be replaced by a window into an enormous laboratory, its pristine white surfaces and glass panels glowing under soft blue lights. A dozen men and women in sleek jumpsuits moved with quiet efficiency, their reflections shimmering on the polished floor. The air on the other side seemed clearer, sterile, a world away from the earthy scent and dust of the barn. No sound came through, just silence. One of the figures gestured toward the window then touched the solid clipboard he held. The rippling glass vanished, nothing but air separating the lab and the interior of her barn.

"I hope I'll see you again, daughter." Her father winked at her, turned, and stepped through the portal with Adelaide, William Tell at his heels.

"Francie. I—"

"No promises, Mitch. I couldn't bear it if ..."

His green eyes bright, Mitch nodded and passed through the portal. She could see them on the other side.

Her hand tightened on the periapt. Its purple light simmered, pulsing with her heartbeat. She could smell the cold, clean air, hear the soft murmur of voices.

It would be so easy ...

She took a step toward the opening—

Orion nickered, bringing her back to the barn. The moment slipped away. She needed to stay. Wanted to stay.

A group of people swarmed Mitch and her father, hiding them from her sight. She strained to find them in the crowd as the portal shimmered then glitched into barnwood before clearing. Mitch pushed his way back to the portal, gazing back at her across time. Francie shook her head. "Don't, Mitch." Her gaze sank to the Minox clutched in his hand.

And she remembered. Her eyes flashed up to his.

"The Minox. 1946. It's inside!" She rushed forward, pointing at his hand. "The Minox!"

The portal flickered and became the rippling window again.

Mitch frowned. His lips moved. She couldn't hear him. He turned the Minox over in his hands, brow furrowed. He spoke again, the movement of his lips calling to her, but the barrier between them swallowed his voice.

"Use it! Use the information." Francie's voice cracked with urgency. "It might save my father! Bring you back to me!"

He touched his ears and shook his head. He couldn't hear her, didn't understand. The Minox slipped in his grip, and he fumbled to catch it, his expression a tangle of frustration and longing. He mouthed her name.

Francie gripped her periapt and charged toward the opening.

The portal closed. Her hand met solid wood. *No. Not now. Not yet.* She was transposed. She could do this. *Use the periapt, use my qubix.*

She screamed, "Shift!" She willed the portal to reopen for her.

The wood, rough and warmed by the sun, didn't change under her hand.

The glimmer had collapsed.

It was over.

Francie slid down, sitting on the hard floor, the periapt cradled in her lap. Its light dimmed. The world made sense when she could break it down into equations—force, mass, acceleration—all predictable, all manageable.

But nothing about this felt neat or solvable.

Something that felt a lot like grief permeated the stillness. She curled in on herself, forehead resting on her knees.

Slowly, the silence around her softened.

First, the faint rustle of wind threading through the rafters, then the tentative trill of a bird, hesitant but growing stronger, weaving through the quiet.

Orion's soft nicker reached her ears—uneasy, but *here* with Francie.

Movement flickered at the edge of her vision. Venus's dark muzzle peeked out over the stall door, wiry whiskers quivering as she scented the air.

The barn breathed with life again.

And in that reawakening, the sadness eased from Francie's chest.

Thirty-Two

Capitan Mountains, Southeastern New Mexico

Rain threatened, heavy in the morning breeze that teased Francie's curls. She hefted Orion's saddle from where it fell before that wild ride through the past. Hard to believe it had been ten days since that ride, since she traveled to Roswell, spoke to Adelaide Baer, and found Sergeant Mitchell Ward at the diner. A fleeting pang stirred, which she suppressed.

Francie set to work, brushing dust off the saddle's leather, straightening the stirrups, checking the underside for prickles or burrs. It was usable, something she'd counted on when she rode Orion out to the site with nothing but a blanket, the periapt slotted in a makeshift sling along his withers.

She'd kept the periapt by her side since her father, Adelaide, and Mitch vanished through the portal. She longed for any hint that they found safety, that Mitch had protected them from whatever awaited. But days passed with only silence.

She might never learn their fate, but small certainties steadied her. Like the disappearance of her father's broken coffee cup. Like the tin of *engelsaugen* on her dining room table and the "convertible" pickup truck. Her drive to Arabela in Adelaide's car, her call to the sheriff to report Adelaide's disappearance. Proof none of it was a dream. Even Eitan Baer's silent tears during the days of fruitless searching. Francie comforted him as he had once comforted her, both burdened by unanswered questions—even though she now held answers he would never accept. Dr. Baer hadn't believed her before, not about the landing, not about what she'd seen. Some truths belonged only to those willing to listen.

As for Sergeant Mitchell Ward, when he failed to return to his post, the Army declared him AWOL. In Roswell, the gossip mill spun wild tales. Most folks were convinced he'd run off with Marsha Hellerman after she'd announced she was through with small-town life and sped away in a cloud of dust the week before. The timing fit too neatly, and people always preferred a story that tied up loose ends, even if it wasn't true. With Sergeant Ward gone and no official report filed, the military's attention never shifted to her ranch. Her land was safe. It was what she'd wanted. A victory. *Her* victory.

But somehow, it fell short. The wind stirred through the treetops, and a quiet restlessness settled on her shoulders along with the sense that something was missing, just out of reach. Francie swung into the saddle and gazed up at the gap between the line of trees crowning the cliff.

Instead of heading home, she turned the horse toward her father's hideout canyon.

Orion beelined into the shadowy slot, and Francie ran her leather-gloved fingertips along the wall. This time, there was no starry sky above, but a cloudy layer that darkened the day. At the camp, she secured Orion, running a hand down his neck. She leaned into him, absorbed his solid, familiar warmth, grounded by the scent of leather and horse. Then she slipped the periapt from the sling and made her way to the cave, memories fresh, betrayal, shock, and excitement, the emotional shadows that followed her.

Pausing at the cave's mouth, Francie lingered in the waterfall's cool mist, the periapt glowing in her hand. In the quiet, Mitch's voice hovered at the edge of memory so real she half expected to see his silhouette at the edge of her vision. The short time they'd shared had changed everything.

She walked to the back room, and the polished granite wall mirrored her reflection. The glimmer had closed, but she had to try.

A deep breath. Palm pressed against the smooth stone.

"Shift."

Her splayed fingers over the surface but met with solid resistance. No ripple of energy, no promise of passage.

She slumped into the stone as she had the barn wall. She'd tamped down hope, thought she'd succeeded, but a tiny fragment had still burned in her chest.

Disappointment weighed on her as she turned to go, but this changed nothing. She'd already packed her belongings and left them in the barn to make way for the hired caretaker and his family. She would load her brand-new truck with luggage and books, and drive from her Capitan Mountain ranch to Socorro to restart her coursework. Her path forward was set, and these memories would fade as new experiences took their place.

"Francie."

The gruff voice—one she never expected to hear again—stopped her in her tracks. She spun around and stared at the glow of light coming from what had once been a black granite wall, now opened into the room she'd seen more than a week ago.

Her father stood inside.

Thirty-Three

Francie didn't remember hurtling herself through the looking glass and into his arms. She broke down and sobbed as he cradled her.

They held each other, the quiet of the room wrapping around them. He tugged a threadbare, cross-stitched handkerchief from his pocket, tucked it into her fingers, then guided her to the table and poured coffee. He sat beside her, holding the mug she'd made for him as a girl in his hands.

"I'll want that back." He gestured at the hankie. "A reminder of your mother."

Francie studied her father as she mopped her cheeks. New lines etched his face, his once black-peppered hair now completely white. A hollow ache settled inside her. He'd aged far more than she expected since he'd disappeared a year ago.

She took a shaky sip. Burnt and bitter flavors flooded her tongue, and she grimaced.

"This is the future, right? You'd think they'd have figured out coffee by now. This tastes like you boiled it in an old sock back in our kitchen."

"Best years of my life. Funny how those little things stick with you." He traced the mug's healed seams.

"I noticed it was gone," Francie said. "When did you take it?"

"When I ate that cookie. All right, two cookies. Even as a younger man, I figured it meant something to you, since you'd left the pieces on the counter. When you gave it to me, I understood at last."

He looked down at the mug, then back at her. He didn't say anything, but his fingers tightened around the handle.

Francie hesitated. "What happened after you took Adelaide back?"

She paused, weighing whether to ask about Mitch, deciding to wait.

He laughed. "They arrested and tossed me in solitary. As for Adelaide, she was admitted to a regen hub. A regeneration hospital. They put her in stasis, an induced sleep, and cured her, last I heard."

Relief welled up inside her. Adelaide had been healed and removed from her world.

Her father swirled his coffee. "I want you to know that destroying those journals restarted my life from that point forward."

"You left my world ten days ago, but you're …"

"My next birthday, I'll turn one hundred and seven. Time isn't linear or constant." He shook his head. "When we shifted from the barn, I didn't drop out of the sky onto the ridge and knock down a tree in frustration like thousands of times before. Instead, I walked through the portal into Mitch's time. It took all of fifteen minutes before I was arrested."

Her gaze flew to his.

"Luckily, someone"—his eyes twinkled—"had scanned *and* deciphered the 1946 journal into the Minox. A perfect bargaining chip, and Mitch played it."

"That was me. I had the journal because you—" She stopped,

eyes narrowing. "You set me up to carry it. Everything that came before ..."

"Came together this time loop. Finally. But I would've kept going ... forever—" His words croaked to a halt.

Francie's chest ached. "Dad."

"I messed up everything so badly with my ... arrogance. My hubris. Adelaide tried to make what we'd done right for the world, but I—" His mouth trembled. "I needed to make it right with you."

Francie picked up his hand and held it tightly, not knowing what to say to make any of what he'd done better. Maybe nothing could.

Instead, she prompted him to continue. "A perfect bargaining chip?"

He squeezed her hand, but his eyes, haunted and filled with remorse, spoke to her, told her *I know what you're doing.*

"Mitch had another fragment from an earlier journal year, too." He sighed and released her to hitch one blue jean clad leg over the other. "So when I offered the rest of my work to my, er, captors, they jumped all in."

"But you hadn't written any of it yet."

"True. But what was on the Minox was valuable enough that, after some ... negotiation, they let me glimmer hop until I could return to your mother so I could recreate my work. The Roswell crash told me another glimmer was open, so I shifted back through the looking glass last year when I disappeared. That was our bargain."

"You didn't take the journals with you."

"I didn't need to. I'd scanned them into my qubix—my pocket watch. I didn't realize leaving the physical ones behind would cause such a mess."

She leaned forward. "Then why are you so much older?"

"Because the first time I ran, I didn't scan my work. I thought I'd be back here in a few days. Instead, I got caught ... and condemned, unless I brought them the deciphered journals. Rumors from when I shifted to Mitch's time as a young man had made them legendary."

"But you just said—"

He raised his eyebrows.

She stopped, repeated slowly, "The *first* time you left. Time is not linear and constant."

"Correct. That first time in 1947, at the starting point of all this, I became caught in a secondary time loop. No one knows why, not even me, because no one had even seen this kind of thing before. They're studying it now. Calling it an Echo Envariance. E-squared. A fancy name for a quantum spillover of causal shells into my own other life-points."

She smiled and shook her head, not understanding, but not wanting to waste whatever time she had with him on a technical lecture, even if it was with history's greatest expert.

"And that's when everything started? The chronoshift, the looping?"

"Yes. To get my journals back, I had to shift-jump until I reached the 1947–48 glimmer. I hit a time-fold, fell out of the sky, and landed on the ranch."

"Ten days ago. But this time, you broke the loop."

"And now it's on record that when I left last year, I took my calculations with me. As part of my plea bargain, I stayed and made my theories real. That was over thirty years ago. They shifted me all over—different times, different jobs. When I turned a hundred, they let me retire. I've been checking the looking glass ever since, hoping. And today, here you are."

He let out a soft laugh. "Strange, isn't it? When I went and changed history, what I got in return was you and her. Maybe that was always how it was meant to be."

Her father bowed his head and took another sip of coffee. The lamplight reflected off the silver in his hair, deepened the lines etched around his eyes, and his expression was caught between vindication and regret.

"I'm sorry for what I put you through." He exhaled, slow and rough. "But if I hadn't, we wouldn't be who we are now."

Francie held his gaze for a long moment before she looked away, jaw tight. She could almost forgive him—if only she understood why he hadn't trusted her.

"What is it, Francie?"

"Why did you keep who you were a secret?"

He hesitated, thumb tracing the rim of his mug. "Your mother knew—"

"She *knew*? That you and your ... " Francie choked on the word.

"Murdered her mother. Yes, I told her everything, even the worst of it. She cried. She screamed. And she forgave me." He paused, as if searching for words. "Francie, I tried to save her, cure her cancer like Adelaide's, but because of what I'd done—"

"Then why didn't you?" Francie's voice came out raw. "You could have taken her forward. You *should've*—"

"She wouldn't go," he said. "Because of what I'd done, and how so much of everything went wrong. She was afraid that saving her might trigger worse events. She forgave me for what happened to your grandmother, but she wouldn't let me risk that again. She stayed in her time, hoping her decision would create a better future for us."

He drew in a long breath and met her gaze. "After she died ... I was afraid that if you knew, you wouldn't understand, so I'd wait until you were older, and I just never—"

"You decided for me."

He flinched. "It wasn't—"

"Yes, it was," she cut in. "You, of all people, knowing what women have in the future, what I could have, and you hid it from me."

"I thought I was protecting you." He lowered his eyes, shoulders hunched. "Perhaps I was protecting myself, too. I'm sorry, Francie. I should have trusted you with the truth."

She let the silence settle between them before leaning in to cover his hand with hers. "I understand why you did it. But when things got hard, I ran away. And you—my own father—hid the one choice that could have changed my life."

He sighed then squared up, chin lifted. "I can't undo that, but you know now. You can stay with me. Here, in the future. It would be ..."

"Easier?" She held his gaze, steady and sure. "In the past, I wanted that. I don't want easy anymore. I'm going back to school in the fall."

"But last time—"

"*This* time," she said, with a small, genuine smile, "I'm not running. I'm ready to fight for what comes next."

Her mother had once chosen the harder path, too, staying where it hurt now for the sake of a future she'd never see.

Her father's expression softened. "I'm proud of you, Francie."

Tears again stung her eyes. She blinked hard, gaze darting around the room, searching to regain her composure, her gaze falling on the dog bed. "Where's William Tell?"

"Heck, that dog makes his own future. Up and disappeared years ago. He'll be back." He shrugged. "Or not."

"You left me the periapt, but why did you hide the cipher?"

"Adelaide," he said. "She hid her anger well about your mother and me. And she was tough, but good to you, until the end. I never trusted her. If she'd gotten both the code and the journals, I figured she might have exploited them. Or turned me in. Turns out I was right about that. Best to keep the two parts separate."

An alarm cut through the moment. He pulled out his pocket watch and grimaced. "This glimmer closes in five minutes. If you're not staying, you need to go." His faded eyes crinkled with a smile, though yearning burned behind them.

"But I thought they lasted a year?"

He smirked. "It's a microglimmer."

"You did it. You finished your calculations."

"And the experimentation. This alone was enough to turn me from outlaw to revered." He sobered, then nodded toward the glasslike wall. "You understand no one from your time can know about this."

"Who'd believe me?"

She held her father tight, memorizing the feel of his arms, the imprint of his scent. Leaving him was another kind of loss, but it was a decision she could live with.

Francie kissed his cheek. Then, clutching her periapt, she crossed to the portal, hesitated, stomach twisting itself into a hard knot.

Her father called after her. "You haven't asked about Mitchell Ward. I take it he didn't come back."

Francie shook her head. "No." Her father was eighty years older. Maybe that much time had passed for Mitch, too, while only days had slipped by for her. Maybe he'd stayed in his own time, deciding not to gamble on a promise they'd never made. Any chance at being together would stay on that far side of time, untested.

"I lost track of Mitch after I shifted to marry your mother. When I returned from 1947, I searched for him but found nothing. I'm sorry. Go Francie, or—"

She stepped through the portal. When she turned for one last goodbye, cold black stone met her gaze. It was done. No turning back.

Everything felt sharper, the air alive with possibility. She took a single steady breath and stepped into the tunnel, watery light shimmering through the waterfall guiding her back into her world. Francie tightened her grip on the periapt.

The future was uncertain and unpredictable, but it was hers to shape.

SCHOOL OF MINES
START OF FALL SEMESTER, 1950

A person's life consists of a collection of events, the last of which could also change the meaning of the whole ...
Italo Calvino (1923-1985)

SOCORRO, NEW MEXICO

"Miss Cortez! Wait!"

Hand on the lecture hall door, Francie turned to find a young woman scurrying toward her, powder-blue skirts bouncing. She skidded on the newly waxed linoleum before catching herself. Light makeup softened her features, and her wavy brown hair was cropped in a short, fashionable style. Cat-eye glasses couldn't quite hide the anxiety in her brown eyes.

"I—I saw your notice about physics tutoring? I have Professor Standley's freshman physics class and ... and. Well, I ... we—" Two other young women huddled behind her now, one in a pretty pink-checked frock, her expression bright and excited, the other in mannish slacks and a white button shirt, a jaunty red scarf tied around her neck, gaze defiant. "We're physics majors, and we'd like to come. I'm Jean Syler." She waved a hand at her friends. "And these girls—"

"Women," Francie said. "These women." She smiled to take away any sting from her correction.

Jean stood up straighter, her face wreathed in a grin. "Yes. These women are Rita Duran and Virgie—uh, Virginia Arrieta."

Francie shook their hands then checked her watch. "Professor Standley's class starts at nine o'clock. Have you read your assignment?"

The three glanced at each other, noses wrinkling. "We haven't," Rita said.

"Chapter one. Take notes, try a few of the problems, and each of you should formulate one good question about the material to ask at the end of class. Professor Standley always leaves time for questions." Francie paused until they nodded. "Make sure you sit at the front."

"The front row?" Rita exchanged a wide-eyed glance with Jean.

"He can't ignore you there," Francie said. "You—we—need to be seen. Show that we want to be taken seriously."

"I do want that. Really. No matter what *anyone* says." Virginia's cheeks reddened, and she tugged on her scarf. "You'll help us, then. If we need it."

Not as tough as she pretends.

"Yes. A career in physics is not an easy road. It's one that's better traveled together." Francie pulled open the lecture hall's door and stepped across the threshold. "See you tomorrow for our first session. Six o'clock in the library. And please, call me Francie."

As their thank-yous faded behind her, Francie skipped down the steps of the sunken lecture hall, her wide, pleated skirt swinging. She nodded to faces she recognized after two years in the physics program, and they nodded back in acknowledgment. No one ignored her anymore. She hugged her books to her chest, unable to suppress her smile.

It was working. She'd gathered her courage and pushed against the prejudice. She'd stayed in her time because the future her decision might build was worth it. *This time, I'm not here to prove a point to anyone but myself.*

That made all the difference.

In those same two years, Francie had also learned to let go of what she couldn't change, including Maury. He'd finished his engineering degree and moved with his wife and daughter to the Pacific Northwest, taking a position with a major aeronautics firm. Francie wished them well, honestly. The old hurt had faded, replaced by relief. Looking back, she knew she'd dodged a bullet. Marriage to Maury would have meant accepting a life shaped by someone else's expectations—his and the world's. She wanted more than that, and maybe, someday, she'd find someone who valued her ambitions as much as his own.

The periapt and her father's 1946 journal sat locked away in the little house she rented off campus. But the wedge key never left her pocket. It was a sliver of the past and the future, small enough to hold, impossible to forget. A reminder of how much her life had changed in one short day.

Francie raised the desk, sat down, and opened her notebook to a fresh blank page before she fished a pencil out of her handbag. The class was to be taught by a recently hired professor no one knew much about. Folding her hands on her desk, she waited for the first class of her senior year to start.

When a distinctive silhouette rippled in the privacy glass of the door to the lecture hall's well, Francie stiffened, her clasped fingers tightening. And when the door opened, she let out a silent gasp.

He looked the same. Maybe his hair was a little longer in the back, but that soft wave still curled over his brow. Even as she stared, forgetting to blink until her eyes watered, he ran his gaze over the small class perched in the hard folding chairs and ...

Nothing. He didn't single her out during the sweep of his eyes, didn't linger for a chronon on her face, didn't acknowledge her presence as the only woman, even though she sat in the front row. He turned to the clean blackboard, picked up a piece of chalk from the wooden well that hung along the bottom edge, lifted a strong arm encased in his tweedy woolen jacket, and wrote his name, Dr. M. Ward, and the title of the class, Physics 400.

When he finished, the writing bold and solid white against the slate, he dusted his fingertips on a handkerchief pulled from a shirt pocket, picked up a clipboard with the class roster from the demonstration table between him and the class, and said, "I'm Dr. Mitchell Ward, and I'm here because a friend solved a major space-time problem for me. With minutes to spare, I caught my flight, which dropped me unceremoniously into Albuquerque a few days ago."

A few students chuckled, not quite getting the joke. But Francie did.

After two years, Mitch stood before her—a specter from a dream she'd tried to forget. He'd returned because her father had cracked the time restrictions of glimmers. Somehow, Mitch had accessed the research—her father's final gift—that had taken so many lifetimes to complete.

A glimmer had opened, and he'd come to her.

"Now," he continued. "Let's see who's read the first assignment on entropy and probability in Georg Joos's *Theoretical Physics*. Can someone explain the derivation basics of the Maxwell-Boltzmann energy distribution?"

He ran a finger down the student list as the men around Francie slumped deeper in their chairs, their attention fixed anywhere but the front of the class.

Mitch looked up. "Miss Francisca Pearl Cortez?"

His green eyes warmed as he held her gaze, his lips curving.

And there it was, that smile.

Her breath hitched.

Oh, that smile.

THE END

IF YOU ENJOYED THIS BOOK...

Wait! Don't go yet. If you enjoyed this story or any other of my books and have a few minutes, please recommend it to family and friends, give it as a gift, request it at your local library, or leave a quick review on Goodreads, Amazon, Barnes and Noble, Kobo, Google, Apple, Book2Read ...

Word of mouth and reviews help other readers find my books in a world where millions of books are published each year. Short or long, your words can make all the difference.

Thank you.

Francie's Cortezian Cipher

A cipher is a rule-driven way of taking a readable message, scrambling it into something that looks like nonsense, and then bringing it back again if—and only if—you have the right key. It does this by swapping letters or groups of letters for other symbols, shuffling their order, or some mix of both. Without the key, the original message stays buried inside the gibberish.

Famous "cipher" examples:
Caesar cipher
The Voynich Manuscript
Zimmermann Telegram cipher
Enigma Machine in World War II
Zodiac Killer's ciphers
Ralphie's Secret Decoder Pin: *A Christmas Story (1983)*

The cipher in *Echo of Lies* is a real, rule-based cipher. Using the letters of the name FRANCISCA PEARL CORTEZ, each character is assigned a number in order of first appearance:

F = 1   R = 2   A = 3   N = 4   C = 5   I = 6   S = 7   P = 8

E = 9   L = 10   O = 11   T = 12   Z = 13

The remaining letters and digraphs (e.g., Th, Ch, etc.) continue the sequence:

B = 14   D = 15   G = 16   H = 17   J = 18   K = 19
M = 20

Q = 21   U = 22   V = 23   W = 24   X = 25   Y = 26
Th = 27

Ch = 28   Gr = 29   St = 30   Bl = 31   Sh = 32   Br = 33
And = 34

Next, every number is "translated" into a Greek letter:

1 = α   2 = β   3 = γ   4 = δ   5 = ε   6 = ζ   7 = η   8 = θ
9 = ι

10 = K   11 = Λ   12 = M   13 = N
14 = Ξ   15 = O   16 = Π
17 = P   18 = Σ   19 = T   20 = Υ
21 = Φ   22 = X   23 = Ψ
24 = Ω   25 = A   26 = B   27 = Γ   28 = Δ   29 = E
30 = Z
31 = H   32 = Θ   33 = I   34 = λ

Example:

"Francisca Pearl Cortez"

F R A N C I S C A   P E A R L   C O R T E Z
1 2 3 4 5 6 7 5 3   8 9 3 2 10   5 11 2 12 9 13
α β γ δ ε ζ η ε γ   θ ι γ β K   ε Λ β M ι N

Hidden message:

Francie U R the key

Francie   U   R   the   key
α β γ δ ε ζ ι   X   β   Γ ι   T ι B

How about this one?

ζαΒΛΧιδΣΛΒιΟΓζηΖΛβΒΛβγδΒΛΓιβΛαΥΒ
ΞΛΛΤηλΡγΨιγαιΩΥζδΧΜιηθΚιγηιβιεΛΥΥι
δΟ

TIME TRAVELER'S POCKET SHIFT GUIDE

Traveler: Please review the following operational guidance post-deployment.

Congratulations on enlisting as a space-time (s-t) shifter as we continue to work to make our program safer both during your shifts and missions. Be assured that current shift-loss statistics fall within the Authority's acceptable variance range for the present fiscal cycle.*

If you're reading this, you've survived your shift to the past, and your mission may proceed. **Keep this guide on your person at all times**. It may save your life.

Primary operational objective: maintain non-disruptive integration with the local environment and population. Local inhabitants are assessed as low-technology, high-vigilance, and non-briefed on temporal transit capabilities. Although you have studied the historical culture and language of your mission's s-t, many of their customs will doubtless shock or surprise you.

Remember, whether your mission is observatory or kinetic, leave only footprints, and residual impact should be confined to traveler memory only.

Section 1: Core Operational Concepts

Glimmers

Transient transit corridors in space-time linking designated coordinates in separate temporal zones. Activation and transit through glimmers require the concurrent presence of a functioning Qubix unit and an assigned Shift Mammal.

- Glimmers designate the subset of historical intervals cleared for limited intervention under current Entropy Compliance Protocols (see *ref.* Butterfly Effect).
- Each glimmer has specific *s-t* entry and exit points, but is flexible within that *specific s-t*. They can be opened at any "place" within the allowable *s-t*.
- *S-t* outside glimmers is closed to time-travel. Initiating shift outside an authorized glimmer pathway is technically feasible but classified as a Category-Omega violation; traveler existence beyond the attempt is statistically negligible (see *ref.* Acceptable *s-t* loss ratios).
- More than one traveler can access the same glimmer from different future dates, but each traveler is tied to their own origin point[1].

Portals

Portals (also: 'looking Glass' portals) constitute fixed, high-stability corridors linking specific, non-adjustable *s-t* coordinates.

2. Your Equipment

Qubix

Advanced genefixed AI support disguised as something ordinary within the traveler's space-time mission. Examples: pocket watch, camera, charm, ecobAInd, etc.

- Tracks your *s-t* coordinates, local time, and entropy risk.
- Negotiates with glimmers and portals so you don't fall into unknown space-time.
- If a traveler elects, the Qubix can be physically implanted[2].

Shift Mammal[3]

Genetically engineered animal companion that allows evolutionary tunneling, aka, pairing deep past encoded in DNA to *s-t* glimmers/portals.

- Shift mammals are a limited asset, and therefore, only the Temporal Registry can assign them for *s-t* missions. Possession of a shift mammal without the proper authorization is illegal and can result in temporal termination (see section 5 below).
- Without your shift mammal, travel is a one-way ticket to what has been euphemistically termed "entropy soup."
- Be aware that your shift mammal may decide to abandon you. That is their right.
- **If your assigned shift mammal refuses to move toward a glimmer or portal, trust their instincts.** They can sense closures and lethal paradoxes long before you can.

Care basics:

- Preferred treats are species-specific. Suggestions: *Felis catus*—dried fish; *Canis lupus familiaris*—peanut butter; *Vulpes vulpes*—grapes; *Mephitis* spp.—dried fruit; *Procyon lotor*—warm beer and cold pizza. (For further food inquiries, see *ref. Snacks for Shift Mammals: A Comprehensive Study.*)

4. Time-Folds, Time-Loops, & Age-Shifts

Time-Folds

Time-Folds: low-probability, high-impact *s-t* wave events occurring at glimmer/portal boundaries that may induce involuntary temporal displacement along the traveler's lifespan.

Possible effects:

- *Mild:* a few days or years shaved off or added; annoying but survivable.
- *Severity Level 1:* regression to juvenile, infant, or prenatal state (memory retention variable)
- *Severity Level 2:* acute progression to late-life condition, including possible terminal senescence.

Field slang:

- *Chronoshift* – any age change caused by a time-fold.
- *Temporal Reversion* – becoming a younger version of yourself, with or without your current memories.
- *Youthalation* – sudden, dramatic age regression.
- *Geriattrition* – sudden, dramatic age progression.
- *Chrono-Drift* – slow, wave-like aging or de-aging over hours or days.
- *Chrono-Shear* – violent, damaging *s-t* shift where

different body parts age via regression *and* progression. Extremely rare.

Time-Loops:

This Authority formally states that 'time loops' do not exist, have not been documented under authorized conditions, and are not recognized within any current operational or theoretical framework.

5. Implants, Chips, and Termination Protocols

Certain travelers may elect to receive *s-t* locator implants ('chips') that continuously broadcast identity, location, and mission-scope authorization.

Chipped Traveler:

- Your chip announces you to the Temporal Registry and to any enforcement node scanning within the vicinity.
- Chips allow remote lockdowns: suspension of your Qubix permissions, forced recall, or freeze at your last safe space/timestamp.
- Any attempt to modify, disable, or obscure chip function constitutes immediate cause for forced recall and mandatory review by Enforcement.

Termination Conditions

Under extreme circumstances, a chipped traveler can be flagged for termination:

- Confirmed attempt to weaponize glimmers or portals for large-scale destruction.

- Repeat violations that destabilize an era beyond repair (multiple timeline breaches, unauthorized paradox experiments, etc.).
- Persistent refusal to exit a critically unstable portal when ordered.

Termination may include:

- Hard severance of chip link and automatic ejection into a non-navigable time-fold (non-survivable).
- Full erasure of temporal access credentials (Qubix link, Registry record, and travel clearance). Traveler's continued existence in last known coordinates is classified.
- *Contract termination:* liability contracts whereby the traveler agrees to termination if they miss shift transport at the end of their glimmer and mission.
- Contract and bad behavior termination account for ~23.65% of the shift-loss ratio.

If your chip begins to burn, buzz, or display a termination countdown, do not experiment. Find a safe glimmer out or report to the nearest authorized node.

6. Rules of Time Travel (abridged)

- You travel only through active glimmers or authorized portals. Initiating unsanctioned transit ("free-jumping") into unindexed time is strictly prohibited and statistically equivalent to self-termination.
- You return to your origin point. Alternate futures are an open problem. Do not attempt unsupervised computational modeling of alternate futures using your own timeline as a test subject.

- Any historical change must be absorbed into the larger flow of entropy. Fixing one disaster usually births another. That is not a bug. That is a Universe feature.
- When in doubt, follow your Qubix and your shift mammal. If they disagree with you, assume you are wrong.
- Standard cover response to local inquiry: adopt non-specific identity, local occupation, and transient status. Under no circumstances disclose temporal origin or mission parameters.

Notes:

1. The primary traveler using their specific Qubix/shift mammal controls the glimmer. Any travelers accompanying them will also shift back to the primary Traveler's designated origin point instead of their own.

2. While physical implantation of the Qubix is preferred by the Temporal Registry, primitive medical procedures of the historical past can interfere with or even inactivate the device. Therefore, liability waivers MUST be signed by the traveler under ALL circumstances before shifting.

3. All sentient mammals are hereby recognized as beings with inherent rights to life, safety, and humane treatment, and shall not be regarded as property, equipment, or expendable assets. They are entitled to adequate food, water, shelter, medical care, snacks & treats, and an environment that supports their natural behaviors and social needs.

No mammal shall be compelled to participate in experiments, entertainment, or hazardous travel—temporal or otherwise—without meaningful, observable consent and the freedom to refuse. Each mammal retains the right to make its own choices about whom to trust, where to rest, and which demands to obey, especially when compliance would compromise well-being, dignity, or the instinct for self-preservation.

References:

Please contact Faye at the main office.

*Statistical analysis of survival rates can be requested after filling out forms TR 4521, TR 7885, TR 027ST, TTA 67G-1, TTA 67G-4, SL F45K, SL 0095, and AO 98B. You can find these and other forms at UIW:TimeRegistry/org/forms_Authority_T-TY711. Ask for Mary.

The Time Traveler's Pocket Shift Guide is issued by the Temporal Registry and updated each cycle

Excerpt: Sting of Lies

A Lies Mystery

The paved road to the Donavan Experimental Farm and Ranch Staff Complex wound through thick fairy-tale forests and wild-flower-dusted meadows, and across burbling streams. She should have expected that people as rich as the Donavans—and they were supervillain-with-a-volcano-lair rich according to the internet, ranked twelfth in the country for accumulated wealth—wouldn't have run-of-the-mill blacktop surfaces. Nope. These roads used *exhaust gas-decomposing, permeable, low-heat absorbing, piezoelectric energy harvesting, noise-reducing materials.* So read the sign at the rest area. These people really liked signs.

Mountains loomed in the distance, dark green and gray against towering puffs of clouds so white they dazzled. Topping a rise, a line of man-made structures appeared through the screen of trees. She sailed over another picturesque bridge covering another picturesque stream and followed the picturesque road to an open and unmanned gate. Her car bumped off the piezoelectric pavement and into an expansive yard of hard-packed dirt bounded by rustic single-level buildings with false fronts. Like an old Wild West town, except for the state-of-the-art solar-capture roofs and electric plug-in stations charging dusty utility terrain vehicles in place of hitching posts.

A large man stepped into the street: black jeans and boots, a Donavan-logoed polo stretching across a broad chest, and wearing a black cowboy hat and aviator sunglasses. Myrna stopped and rolled down the window. He strode around to her driver's side and braced a hand against the roof to lean in.

"Dr. Lee? Glad you could make it. Dillon Bard, head of security. If you'll park by the side of that red brick building, I have some paperwork you'll need to sign inside, then we'll get you out to the site."

She pulled out the folder tucked under her computer bag. "But I've already—"

"Yes, ma'am. Just a formality." His sharp-edged jaw relaxed into a reassuring smile. He backed away and waved a guiding arm.

Myrna cranked the wheel and pulled into the spot. It was shaded by a huge cottonwood tree, bright green leaves fluttering in a gentle breeze. She set the brake and powered the driver- and passenger-side windows all the way down, letting the scent of dust and flowers invade her car.

"This will keep you cool for the few minutes I'll be insi—"

William Tell barked his *I have to pee* bark.

She twisted in her seat to glare at him.

"You just went," she hissed. "So I don't even believe you. You're making trouble because I forgot Tan Turtle."

He tilted his head, his arrow-shaped bat ears perked at the mention of his favorite toy.

Dang it, she shouldn't have reminded him. Scowling, Myrna snatched up the folder and her backpack and exited the car—

Right into the hard chest and arms of a handsome brown-haired, green-eyed cowboy. Smile crinkles fanned from the corners of eyes topped by brows lighter than his tanned skin. Young, maybe early twenties.

"I'm Paden, ma'am. If you'll point out what you'll need at the die-off site, I'll get it stowed in the truck."

"Oh. Uh, I'd like to take my car." She remembered to lower her voice.

His smile turned rueful. "Terrain's rough, and it's a long drive. If you'll just show me the gear you'll need."

She chewed her lip as she opened the hatch and pointed to two rectangular chests, both secured by metal latches, and plastic pouches containing disposable white forensic coveralls and purple nitrile gloves. A head covering with a plastic face shield sat on top.

"I'll also need dry ice if you have it. If not, wet ice will do. And I'll need a place to change." Myrna gestured to her pink pedal pushers and knock-off Keds.

"There's a bathroom inside." Paden smiled. "And don't worry, ma'am. I'll watch your little dog."

He hauled out the two chests and stacked them on the wooden slats of the covered porch that ran the length of the red brick building. Leaning into the back of her car, Myrna unzipped her duffle bag, pulled out jeans, socks, and her old, dusty hiking boots that she'd had to dig out of the back of her closet because she'd never wanted to ever wear them again. As she zipped up her bag, she casually adjusted it to hide the edge of the hard case below.

Clothes hugged against her chest, she scuttled across the porch to the screen door. Two more cowboys nodded and smiled as she approached. Neither wore the Donavan polo. Instead, they were dressed in blue chambray work shirts, worn jeans, and laced-up leather work boots. One was tall and lanky and a little stooped, early fifties. He introduced himself as "McJunkin, ma'am, but call me Webb."

The other man was shorter with a whip-cord leanness, midforties, close-cropped blond hair, and a smirky mouth. "Jessup, ma'am."

He caught her eyes in his crystal-blue gaze. Myrna faltered, stomach somersaulting with attraction, her shoes seemingly stuck to the wooden platform for endless seconds before the lanky cowboy stepped between them and politely opened the door. She unstuck herself and hurried through. Both men followed her inside.

The interior walls of the building were pleasantly wainscoted a creamy white, but the mesh-covered windows screamed security. Behind a counter built like it had been plucked from an old-timey Western bank—including lacy ironwork teller cages—plasma video monitors covered a wall. Each screen rotated through multiple views of forests, meadows, ponds—even a manicured golf course and lodge—every few seconds. The displays were manned by a dark-haired woman who didn't turn around. Myrna had seen this type of setup before. Artificial intelligence monitored movement and signaled anomalies across the ranch. It learned to ignore foliage stirred by weather or the wanderings of wildlife.

"This is a standard nondisclosure agreement, like the NDA you signed in Dr. Kelly's office." Dillon Bard handed her a large tablet and stylus. "If you'll scroll through and initial the Xs. Oh, and there's a fingerprint page. Again, standard." He nodded to a scarred wooden rolltop desk and chair against the far wall. Myrna wandered toward it, speed-reading as she walked.

Deep, ugly growling yanked her head up. A huge wolf-dog, shoulders hunched, head down, and lip curled up on one side of a mouth filled with sharp teeth emerged from behind the counter. Myrna froze, pinned by malevolent yellow eyes.

"Briscoe, nein." Dillon Bard spewed a spate of German commands at the animal. Its ears drooped, the ridge of fur along its back flattening. It skulked across the floor and dropped to sit next to a bowl of water by the front door. Fierce eyes remained vigilant.

"Hey, Bard, your damn dog's gonna kill somebody one of these days," the blond cowboy, Jessup, said.

"I can handle him. Besides, he keeps this place free of tres-passers."

The exchange between the two men was rote, even practiced. A warning directed at her?

The lanky cowboy, McJunkin, pulled out the chair for Myrna. As she sat, a faint gruff bark sounded through the screen door. Myrna set her teeth, determined to ignore it, but Briscoe's flattened ears flicked. She pressed her thumb on the last page of the agreement when William Tell barked again, this time louder, like he was right outside. But of course, that couldn't be ri—

Paden pulled open the door. William Tell trotted inside the room.

"Dr. Lee, this guy was scratching and— *Oh, shit.*"

With a wild snarl, Briscoe lunged at the smaller dog, teeth barred. Horror stamped every man's expression until they realized Briscoe had stopped mid-attack. His snarl receded into a high squeak.

William Tell swiveled his tan piggy butt with its knotted tail. Bat ears pitched forward, head tipped to one side, he stared down the wolf-dog, who practically folded in half, a puddle forming beneath his shaking back legs. William Tell ambled to Briscoe's water dish, dipped his head, and lapped noisily. Pivoting, he musically broke wind directly into the larger dog's muzzle, then trotted toward the three men—Bard, McJunkin, and Jessup—standing side by side along the counter, blinking in astonishment. Briscoe slunk through the screen door, still clutched open by a slack-jawed Paden. Even the woman at the monitors stood to watch.

But William Tell wasn't finished. He sniffed Bard's foot, lifted his back leg—

Myrna pleaded, "*No, no, no.*"

—and proceeded to hop down the row of boots, arcing a precision stream of pee as he traveled. Myrna hunched her shoulders, cheeks red-hot with embarrassment.

He always made her pay.

Bard and McJunkin danced back, Bard cursing in German as he shook the urine off shiny black leather. William Tell ran out of pee before he hit his final target. He dropped his leg and plunked down to sit on top of the only dry boot.

The owner of that boot—Jessup—shook with silent laughter. "Guess this guy showed us who's boss." His voice was a rich baritone. "Didn't you, boy?"

William Tell tipped his head back, beady eyes staring up at the genesis of sound. The cowboy extended open hands and, as if in slow motion, bent down to wrap his fingers around William Tell's torso. Myrna froze, eyes widening until they burned. Jessup straightened, the dog secure in his grasp, back legs dangling.

And his face changed, his brows contracted—

"*Don't pick him up!*" It came out as a screech, but such was her panic. Myrna launched up, her chair toppling with a *thunk* behind her. She dashed to the man, remembered to close her eyes at the last second, and groped for the dog, her fingers dislodging the cowboy's work-callused hands. Eyes still closed, she placed William Tell on the floor before she cracked open a single lid.

The little dog stood for a moment, shook himself, then trotted past Paden and out the still-open screen door. With a wheezy sigh, he plopped down in a strip of sunshine, one back leg stuck out behind him. Briscoe, tail tucked, skulked off the porch across the sunlit dusty street and into the shadows between buildings.

Jessup stared at her, eyes wide, brows practically pegged in his hairline.

"He's, um ... afraid of heights." Myrna cringed at the high squeakiness of her voice.

She swiveled on the ball of her foot, hurried back to the table, and grabbed the tablet and stylus. Shoving them into Dillon Bard's hands, she babbled brightly, "Let me just put his harness on—and leash—because he can be hard to catch. Ha ha. Then I'll get changed, and we can go. Samples to collect. Right?"

～

"Potenza (the Nicky Matthews series) pairs an idiosyncratic sleuth with a rip-roaring plot ..." **Publishers Weekly Review**

A Killer Nashville Silver Falchion Finalist

Can solving a mysterious poisoning save her career? Oh, and lead her to a long-lost buried treasure? Wait. AND thrust her into the arms of true love?

Ice Age paleontologist and poisons expert Myrna P. Lee only took the job on the sprawling northern New Mexico ranch to revive her disaster of a career, solve an environmental poisoning, and dig up a mammoth. She didn't expect a cold case murder mystery, a hidden treasure, layers and layers of secrets and lies, or a handsome cowboy assigned as her minder who moseys up to her side and sets her heart pounding.

And it's hard to stay focused on solving the poisonings when everything she discovers places her in the sights of villains who don't care who they hurt in pursuit of the treasure.

Luckily, she has her faithful little dog William Tell at her side to help - if he decides to cooperate, the little *sh- ... sweetheart.*

If you like stubborn smart heroines, rugged cowboys with slow and sexy smiles who get caught in their own web of seduction, and a small dog who surprises the heck out of people when he's picked up, then you'll love *Sting of Lies*.

ALSO BY CAROL POTENZA

Nicky Matthews Mystery series

Hearts of the Missing

The Third Warrior

Spirit Daughters

Sacred Ghosts

De-Extinct Zoo Mystery Series

Unmasked

Signs

Ambushed

Shattered

Lies Mystery Series

Sting of Lies

Echo of Lies

Non-Fiction

Demystifying the Beats: How to Write a Killer Book

Author Survival Guide: How to Plan, Prevent, and Recover from Writing
Disasters

Podcast

Periodic Table of DEATH and Mystery

About the Author

Carol Potenza is the award-winning author of *Hearts of the Missing*, a Tony Hillerman Prize winner, *Spirit Daughters*, a Daphne du Maurier Mainstream Mystery/Suspense winner, and *Sting of Lies*, a Killer Nashville Silver Falchion Finalist. She was a genetic engineer and taught biochemistry at New Mexico State University before transitioning to a full-time mystery writer. Carol loves the combination of strong women sleuths, paranormal and murder, mixed with science or, as she likes to call it, *Biochem-Mystery*. She sets all her mysteries—historical, contemporary, and futuristic—in the beautiful state of New Mexico, her adopted home.

Please visit Carol at her website: https://calypza.substack.com/

www.ingramcontent.com/pod-product-compliance
Lightning Source LLC
Chambersburg PA
CBHW061736310726
48969CB00002BA/509